"Congratulations, you're the third caller."

The first thing Kaitlin heard was the sharp intake of breath. Then she heard the whisper. "Hello, Moon Lady. I'm calling to discuss the matter of your farewell."

"I'm not going anywhere," she replied between clenched teeth.

The caller made a clucking sound. "You ought to take me more seriously. I don't particularly like staying up this late to remind you to get the hell out of town. I have better things to do with my time."

"Then go do them!" she shouted, ready to hang up. Then she heard something that turned her blood to ice.

"Kait . . . lin."

"H-how did you know my name?" she gasped.

"My, my, we are slow to catch on, aren't we? How many times must I tell you we know each other?"

Kaitlin panicked. "Who are you?" she yelled into the phone.

Her only answer was the sound of the dial tone.

ABOUT THE AUTHOR

Elaine Stirling was "born in a suitcase." She
has traveled all over the world, but now lives in
Toronto with her two young sons. When she
chose a radio station as the background for her
book, Elaine looked up a childhood friend who
has been a successful disk jockey for the past
eight years. After receiving the royal treatment,
Elaine says if she weren't so happy writing for
Harlequin, she'd become a disk jockey herself!
But Elaine is a most successful romance
novelist. In 1985 she won the Romance Writers
of America's Golden Heart Award. The book
she submitted became her first published
Intrigue, *Unsuspected Conduct*.

Books by Elaine K. Stirling

HARLEQUIN INTRIGUE
28–UNSUSPECTED CONDUCT

These books may be available at your local bookseller.

Don't miss any of our special offers. Write to us at the
following address for information on our newest releases.

Harlequin Reader Service
901 Fuhrmann Blvd., P.O. Box 1397, Buffalo, NY   14240
Canadian address: P.O. Box 2800, Postal Station A,
5170 Yonge St., Willowdale, Ont.   M2N 6J3

MIDNIGHT OBSESSION

ELAINE K. STIRLING

Harlequin Books

TORONTO • NEW YORK • LONDON
AMSTERDAM • PARIS • SYDNEY • HAMBURG
STOCKHOLM • ATHENS • TOKYO • MILAN

To Ingrid Schumacher of CHUM-FM for making
it look so easy. You've done us proud, kid!

———————◆———————

Harlequin Intrigue edition published February 1986

ISBN 0-373-22035-9

Prologue

At an open window stood a solitary figure, hardly aware of the cool evening breeze rippling through the curtains, oblivious to the twinkling lights of Toronto's skyline. Only the heavens held the observer's interest.

The moon was new, a fledgling enchantress taunting Mercury with her silver charm. But the evening star would have his way with her in the end, for he was a planet—Mercury, Roman god of eloquence and cunning, a master of seduction. The moon, though alluring, was neither planet nor star but a satellite, reflecting the light of others far more worthy.

It was pleasing, on the nights that sleep would not come, to watch the orderly progression of the heavens. Each celestial body had its place; each knew its limitations and its spheres of influence. People could learn from them, if only they would take the time.

A journal lay waiting on a nearby table; it was opened to a clean page, a virginal, unsullied page. Clean pages were best. They sparked one's thoughts with their freshness and hinted at the promise of fulfillment, like an untried lover. The keeper of the journal turned away from the window, sat down and began to write.

I can sense it in the movement of the stars. Soon, after all these years, I'll be able to reach out and claim what's due me. Until now, people have gotten in my way; they've held me back. But they can't do it much longer. I'll win out in the end. I'll reach the sky, and no one can stop me . . . not even the moon herself.

Chapter One

Kaitlin Harper tipped the porter who had brought her bags to the taxi stand outside Toronto's Pearson International Airport. She tried to ignore the lascivious look he was giving her as he stood there, hand outstretched. Some men had no couth at all, she thought disgustedly, wondering whether she should forget about tipping him altogether. It would serve the old lecher right.

Just then, the driver of the first cab got out and came around to the sidewalk. "Hi there," he said. "Let me put these bags in the trunk for you." The glare he leveled at the lingering porter plainly told the man to get lost. To Kaitlin's amazement, he did.

"Thank you," she said gratefully, pushing thick, sunstreaked brown hair away from her face and tossing her carryon bags into the back seat before climbing in.

"Don't mention it." The pleasant, sandy-haired young man got back into the taxi, glanced at his passenger through the rearview mirror and gave her a friendly grin. "You must be used to a lot of unsolicited attention. Are you in show business, by any chance?"

Kaitlin knew what he was implying, and if he hadn't already demonstrated his chivalry, she might have sweetly told him to mind his own business. A combination of green eyes that tilted upward, a full mouth and a figure generally described as voluptuous had proved to be as much of a curse as a blessing. Some men took one look at her and immediately lowered their estimation of her intellect a notch or two; women, on the other hand, became defensive, clutching their husbands as if Kaitlin were a scheming homewrecker.

"No, thank goodness, I'm not in show business," she answered, resting her elbow on the edge of the open window and looking out as they drove away from the terminal building.

"Sorry, didn't mean to be nosy," the driver said. "Where can I take you?"

Kaitlin gave the address of a luxury building off Avenue Road where she'd leased an apartment on an earlier house-hunting trip. The rent was steep, but the location was worth it. At the age of twenty-seven, she'd decided it was time to start pampering herself a little.

"Have you been away on holidays?" the cabbie asked as they sped along the multilaned Macdonald-Cartier Freeway.

"Holidays...oh, vacation, you mean. You'll have to excuse me; I'm still trying to get used to your Canadian expressions. No, I'm moving to Toronto." She made a point of pronouncing the name of the city in two syllables—T'ronno—the way the locals did. It was important that she sound like one of them.

"Is that right? Where're you from?"

"Sandusky, Ohio."

"How about that? I did some summer stock in Ohio once, a place called Canton."

Kaitlin began to relax her well-entrenched defenses and respond to the driver's friendly manner. "Canton's a nice town; I have relatives there. You're an actor, are you?''

He laughed. "Between fares, you might say. It's a tough business, but so far I've been fairly lucky. I've done some understudy work at the Stratford Festival, and right now I'm up for a role at the Royal Alex. That's a great old Victorian-style theater here in Toronto. You ought to catch a play there sometime.''

"I will. I love the theater." She watched the clusters of apartment buildings whiz past her window and read the exit signs bearing street names that told her nothing. She wondered how long it would take before such a sprawling metropolis felt like home. "You must know Toronto well, driving a cab."

"Yeah, but I was born here, too. Between pounding the pavement for auditions and picking up fares, I've probably covered every square inch of this place at one time or another.''

Their conversation temporarily exhausted, the driver reached out his hand to turn on the radio. Kaitlin leaned back and let her mind drift along with the popular ballad that was playing. When the song was over, she heard "See sky high...C-S-K-Y!" delivered in an upbeat rock rhythm.

She sat up. "That's my station! That's where I'll be working!"

"As an announcer?"

"Yes!" Then she sat back, feeling sheepish because she had just contradicted the firmly negative answer she'd given five minutes earlier when he'd asked her that innocuous question about show business.

The cabbie, however, was polite enough to overlook her dramatic change of attitude. "I should have guessed you'd be in radio. If you didn't act or sing torchy love songs for a living, radio would be the only logical alternative."

"I know," Kaitlin said and laughed. "It's my voice. I used to get so embarrassed in the high-school glee club. Even the alto parts were too high for me."

"Don't be embarrassed. You've got a great voice— take it from me. I've always wanted to have a voice like Laurence Olivier's and I even got my name legally changed, but I still don't sound like him."

"You changed your name to Laurence Olivier?"

He chuckled. "Not quite. Eugene O'Neill, the playwright, is my other hero, so I combined their names and came up with Laurence O'Neill. My friends call me Larry. You can, too, if you like."

Smiling, she took the hand he extended over the seat. "Pleased to meet you, Larry. I'm Kaitlin Harper."

"Pretty name for a pretty lady," he remarked. "Welcome to Canada, Kaitlin Harper."

A few minutes later, they pulled up in front of an eight-story red-brick building set back on a quiet residential street lined with stately old maples. It was late May, and the leaves still glistened with the brightness of spring. Larry turned off the engine and jumped out of the cab to open Kaitlin's door.

"I'll help you bring up your bags," he offered.

"Oh, would you, please? That'd be wonderful."

Inside the cool marble lobby, Kaitlin held the elevator door open while Larry brought all the suitcases from the car.

"Has your furniture arrived yet?" he asked as they ascended.

She shook her head. "Not until later this week. But it doesn't matter. The apartment has decadently thick carpeting I can camp on till my things arrive."

After he had carried in the luggage, Larry glanced around the spacious living room and gave a low, appreciate whistle. "Nice place. Deejays must do all right."

"I can't complain." Kaitlin pulled out her wallet. "Thank you so much, Larry, for helping me with this stuff. I was sure I'd end up getting some driver with a bad back and a rotten temperament. How much do I owe you?"

He quoted the amount that had registered on the meter, to which Kaitlin added a generous tip. Thanking her, he drew a business card from his shirt pocket. "Keep this in a safe place, and if you ever need a taxi or a sympathetic ear, give me a call." He thought a moment. "In fact, why don't you let me show you around the city myself? Toronto can be pretty intimidating to a newcomer."

Kaitlin took the card and smiled. "That'd be nice, thank you. I don't have a phone yet, but you can call me at the station or leave a message if I'm not there."

"I'll do that."

"Oh, and good luck, by the way, at the…Royal Alex, is it? I'll be watching for your name in the entertainment section of the paper."

He looked pleased. "It's the Royal Alexandra, actually, and when you do come and see me, be sure to come backstage afterward."

"I will. Bye, Larry."

"Take care. I'll call you soon." With a wave he was off, and Kaitlin, still smiling, shut the door behind her.

THE UNIQUE PHENOMENON of radio did not require a pricey, high-profile location on Bay Street or the Harbourfront to command respect. CSKY FM reached the airwaves from an unassuming brick building at the north end of Yonge Street, where the neighborhood businesses were small and still bore the names of their long-time proprietors. Santini's Bakery was on one side of the station, Bradley's Shoe Repair on the other.

Kaitlin put on dark glasses against the midday sun as she climbed the stairs from the subway to the street. She knew that the numbers on Yonge Street got smaller as one went south toward the lake, so she scanned several storefronts to get her bearings. Then, turning right, she walked the remaining two blocks to the station.

A sense of anticipation quickened her heartbeat and her pace, though now and again she still wished she were back in Sandusky with her own little show and her tiny apartment. But it was nothing more than nerves that made the memories so enticing. *This* was what she really wanted: a chance to work alongside some of the industry's finest announcers and perhaps become a radio legend in her own right. As comfortable as her hometown job had been, it was only a stepping-stone, and Kaitlin had always known that at some point she'd have to leap to the next one.

Glancing down at her raspberry-colored silk suit, she touched the pearls at her neck and decided the ultra-feminine image would do for now. Once she was in the control room, she could go back to being her casual, unnoticeable self. She entered the glass doors at the front of the building and went to greet the receptionist, whose semicircular desk took up most of the small lobby. The woman was older than Kaitlin, probably in her late thirties, though she dressed as if she were twenty years younger. Her T-shirt, on which the station logo had been silk-screened, was two sizes too small for her less-than-ideal figure, and her hair was overbleached to a garish lemon yellow. She might have been attractive if she hadn't been trying so hard.

For the life of her, Kaitlin could not remember the receptionist's name, though she had met the woman on her first visit to Toronto a few weeks earlier. She held out her hand and said, "Nice to see you again. I'm Kaitlin Harper."

The blonde's handshake was indifferent. "I know who you are. The fellows are waiting for you in Mike's office. Do you remember where it is, or am I gonna have to show you?"

Kaitlin did remember, but she had determined that this was a situation requiring more diplomacy than truth. "I'm afraid I don't. I'm terrible with directions and even worse at names. What *is* your name again?"

"Lorna—Lorna Barnett."

"Yes, of course, Lorna," Kaitlin said, as if it had been on the tip of her tongue. "Have you been with CSKY long?"

"Fourteen years."

"Oh, my, I'll bet they could never run it without you."

Lorna shrugged. "Prob'ly not."

"Then would you mind if I came to you with my questions about this place? I'm going to make all kinds of mistakes at the beginning, and it would be so reassuring to know there's another woman to confide in."

At first the receptionist reacted as though she'd been asked to surrender part of her paycheck, but finally Kaitlin's steadfastly pleasant expression won out. "I guess it wouldn't be too bad having another girl around." She examined a chipped fingernail. "Yeah, sure. If there's anything going on in this station that you want to know about, come to me. I'll be able to tell you.'' Kaitlin didn't doubt it.

Station owner and manager Mike Andretti was seated behind his cluttered, oversize desk when Lorna ushered Kaitlin in. He grinned widely, hoisting his girth over the desk to lean forward and hold out a pudgy, bejeweled hand. "Kaitlin, sweetie, great to see you again! Welcome aboard. You're looking terrific. Isn't she looking terrific, Charlie?"

"She's looking terrific, boss." Charlie Carr, the ferretlike little man echoing Mike's sentiments, was the station's special-projects person. He was the one who had heard Kaitlin's show in Ohio and recommended her to CSKY.

Smiling inwardly at the physical contrast between the two men, Kaitlin greeted them and slowly became aware of a third person in the room. He was off to her right, just at the edge of her field of vision. But because her employer was talking to her, it would have been rude to turn and look. All she could make out was dark hair and long legs... and eyes. Eyes so intense in their regard that she could nearly feel them. Admiring gazes she was accustomed to, even out-and-out leers, but this was something different. It was as if he had already summed up her physical attributes and were now homing in on her deepest thoughts. Unexpectedly, she felt a sweep of color move along her neck and spread over her face. The realization was particularly starting, since she couldn't remember the last time she had blushed. And she couldn't really understand why she was blushing now.

"Hey, Charlie, we better stop buttering this little lady up," Mike said with a guffaw. "She's turning red as a beet."

Kaitlin blinked, all too aware that she'd hardly heard a thing they were saying, and smiled in what she hoped was an appropriate response. Then, taking advantage of the conversational lull, she finally turned to the third man in the room.

Their eyes met. He stood up and reached out for her hand. He was tall, even taller than she'd imagined him to be, and a touch on the lanky side—or at least that was how he looked in his loose-fitting, pencil-striped shirt and navy slacks. While his clothes weren't exactly wrinkled, they did have a rather rumpled appearance, which gave her the impression that external trappings mattered very little to this man. She guessed he was somewhere in his mid-thirties.

"Miss Harper, I'm the program director, Elliot Jacobs. How do you do?"

She nodded, noticing that his hand clasped hers with just the right amount of pressure. "Mr. Jacobs."

His introduction was formal, almost quaint—and oddly out of place in the presence of men like Mike and Charlie. Yet Kaitlin felt herself responding to his lead as though she'd been swept onto a dance floor in another age, the two of them partners in the courtly, gentle ritual of a first meeting. She lingered on his face for what seemed like minutes, though surely it could not have been that long.

There was nothing outstanding about his features, though nothing unattractive, either. They were cleanly defined, quietly handsome. He had thick hair, nearly black, that fell in a wave across his forehead and was cut conservatively to temper any unruly tendencies. His eyes were a deep shade of midnight blue, the lashes surrounding them long and black. No wonder his gaze on her had been almost palpable, she thought as she watched the light reflecting from his eyes. Their steady blue brilliance reminded her of polished lapis lazuli.

"I'd like to meet with you this afternoon," he said. "We'll be working fairly closely together for a while, until you feel comfortable in the control room on your own."

"I'm looking forward to it," Kaitlin replied quietly, flinching with a strange annoyance when Mike Andretti's booming voice broke in.

"How 'bout we take this little lady for some lunch?"

The restaurant, Mike's favorite, was loud and trendy, with glossy, oversize menus and portions large enough to feed three. Charlie and his boss ordered strip-loin steaks and Scotch. Elliot requested broiled sole; Kaitlin, the Greek salad. Despite her objections, Mike insisted on ordering champagne to celebrate her arrival.

Elliot poured ice water for Kaitlin and himself. "Has Charlie given you any idea of what we're attempting to do with the all-night show?"

She took a sip of water before answering, not only to cool a suddenly dry throat but to allow herself a chance to think. There were underlying tones of sarcasm in the program director's voice, and it was unsettling not to know why. She gave him a noncommittal smile.

"Charlie hasn't gone into a great deal of detail, but from what I understand, you hope to tap into a largely ignored audience with an entertaining, live, all-night show."

"Basically, that's it," Elliot said. "We're one of the few stations in the area that appeal to an age range of fifteen to forty-five. Our weekend format is geared to the younger crowd, and thanks to the Duke's unique style, our evening show brings in the young ones and the yuppies. But we feel there's still room for growth."

"I'm looking forward to meeting the Duke of Rock," Kaitlin remarked. "He's been an idol of mine for years."

Her program director merely smiled, while Mike let out a chortle. "You and a billion other females, sweetie. Charlie, why don't you tell her what we've come up with?" Kaitlin couldn't help thinking that the station owner had deliberately snatched attention away from Elliot. She glanced at the younger man, whose only reaction was to steadily tap a book of matches on the table. His dark blue eyes were fixed on Charlie.

The special-projects man cleared his throat. "What we find is that most all-night programs are designed to help people relax or go to sleep, which makes it easy to understand why advertisers aren't too keen on purchasing airtime. But if you think about it, the folks who are out there at night need just the opposite. They're truck drivers, nurses, ambulance attendants, bakers, security guards—and they need something to keep them moving. There's nothing worse than turning on the radio to a taped album of watered-down Mantovani, especially when you know there's no one manning the control room. It makes you feel like the only sucker awake in the whole city."

"So you want me to keep them awake and make them feel that they're not alone," Kaitlin said.

"You got it, baby," Charlie agreed, lifting his small hands.

Elliot dropped the book of matches. "Not quite. What he's neglected to mention is that it won't exactly be Kaitlin Harper who'll be keeping Toronto company after midnight."

She turned to him. "What do you mean?"

This time, Mike's interception was more obvious. "What these guys are trying to say is that we've created a special image just for you, the way we did with the Duke. You'll be CSKY FM's Moon Lady, and we've got a hunch you'll be the hottest thing on radio since 'War of the Worlds.'"

"That sounds interesting," Kaitlin said, sensing from Mike's pause that she was expected to display some enthusiasm. Up until now, she had understood that the program was to be entertaining and informative, similar to her show in Sandusky. This was the first time she'd heard any reference to the show as "hot."

Mike pressed on. "As soon as Charlie described your dynamite voice and your natural style with a microphone, I knew we had the person we were looking for. There'll be an aura about you, and all those tired, lonely folks out there are going to think of Moon Lady as their tooth fairy, guardian angel and Tokyo Rose all rolled into one. You'll make this town sizzle."

Kaitlin felt Elliot's penetrating eyes on her, and any doubts she might have had about his opinion immediately vanished. Mike, as if to counterbalance his program director's ill will, assumed a convincing expression of excitement, while Charlie, of course, mirrored his boss. Kaitlin wasn't sure whether her own reaction was based on majority opinion or on the unexplained antipathy of Elliot Jacobs. Then again, perhaps it was the simple, hypnotic allure of a challenge that made her eyes light up as she raised her glass.

"Moon Lady sounds wonderful," she said. "I can't wait to get started!"

ELLIOT'S OFFICE was as rumpled as he was. There was a plaid sofa that sagged in the middle, with a well-worn blanket and pillow piled at one end. Above the sofa, where anyone else would have hung a framed print, he had a bulletin board tacked three layers deep with notices of concerts, premieres and charity functions sponsored by the station. How one made sense of it was beyond Kaitlin. She sat in his office, looking around her, studying his private environment as she waited for him to resolve a crisis in the control room. On the wall adjacent to the window were floor-to-ceiling shelves crammed with books of all kinds, record albums—mostly classical and jazz—and back issues of periodicals ranging from *The Scientific American* to *Sports Illustrated*. Either this was the station library, or the man was extremely well versed in almost everything.

The only uncluttered place in the entire room was his desk. There was nothing on it but an AM-FM radio, a pencil holder and a desk calendar, which dominated the whole space. From where Kaitlin sat, she could see the meticulous entries, all listed according to time, place and order of importance. His handwriting was terse and without flamboyance or affectation. Kaitlin reflected that everything about Elliot suggested he was a man who was comfortable with himself, a man who made no apologies for what he was. Kaitlin strained to read the calendar upside down, for lack of anything else to occupy her time or her thoughts. She noticed a series of letters and numbers at the bottom of the page, some hyphenated, some bunched together like a code. Curious, she got up from her chair for a closer look.

The radio was playing a current hit, so Kaitlin didn't hear the door open. As she leafed through the pages of cryptic entries, she didn't realize she was being watched.

Kaitlin's nicely rounded bottom was planted on the corner of his desk, her mass of golden-chestnut curls spilling over her shoulder. One foot was swinging blithely in the air, the other poised against the floor to reveal slender ankles and shapely calves to their maximum advantage. Of course, Elliot knew she wasn't trying to be seductive, even though her clingy silk skirt was riding up one thigh. It just so happened that while she was busy invading his privacy, she looked as sexy as hell. It was tempting to stand there and enjoy the view for a while, but he really couldn't spare the time. He had a meeting with a record producer in an hour, and there was still a lot of ground to cover with this supposed girl wonder.

"Looking for something?"

Kaitlin whirled around and jumped off the desk. "Oh! Oh, dear! I...uh, I didn't hear you come in!" Her cheeks were a fiery red as she waved in the general direction of the diary. "I don't make a habit of doing things like this. In fact, I generally make good first impressions..." Oh, hell, why bother? It was a little late to be gathering up the shreds of her dignity. At least there'd be no desk to clean out when she was sent back to Sandusky. She hadn't been at CSKY long enough to even have a desk.

Elliot walked toward her with his easy fluid gait, unusual in a man of his height. He motioned her to sit down across from him, and with a look of dismal anticipation, she sank into her chair.

"I'm awfully sorry," she said. It was the truth, but she didn't think that would make any difference.

If Elliot was at all aware of the depths of her humiliation, he was doing an admirable job of concealing the fact. "What were you looking for?"

"Nothing, I—that is, I was just glancing around the office, and I saw your desk calendar across from me. At first, I was intrigued by your handwriting; it's very, er, compelling. Then I saw the entries on the bottom of the page.''

He rubbed his lower lip with his thumb and forefinger, and Kaitlin found herself curiously drawn to the gesture. There was no earthly reason for her to be studying the black hair that sprinkled his tawny fingers, or the masculine outline of his slightly parted lips. No reason whatsoever.

''Did you come to any conclusions about what you saw?''

She pulled her eyes away and looked down at the clammy hands in her lap. ''I didn't get a chance.'' She looked up once again. ''Is it a hockey pool or something?''

For the first time since she'd met him, Elliot revealed a trace of humor. Kaitlin noticed that he didn't actually smile—he hadn't gone quite that far—but there was an amused quirk to his upper lip, and his eyes crinkled slightly at the corners.

''It's not a hockey pool,'' he said at last, ''though I suppose it's a reasonable assumption to make of a Canadian. It's a shorthand system I use to monitor the announcers' performances.''

Kaitlin covered her face and groaned. ''Wouldn't you know it?''

''I'm not going to fire you, Kaitlin.''

She peered through dark lashes. ''You're not?''

He lifted his foot to rest on the opposite knee, and his thigh strained against the lightweight wool of his slacks. He wasn't so lanky after all, she realized; he was streamlined, like a jungle feline—and equally adept at sneaking up on his prey.

"If I fired every deejay who made himself at home in this space that's supposedly my office, we'd have to close the station. I won't go so far as to say I'll knock next time, but we can forget this ever happened."

Kaitlin had to stop herself from leaping up and throwing her arms around her program director's neck, even though he was easily the kindest, most understanding man in the entire world. The last thing she needed now was for Elliot to think she found him attractive, so she confined her reply to a heartfelt, "Thank you."

He nodded briefly before changing the subject. "Let's talk about your show. By now you've probably gathered that we all have different opinions about the format."

She was careful to keep her response impartial. "Yes, I've noticed."

"If you're serious about making a career with CSKY—and I believe you are—I think it only fair to give you some understanding of the personalities you'll be working with. We're an intense group working in close quarters; sometimes it gets testy. Of course, I'm speaking strictly off the record."

"I understand." To be taken into his confidence so soon was more than she could have hoped for. She felt a growing sense of gratitude and vowed then and there that she'd gain Elliot's respect if it killed her.

"Charlie, these days, is on cloud nine now that he's finally got another woman—any woman besides Lorna—into the station. When he caught your show in Ohio, he came back raving; you were all he talked about. He really stuck his neck out to get Mike to hire an unknown, and Charlie doesn't usually take chances with his job. CSKY is his life."

"I see. I had no idea." Kaitlin wished she hadn't thought of Charlie as a ferret and promised herself she'd make it up to him.

Elliot went on. "Then there's Mike. He started with nothing and built this station up to become the second largest in the city. His biggest motivation is money, to put it bluntly, and he'll go along with anything that brings it in. The trouble is, when he and Charlie get together on an idea, they go overboard. It's going to be up to you to set limits on the publicity aspect of your image. Otherwise, they'll run you ragged."

She shifted uneasily in her seat. "What about you? What's your objection to Moon Lady?"

He tilted his head. "Do you want the truth or do you want me to pay lip service to our boss and say I like it?"

"I want the truth."

"All right. I think the idea is cheap and exploitive. The whole image is an outdated caricature, a parody of women. If you're going to be taken seriously in this business, you have to gain the respect of your colleagues and your listeners. An offbeat image can only work against you."

"I disagree," she said, wondering what it was about him that appealed to her combative nature. "The Duke's image is offbeat, and look at what Wolfman Jack created in his day. Even now, his voice and his face are inimitable, and I'm sure he's taken seriously in the business."

"You're right, but the difference between them and you is that you're a woman."

Kaitlin's mouth fell. Who would have believed Neanderthals still walked North America in this day and age? "What is that supposed to mean?"

"I mean that characters like the Duke and the Wolfman are unlikely to trigger the same aggressive urges among their... let's say, unbalanced male listeners, as Moon Lady might. I remember hearing about an incident in Seattle."

"What happened?"

"A female announcer on a local station started giving advice to the lovelorn on her show. A month later they found her behind the station with her throat slit."

"So? What does that have to do with me? Those things happen."

"They say it might have had to do with some advice she gave, which was never meant to be taken seriously. It's the same kind of thing Mike and Charlie want you to do: play up the tease and titillate your listeners."

"Oh, come on," Kaitlin said, hoping Elliot wouldn't notice the goose bumps on her arms as she tried to get her mind off the female announcer. "There could have been any number of motives for the killing."

Elliot shrugged. "Go ahead and take it lightly, but I've heard of similar incidents all through the entertainment industry. Why do you think most rock stars travel with contingents of bodyguards? Their music appeals to people's basest instincts about life and love and lust. It doesn't pose any problem for their normal fans, but what about that one disturbed person out there, that anonymous fan who can't separate his violent fantasies from reality? All I'm saying is you could put on a good respectable show as Kaitlin Harper and never have any problem, but as Moon Lady there's always a chance—however slight—that someone, somewhere, is going to take you the wrong way."

A shiver raced up Kaitlin's spine despite herself, but she found small consolation in Elliot's devastating midnight eyes.

Chapter Two

"Do you have time for a coffee before you go to work?"

Kaitlin leaned toward the window of the taxi to look at her watch. "I think so, but it'll have to be a quick one."

Larry parked the cab in front of a doughnut shop. It was raining steadily now with the water reflected like bright streaks in the headlights of passing cars. Kaitlin dashed across the sidewalk to the entrance of the shop before she pulled off her cotton sailing hat and shook out her hair. When Larry had locked the doors of the cab, he joined her and they chose a booth.

"Would you like a doughnut or a sandwich?" he asked as he scanned the display cases.

"Just coffee, thanks."

The waitress came and took their order without giving Kaitlin so much as a glance. After she left, Larry leaned across the table. "Can you believe it? Your poster is right above the cash register, and she didn't even recognize you."

Kaitlin turned around and saw herself in a diaphanous gown, black lace gloves and a veil shadowing her face. She was standing at a castle window in three-quarter profile, holding out her hand as if to touch the moon. The beauty and sensuality of the photograph came not so much from Kaitlin herself as from its fanciful, illusory setting.

She turned back and shrugged. "What's there to recognize? It took six people and eight hours at Casa Loma to make me look like that. This, on the other hand—" she pointed to her baggy industrial-strength jeans and man-size jacket "—took me five minutes."

Larry gave her outfit a polite appraisal, the contrast between it and his crisp slacks and shirt needing no elaboration. "I've been meaning to ask you about that. This is the third time I've driven you to work since you started...what, six weeks ago...and you're always dressed like The Little Tramp."

"I know," she said with a giggle. "Sometimes I think I'm overdoing it, but I take the subway to work—unless it's raining, in which case I call you—and I feel more comfortable dressing down after dark. What's even worse is the two-block walk to the station when I come out of the subway. It always unnerves me."

The waitress brought their coffee and still paid no attention to her customer's identity.

"If you ask me," Larry said, "you're just trying not to be recognized as Toronto's reigning radio goddess."

Kaitlin gave an offhand wave. "Oh, come on, don't exaggerate. I'm not that famous."

"I beg to differ," her friend said. "I'll bet every locker in our garage has your poster inside its doors not to mention subway billboards and who knows how many bachelor apartments."

"I'm a fad; I'll wear off. But you're right, I try not to be recognized because that's the way my employer wants it. He says the appeal would be lost if people knew me as Kaitlin Harper, Moon Lady.'' She stirred cream into her coffee and took a sip. ''Who knows? Maybe he's right. But enough about me. How's your career going? I haven't had a chance to catch my breath in weeks, let alone chat with a friend.''

''It's all right, I guess. I didn't get the part I was after at the Royal Alex, but something may be coming up at a dinner theatre in Mississauga.''

Kaitlin felt a pang of sympathy for Larry; she knew how much the part had meant to him. ''Dinner theatres do well. A lot of famous actors play them between stage productions, don't they?''

''I suppose, but I was looking forward to getting the lead in *Deceptions*. It's the best Canadian play to come out in years.''

''*Deceptions*? Was that the Royal Alex production you were auditioning for? I'll be hosting the premiere performance next week, or rather, Moon Lady will.'' She reached over to pat Larry's hand. ''I wish you were going to be there. It's their loss, you know.''

''Sure,'' he said. ''I like to tell myself that. Anyway, I'm glad to see you're doing well.''

She smiled dubiously. ''There are times I wonder if it's worth it. I'm beginning to think I left my private life in Ohio. Not only do I have the show to do, there are photo sessions, publicity appearances and the most boring dinners with my boss and our advertisers. I know next to nothing about advertising and commercials, but he insists I accompany him in my Greta Garbo finest just to impress the sponsors. There's nothing worse than squeezing into those costumes on my own time.''

''Why don't you let me take you out to dinner? You can wear whatever you like.''

Kaitlin glanced at her watch. "Soon, Larry, I promise. This pace can't keep up forever. Listen, I have to get to work. The Duke gets nervous if I'm not there at least fifteen minutes early."

"No problem." Larry tossed a dollar and some change on the table and rose to leave. "Are you getting along with everyone at the station? I hear radio people can be even harder to deal with than actors."

Together they dashed through the rain to the taxi. "Sometimes they can be," Kaitlin replied from the back seat, "but I get along with them all, except occasionally for my program director. He's great, but he worries too much; it's too bad because when he loosens up and smiles, he's gorgeous."

Larry made a quick U-turn in the direction of the station. "Do I detect a hint of chemistry brewing?"

"If there is, I doubt that Elliot's noticed." She took out money from her wallet. "Sometimes I think he believes I'm as vampy as my image."

"Well, to quote a famous radio personality, it's his loss." A few moments later, Larry parked the cab in front of the station and turned to look at Kaitlin. "How about tomorrow night for dinner?"

She handed him the fare, then opened the door. "I'm sorry, Larry, but I'm exhausted, and I only want to see the four walls of my apartment this weekend. Another time, maybe. Thanks for the coffee. I'll see you."

When Kaitlin entered the control room, she found the Duke pounding an imaginary keyboard in time to the record, his long red curls bouncing. He waved to her on an upbeat and swiveled his chair around to the turntable, anticipating the end of the song.

"How ya doin', sexy?" One foot was still pounding the bass while his fingers were poised over the record.

"Not bad, thanks." Kaitlin lifted the pullover jacket over her head and tossed it onto a nearby chair, then tucked in her plaid shirt and sat down as the call letters came over the air.

"See sky high . . . C-S-K-Y!"

The Duke leaned into the microphone. "That was the indomitable Jimi Hendrix. For those of my friends too young to remember, take it from me, he was the greatest. If you *are* too young to remember, then it's way past your bedtime at 11:54."

Kaitlin browsed through a fashion magazine she'd plucked from a nearby pile as she listened to the Duke wind down his show. "Moon Lady's standing by. She just soared in from Jupiter, ravishing as ever in crimson satin and starlight." He rolled his eyes and tossed Kaitlin a grimace, which she returned with one of her own. It was one of their private jokes, the Duke dreaming up Moon Lady's attire each night, laughable because the fantasy was such a complete contrast to the real thing.

"This is the Duke of Rock Stevenson bidding you farewell until tomorrow. Remember, love makes the time pass and time makes love pass, so why don't you all go out and pass some love around while you still have time?" At that, John Lennon followed with "All you need is love . . ." The Duke wheeled away from the board and Kaitlin took his place.

"So how about you?" she teased. "Going out to pass some love around tonight?"

The Duke was dressed in skintight satin pants and an epauleted, gold-fringed jacket that called to mind the Prussian aristocracy. From a hook behind the door he lifted a plumed hat and positioned it carefully on his curls

"Hope so," he said, checking his reflection in the mirror. "A buddy of mine is having a housewarming bash at an old place in Cabbagetown he just had gutted for three hundred grand. It's five stories high and six feet wide. If I do meet anyone promising, it'll have to be in a standing position."

"Duke, you're disgusting," Kaitlin said with a smile.

He returned her grin. "I know; I've spent years perfecting my infamy. A decade ago, wimpy Luther Stevenson couldn't get a date to save his soul. Now I have to beat them off. Speaking of which, what are you doing tomorrow night?"

Lord, why me, she thought and pulled out the music logs she'd prepared earlier. "With any luck, I'm going to expire in my living room."

"I think it's time you and I got to know each other better, considering everything we have in common." He leaned across the counter toward her, red curls framing his face.

Kaitlin didn't bother to point out that she couldn't possibly have anything in common with a man who wore more makeup than she did. The Duke was good-looking in a flashy sort of way, but she wasn't sure there was anything worthwhile beneath the trendy exterior.

"I'm sorry, Duke, but I've had an awful week, and I'm looking forward to sleeping and washing my hair." She examined a thin spot on the knee of her jeans. "Who knows? I might even get some shopping done."

"How about next weekend?" he urged.

Sighing, Kaitlin looked up at him and tugged the lapels of her shirt. "Look at me; I'm a drudge. What would it do to your image to be seen with a bag lady?"

Duke gave her clothes a distasteful glance. "I assumed you'd have enough breeding to get dressed up for a date. In fact, what I had in mind was the two of us showing up at October's in full regalia. The Duke and the Lady. Think of the publicity!"

"No, thanks. To me, Moon Lady is work, and the weekends take too long to get here as it is."

He brushed his finger along her chin. "It wouldn't be work when you're with me, babe. It'd be sheer, unadulterated . . . party time."

Kaitlin tilted her head far enough back to escape his touch and get the message across. "Look, I appreciate the fact that you are the Duke wherever you go, and that you actually manage to rock around the clock like your fans expect you to, but I'm not like that." She pointed at the poster on the wall. "That's not me over there. It's a fabrication, an illusion. I'm flattered that you'd want to take Moon Lady out, but believe me, Kaitlin Harper's a real bore in comparison."

The Duke straightened and tossed his hair. "Is this your way of saying you'll never go out with me?"

"I think so," she said as gently as she could, wondering why anyone would want to have the truth so clearly spelled out.

He pursed his lips, as if debating whether to pursue a different tack. Then he shrugged. "Okay, you had your chance, but my guess is Moon Lady's gone to your head. You're not a bore, Kaitlin Harper; you're a clever little ice princess." Pivoting on one boot, he marched out the door.

Under other circumstances she might have chased after him and made him retract his cruel comment, but the Beatles song was nearly over, and she had a show to do. She'd deal with the Duke tomorrow night.

"Good evening, this is Moon Lady coming to you at the witching hour. It's midnight, and I'll be with you for the next five hours, till the sky lightens and the moon goes down." She pulled a commercial cassette from a revolving rack and slipped it into the tape player. "Tonight our show takes you to the far reaches of the universe, where life is not as we know it, but something mystical...transcendent...unlike anything you've ever experienced... Don't go away."

Three hours later, Kaitlin was timing her breaks around yawns. Just her luck that the music she'd selected for that night's theme was mellow, too mellow to keep her awake. She slapped her cheeks to revive circulation and donned her headphones once again.

"Emerson, Lake and Palmer is the group you just heard, giving us their illustrious opinion of the nighttime. Do you ever wonder why night is so fearful to us, the one time when we can see the farthest, hear most clearly...and love at our best? It should be anxiously awaited as a time to cleanse ourselves of the tension and the worry and the stress of the day, not a time to turn on all the lights and turn up the TV to drown out the silence. I've traveled to a dimension where creatures dread the sun and shrink from its deadly rays and blistering heat. And not only are they sensuous, beautiful creatures, but they live to be five hundred years old. Care to accompany me the next time I visit?" She switched on the turntable. "Let's hear what Cat Stevens has to say about darkness, and by the way, if any of you know what became of that legendary musician, give me a call at 555-CSKY. Maybe Moon Lady can persuade him to come out of retirement." The gentle rocking sounds of Cat's acoustic guitar filled the control room, and Kaitlin hummed along as she worked her way through the commercial log.

"I wouldn't mind accompanying you," said a voice from somewhere behind her.

Kaitlin shrieked, jumping from her seat at Elliot's unexpected appearance. "Are you trying to give me heart failure, sneaking up on me like that?"

Elliot laughed, and she was struck, as always, by the way it lit his whole face. His teeth were perfect and white, the sound of his laughter deep and vital. "I'm sorry. I didn't mean to scare you; it's this intense power of concentration you have. A herd of elephants could sneak up on you."

His hair was ruffled across his forehead, giving his face an appealing boyishness, and he was wearing jeans and a dark T-shirt—a rare casual departure for him. Kaitlin liked the way he looked.

"Isn't this your day off?" she asked.

"Yesterday was. I've been getting some paperwork done."

"Until three in the morning?"

"My air conditioner's broken, and it was too hot to sleep. Anyway, I like getting the routine work done when there's no one around."

Kaitlin seldom had any visitors during her show. Occasionally, the janitor would come in to vacuum, but for the most part he preferred to do his cleaning at a more civilized hour. When Kaitlin had first started the job, Elliot had spent a few nights in the control room with her, but she'd caught on quickly, so there was no need for him to stay. At the time, she'd wondered whether she was doing her job a little *too* well; it had been nice having him there. It tended to get lonely in this blue-carpeted box of a room, sitting there night after night with only the microphone and the telephone to keep her in touch with the world. And yet she hardly ever gave her solitude a thought. Except now, of all times, when Elliot was with her. Strange how contrarily the over-taxed mind behaved at times. Suddenly she noticed that his arms were behind his back.

"What are you hiding?" she asked.

He brought out a flat, rectangular parcel. "A peace offering."

"What for?" She lifted her arms and mussed up her hair, a habit she'd developed to perk herself up; unknown to her, it never failed to stir her program director's blood. Even in her androgynous plaid shirts and oversize jeans, she still managed to look like a movie bombshell from the forties. He wondered if she was aware of just how miserably she failed at looking inconspicuous.

"It's my way of apologizing for not believing in you," he answered.

"You're not supposed to believe in me," she said, aware that her heart was skipping suddenly. "There's no such thing as Moon Lady, and I've never really traveled to other dimensions."

He moved closer, an arm's length away, and handed her the parcel. "I know, but it was Kaitlin Harper I didn't believe in. I should have."

She took the parcel and looked up at Elliot. "What brought on the change of heart?" Perhaps "heart" had been a poor choice of words, she thought, wondering when her own would cease its palpitations.

"I listen to your show, and whether you realize it or not, there's a lot of Kaitlin Harper that comes through. I like what I hear."

She didn't know what to say. They had worked side by side for weeks, putting together the best night show in the city, and he'd never before praised her abilities.

Not that she had expected him to; he'd already let her know what he thought in so many other ways. He'd help her with her research when she was too exhausted to pick up a pen; he'd have it out with Mike and Charlie if he thought they were working her too hard; he'd make excuses for her so she wouldn't have to attend production meetings as often as the other announcers. If he never actually promoted her image, neither did he belittle or discourage her from taking it to the limits of her imagination. In some ways, Kaitlin sought Elliot's tacit approval more eagerly than she did Mike's effusive praise.

Her eyes sought his, and they held. "You didn't have to do this, you know," she said. "I've never enjoyed working with anyone quite as much as I have with you."

Elliot raised an eyebrow. "I'm surprised to hear you say that, considering our unlikely beginning, but I am glad to hear it." More than he cared to admit, since it wasn't the heat keeping him up most nights—it was Kaitlin. When she was on the air, he found that he couldn't bear to miss the sound of her voice; often he would doze fitfully with his bedside radio on, telling himself he was only monitoring her program.

The trouble was, he knew all too well that Kaitlin didn't need another lusting male. She was surrounded by enough of them as it was. Besides, she was too precious a commodity to the station—and to his own plans. He couldn't risk jeopardizing future prospects for the sake of sensual gratification—however tempted he might be. There were plenty of other women in the city who were far more accessible and nonthreatening than Kaitlin; and as he'd discovered, he could close his eyes at the right moment and almost forget he wasn't making love to a woman with green eyes, sun-streaked chestnut hair and a voice like hot molasses.

"Go on," he urged. "Open the package...as soon as you put on some more music."

Horrified, Kaitlin realized she was a scant few seconds away from dead air. She swung around and switched on the second turntable before returning her attention to the parcel.

Tearing off the brown paper, she lifted the lid of the box. Inside was a framed color photograph of a lighthouse on a rocky shore, a full moon illuminating the night sky. A solitary figure was silhouetted in the distant lighted window, and at the bottom of the picture, a caption attributed to Carl Sandburg read, "The moon is a friend for the lonesome to talk to."

Kaitlin didn't stop to think as she laid the gift down; she was merely acting on impulse when she threw her arms around Elliot's neck and kissed him. It was a light brush of the lips, a simple thank-you—nothing more. Yet she staggered back half a step and touched her fingers to her mouth as though she'd been scalded, and the two of them stared at each other for what seemed like forever.

"Th-thank you," she stammered. "It's...a lovely gift."

He couldn't take his eyes off her, not because she'd kissed him—it had been spontaneous and innocent enough. But because of the spark, the lightning flicker of desire that had passed through them and startled them both. If she hadn't jumped back the way she had, if he had had the wherewithal to take her in his arms during that instant, their mouths would still be together. Had he not stood there like a starstruck farmboy, they'd still be tasting each other, discovering the sensations of their bodies touching, exploring the depths of their unexpected arousal.

Elliot reached out and drew his hand through her hair, briefly crushing the thick mass of curls before releasing them. His movement was as impulsive as her kiss had been, and as irresistible as a book of matches to a man obsessed with fire.

"I have to go," he said in a low voice.

"Do you?" she asked too quickly, breathlessly. "Couldn't you . . . would you like to stay for tea?"

He nearly said yes, but that would have been a mistake. This wasn't a living room; it was a radio station. And even though the door was closed and there was no one else in the building, they would have no privacy. This was a room shared with thousands of listeners. She was here because she had a job to do; he'd already finished what he'd come here for. If he were to stay, he'd want to take her into his arms and find out if that fleeting spark could be repeated . . . and prolonged.

"I can't," he finally answered. "I've got to be back here in a few hours as it is."

She nodded. "I understand. Thanks again for the picture; it's the nicest peace offering I've ever gotten."

"Goodnight, Kaitlin." He went out the door and left her more alone than she'd been all night.

JUST BEFORE DAWN when the night was at its blackest, the light on the telephone console began to flash. Kaitlin jumped at the intrusion; she was tired, and calls generally stopped coming by three.

At first, there was no sound when she picked up the receiver and said hello. Then she heard the slow, heavy intake of breath. Oh, great, she thought, an obscene call. Just what she needed.

A moment later, a voice said, "Is this...Moon Lady?" It was a harsh whisper, a raspy sound that might have been made by a man or woman of any age.

"Yes, it is," Kaitlin replied in the most detached, officious tone she could muster.

"I've been thinking about you." The caller dragged out each word, no doubt trying to simulate passion.

She tried not to sound as disgusted as she felt. Didn't kids have anything better to do than make crank calls in the middle of the night? "Is there anything I can do for you?"

"Yes," the voice hissed.

Kaitlin yanked the phone from her ear as if she might contract something infectious from the creep's heavy breathing. Holding it a safe distance from her mouth, she said, "Do you have a special request you'd like me to play?" *Something to do with lunatics, perhaps?*

"Mmm...a request? No...I don't have a request. I only wanted to talk to you. I saw you tonight, Moon Lady...I did...I saw you soaring in from Jupiter. You're always so beautiful, even when you try not to be...but you're too beautiful...it makes me angry. I want you—"

Enough! Kaitlin slammed the receiver down. Sliding her chair as far away from the phone as the U-shaped desk would allow, she turned up the volume of the music in the control room to drown out the thumping of her heart. She wasn't frightened, just revolted by the poisonous sound of that voice. It had been so ugly, so intrusive. She stared at the silent telephone as if willing it not to ring again.

Despite her fatigue and the knot of tension in the pit of her stomach, she finished her show. There were two more calls before five, and she practically attacked the console each time she answered. But one call had been a song request for a nurse's birthday, and the second had been a policeman suggesting law enforcement as a theme for her show. She'd been tempted for a moment to tell the policeman about the heavy breather, but that would have been silly. She was safely locked in the station; a voice, no matter how offensive, could never hurt her. In any event, whoever it was hadn't bothered her again that night.

A PAIR OF TIRED EYES watched as dense clouds obliterated the moon. It was nearly dawn, too late to sleep, but the time could be spent writing. The journal was often more satisfying than rest. Even on the rare occasions sleep came for an entire night, it never brought dreams and without dreams, there was no escape, no relief. Maybe meditation would help. Climbing out of bed, the haggard figure picked up a pen and sat at the desk.

Even though it rained, it was stifling, and lying down made me jumpy. I keep thinking about my plans, how they've been stalled. Everything had been going along so smoothly until Moon Lady arrived. She's all they talk about. She smiles, she flirts, she can do no wrong. Everyone has fallen in love with her, except me. Don't they see she's not real? She is beautiful, but I know what she's really like, deep down. She's just a satellite that doesn't give off any light of her own. I can't let her take away my light. I've worked too hard to get this far. Moon Lady needs to be taught a lesson, and I'm the only one who can teach it to her.

Chapter Three

Kensington Market was colorful, noisy, vibrant, a profusion of sensual delights. Stocky Mediterraneans jostled shoulder to shoulder with long-limbed West Indians for the ripest melons, the juiciest tomatoes and the fresh loaves of crusty Italian bread. There were fishmongers from the Azores and greengrocers from Korea. Long-haired potters in a sixties time warp tended their open-air stalls and tiny shops. The crowded streets resounded with shouts of laughter and the excited din of buyers and sellers haggling over prices. It was a cacophony of languages, a marvelous babel of gestures and dialects, and to Kaitlin it was Toronto at its most exciting. There were places to shop closer to home, but none that rejuvenated her like Kensington Market on a Saturday morning.

Across a bank of lush red strawberries, she saw Lorna filling a basket with ripe tomatoes and shiny green peppers. The woman looked pale and tired, but then Kaitlin realized it was because she wasn't wearing her usual layers of makeup.

"Good morning, Lorna."

She looked up. "Kaitlin! I didn't know you shopped here."

Kaitlin shifted her own bag of fruits and vegetables to the other arm. "Rain or shine, every week. I love this place. Do you live nearby?"

"No, but my fiancé is coming for dinner tonight, and he likes his produce fresh." Lorna stepped back to make room for other shoppers while Kaitlin sidled closer to her.

"You're engaged. How nice!"

Lorna's face filled with color, and for a moment she looked almost pretty. "I am, but . . . well, we haven't exactly set a date. He . . . that is, we don't want to rush into things."

Kaitlin glanced down at the woman's left hand and saw the noncommittal garnet in its simple gold setting. She could picture the kind of man Lorna was in love with, the irresponsible, all-too-common breed who gladly took what was offered with no compunctions, no commitment. Men like that never realized how lucky they had it, while women like Lorna never admitted they were shortchanging themselves. Instinctively, Kaitlin's heart went out to her. At the same moment, she realized it had been a long time since she'd had any old-fashioned girl talk.

"Lorna, have you finished your shopping yet?"

The receptionist eyed her warily. "Not quite. Why?"

"I thought if you had the time we could eat lunch somewhere—my treat. Afterward, I'd like to look for a bedspread and curtains for my bedroom, and I'd love a second opinion." Lorna was regarding her warily, as if she were expecting a hidden catch. How long was it going to take, Kaitlin wondered, to earn the woman's trust?

"I don't know," Lorna said.

"I'd really love your company."

Her shell of resistance cracked. "Guess I could spare the time. I know some factory outlets where you can get drapes and spreads for half price."

"Wonderful," Kaitlin said. "I never pass up a good bargain."

A short while later, they found themselves in a pleasant neighborhood restaurant, munching on crusty rolls and sipping Brio while they waited for their lasagna.

"You're a Sagittarius, aren't you?" Lorna asked.

"Aquarius."

"Hmm, Aquarius." Lorna nodded. "It would have been my second guess, with your ascendant in Aries, I'll bet."

Kaitlin took a sip of her drink. It had been a lot of years since she'd had one of these occult conversations. "I honestly wouldn't know what my ascendant was." Then to be polite, she added, "What's your sign?"

"Try to guess."

Kaitlin held out her hands. "Sorry, I don't know much about astrology..."

"I'm a Scorpio. Scorpios have a sixth sense about people, you know."

"Do they?" Kaitlin murmured. Maybe there wasn't too much hope of their becoming friends, after all. She'd never had much patience with self-proclaimed psychics and their vague, mysterious pronouncements. Still, it might make for an interesting lunch, she realized on further reflection. "What does your sixth sense tell you I might find interesting?"

"Elliot's attracted to you."

Kaitlin sat back in astonishment at the woman's bold remark. One certainly had to give her credit for directness. Mercifully, the lasagna arrived just then, and

Kaitlin made a studious production of adjusting her napkin and sprinkling on the cheese. "Why do you say that?" she finally asked.

"He hasn't been himself since you arrived."

"Oh? That doesn't tell me much, since I don't know what he was like before."

Lorna stabbed at her pasta. "He used to be much too serious."

"*Used to be?* Are you saying he's lightened up since I came? You could've fooled me."

The older woman riveted Kaitlin with an accusing look. "He'd probably lighten up even more if you didn't play with his affections the way you do."

"I don't!" Kaitlin protested.

"Yes, you do. Every time you flirt with Charlie or take Mike's arm—"

"Lorna, come on! Just because I'm friendly does not make me a tease. I don't mean anything by it."

"Maybe not, but I think you should know some people might misunderstand your intentions. Especially Elliot. His biorhythms are at an emotional peak right now."

Kaitlin cast a despairing look at the ceiling. "You study that, too, do you?"

"Faithfully."

"How do you know Elliot's?"

"I know everyone's," Lorna declared smugly. "I handle the personnel files, so I know your birthdays. And I have a good memory for little facts like that."

That struck Kaitlin as a most unprofessional use of company records, but she doubted that she could appeal to Lorna's conscience by mentioning the fact. "Okay," she said with a sigh. "What does that mean—his emotional peaks or whatever?"

"It means he should act on the impulses of his heart. It's a difficult thing for a man like Elliot to do."

"Oh, I see," said Kaitlin, not really seeing at all.

"Don't you want to know about yours?" Without waiting for a reply, Lorna plunged on. "Your emotions are at a low, but your intellect is high. You have to think things through. Don't follow your instincts; they might deceive you."

Kaitlin motioned for the waiter to bring more coffee. Thank goodness they hadn't picked a restaurant that handed out fortune cookies.

WHEN KAITLIN SHOWED UP at the station for Monday morning's production meeting, there were a dozen long-stemmed ivory roses on Lorna's desk. "Oh, how beautiful!" she exclaimed, going closer to breathe in their heady scent. "Are they from your fiancé?"

Lorna looked up, the expression of wary reserve planted fixedly on her face again. Kaitlin was surprised; they'd got on so well during their shopping expedition the other day. "They're for you," the receptionist said. "Here's the card."

Kaitlin took it out of the envelope and read it aloud. "To Moon Lady." She looked at the back of the card. "That's all it says. It doesn't say who they're from."

"Don't tell me you have no idea," Lorna said.

"I don't. I've been sent cards and letters by fans before, but nothing this expensive."

The receptionist sighed in overt exasperation. "It's not from one of your fans."

Kaitlin raised her brows. "It's not?"

"The flowers are from Elliot."

"No-o-o," protested Kaitlin. "Elliot wouldn't do something impulsive like this. Besides, he already gave me a—'' Hastily, she closed her mouth, but it was too late.

"Aha! He already gave you something, didn't he? I knew it; it's his emotional peak. What did he give you?"

"Lorna! It's personal!" Then, realizing how misleading the statement sounded, she tried again. "It's just a picture of a lighthouse at night. Nothing fancy, but it's very nice, and…it sort of…relates to my job."

Lorna's romantic streak was beginning to conquer her sullenness; her eyes positively glistened. "He's showering you with gifts, trying to win you over! Take it from me."

Kaitlin waved her hand dismissively and headed in the direction of Mike's office. "If he were, I'd be embarrassed to death. Anyway I've got to go; the meeting's probably started already. Would you look after the roses for me?"

"Of course." Lorna was touching one of the blooms as if she wished it were hers.

Kaitlin could hear the argument between Elliot and the Duke even before she entered Mike's office for the meeting. Her mind was still on the flowers, though she was certain Elliot hadn't sent them.

"I'd sooner sell pencils outside the Eaton Centre!" the Duke declared, his arms folded stubbornly across his silk-clad chest.

"I'm not asking you to play an entire album of his," Elliot explained with only the faintest hint of impatience, "but he is the first Spanish singer to successfully cross into the North American market. Don't you think it might be nice to give your listeners a cut or two occasionally? From what I understand, women are crazy about him."

"Oh, yeah?" the Duke said. "Well, they're crazy about me, too, and maybe I just don't need the competition!" He turned to Kaitlin. "What do you think of the guy?"

She barely managed to suppress a grin. "I can't argue with a smile and a tan like his. Go on, Duke, play his music. It won't hurt." From the corner of her eye, she saw Elliot relax and felt a flutter of pleasure knowing he approved of the way she handled the Duke. "Good morning, everyone," she said, glancing around the room and looking at Elliot last.

His clothes were freshly ironed; he must have slept at home last night, she decided. His cotton shirt was light blue, his slacks dark, and his burgundy necktie with its single diamond pattern was pulled loose from his neck, as if in frustration at the Duke's recalcitrance. Formal as always, she thought as she sat down in the only available seat. A love seat shared with Elliot.

"That's a terrific dress you've got on," Charlie said, beaming. "It's a nice change from your jeans."

"Thank you, Charlie. It's a real scorcher out there today. I couldn't stand the thought of being swaddled in denim." She could feel Elliot's eyes taking in her bright yellow T-shirt dress with the cutaway shoulders and the shiny blue belt. Of course, since Charlie had mentioned the dress, everyone was looking at her, but it was only Elliot's eyes that she could feel. She even found herself wondering if he approved of the way the dress hugged her breasts and followed the curve of her hips. Not that it mattered, and *not* that she'd worn the dress to make an impression! It was summertime, and all the women dressed this way.

The meeting dragged on for two hours and by the time it was over, tempers were severely frayed. Kaitlin was sure that if it weren't for Elliot's calm, unruffled manner, the station would fall apart. Mike was a nice guy, but hopeless as a manager.

After the meeting, Elliot caught up with Kaitlin in the hall. "I know you want to get home to sleep," he said, "but I'd like to see you in my office for a minute."

She looked up at him, at warm caring eyes that were ringed with fatigue. "Sure," she replied softly, all too aware that she was pleased at the thought of being alone with him. A silly reaction, admittedly, since he could very well be calling her in for a reprimand. Program directors were known to do that on occasion.

"Nice roses," was the first thing he said when they were alone in his office.

"You saw them?" she asked, wondering whether he was fishing for thanks. Not that Lorna's unflagging certainty had any basis in the truth. Elliot couldn't possibly have sent them; he wasn't the type.

"I was at the front desk when they were delivered." He did seem to be leading up to something, however.

Kaitlin turned to browse the bookshelves. "They are lovely," she agreed. "I've never seen roses quite that color before." Idly, she scanned the titles: books by Byron, Dickens, Emerson...heady stuff. Okay, Elliot, the ball's in your court now.

He didn't disappoint her. "They must be from a special friend." The silence that followed felt like an unasked question.

Would it bother you if they were, she wanted to ask. Her back was toward him, but she could feel him studying her, willing her to give him the answers he wanted to hear. Why couldn't he come right out and ask her? If he was attracted to her, why didn't he just admit it? Didn't he realize he'd be a worthy rival to any man?

She turned to face him. "Actually, I don't know who they're from," she admitted. Something in his eyes told her the answer came as a relief. Then he frowned.

"Doesn't that worry you?" he asked.

"No. Should it?"

Elliot rubbed his chin. "I don't know. It strikes me as odd for someone to send something so expensive without acknowledging themselves. A normal person wouldn't do that."

For some reason, his doubt bothered her, and she spoke without thinking. "There's nothing threatening about an anonymous gift, believe me. I think it's romantic. Heaven knows, people don't often give gifts these days without expecting something in return—" As she realized her inadvertent insinuation, her hands flew to her mouth. "I'm sorry, I didn't mean—"

A dark emotion passed across his face. "Forget it. You're probably right, anyway. I must have bought that ridiculous picture to ensure your continued goodwill, and who knows, maybe I did want more in return."

He moved toward her, and before she realized what was happening, she was in his arms. There might have been an instant when she could have resisted and pulled away, but it was gone now. And with her head tipped back, Elliot claiming her mouth with his, she knew why hesitation had never even crossed her mind. This was the culmination of something that had been taunting her for days, the rekindling of the brief spark that had flickered between them once before, an ember now fanned to a flame as their mouths parted and they drank in each other's passion.

They were greedy kisses, unbridled and full, seized by two people who had fought shy of each other for too many weeks and had ignored too long the emotions that simmered beneath the surface of civility. Locked in his embrace, she could feel his hard broad chest through the cotton coolness of his shirt; as her arms rested on his shoulders and her fingers curved around his neck, she felt his strength, his implacable masculinity. His hands moved down her back, sliding over the smooth knit of her dress. His fingers touched the bare flesh at her shoulders, sending white-hot currents along her spine to reach deep and intimate places within her. He spoke her name against her mouth in a husky, ragged voice.

"Yes, Elliot," she whispered back, instinctively accepting the feelings between them.

Gripping her shoulders with steely fingers, he pushed himself away. His eyes were like cobalt fire as he stared down at her, his face flushed tawny with desire. She could feel the responding crimson on her own face and realized how ill-timed this interlude had been. Here they were, in the fluorescent harshness of his office on a weekday morning, a closed door the only barrier between them and their colleagues. Elliot, no matter how attractive, no matter how compelling, was her superior. He was important...no, essential to her career success; it would be professional suicide to risk everything for the sake of a few hurried moments of passion.

"I didn't intend to get carried away like that," he said, running his fingers through his dark hair and looking almost as unsure as she felt.

Kaitlin made a fumbling attempt to straighten her clothes. Her dress had worked its way up the length of her thighs; her hair was in disarray. "It's all right," she said. "I shouldn't have..." The words fell away, meaningless. She shouldn't have what? Responded? How the hell could she have done anything else?

A smile played at his lips, lips that were still moist from kissing her. "Believe it or not, I asked you here to talk about your show. It must have been your yellow dress that distracted me."

Kaitlin felt a rush of pleasure at his quiet compliment. "I'll try to remember not to wear it around you anymore."

"Don't do that," he said, and caught her fingers lightly in his. "I'd go crazy if I thought I couldn't see you in it again. Kaitlin, you'll have to excuse me if it seems I worry too much. You're new to this city; you haven't had time to develop close friendships. Meanwhile, your professional reputation is growing by leaps and bounds. For most people, things happen the other way around. The way they've happened to you is not a natural progression of events. It means you're more vulnerable, so please be careful."

She closed her eyes briefly and lingered on the soothing sensation of their fingers touching. He made her feel so safe, so special. "Thank you for worrying, but there's no need to. I've looked after myself for a long time, and I can handle the adulation, believe me. I've worked eight years to get it, and it certainly doesn't frighten me."

This seemed to put him at ease, and he nodded. "Just remember, you have a friend here. Don't ever be afraid to come to me."

Kaitlin smiled from the bottom of her heart. "I'll remember," she said.

LATE THAT AFTERNOON, after she'd had a long sleep, Kaitlin went out to run errands. Nearly everything she needed was within a few blocks of her apartment. She dropped off her silk suit at the cleaners, bought some light reading material at the corner variety store and spent twenty minutes waiting in line at the bank to cash her paycheck.

It was still too early to get ready for work, and somehow the thought of spending the entire evening alone before going to the station—where she'd again be alone—seemed particularly unappealing. It was a people-watching kind of day, so she picked an appropriate sidewalk café on Yorkville Avenue.

The white umbrella tables were roped off from the sidewalk, and most were filled with well-heeled shoppers and business types who had finished their workdays and were unwinding with drinks. Kaitlin felt a momentary twinge of envy for people who went home to sleep at night, then she brushed self-pity from her mind as the maître d' took up a menu and led her to a table.

"I'm not very hungry," she told him when he handed her the menu. "Just an iced tea would be fine."

Haughtily he bowed, pressing his lily-white hand to his shirtfront. "Perhaps you would care to peruse our fine dessert selection while I summon the waiter to take your order? Madame might find she'll change her mind."

"Well, pardon me," she mumbled, but he'd already waddled off. If there was anything she couldn't abide, it was snooty restaurants with inflexible pecking orders. Why couldn't he have relayed her order? All she wanted was a damned glass of tea, for Pete's sake. And it wasn't as though she'd intended to hog the table from more lucrative business, either!

Still simmering, she yanked open the menu, if only to determine for herself whether the dessert selection was as fine as that glorified busboy had claimed. Her eyes skimmed the pages then moved up to the daily special clipped to the top of the page. As she read it, her mouth dropped open and she gasped aloud.

The card read simply, "Did you enjoy the roses, Moon Lady?"

Her head shot up and she looked around, but for whom or what she had no idea. No one, as far as she could tell, was paying her any attention, and there were no suspicious passersby.

"Are you feeling all right, miss?" a young voice asked.

Kaitlin turned in the direction of the voice. It was the waiter who'd been sent to take her order, and he was looking at her as if he feared she might be experiencing heart failure at his table.

"I—I'm all right," she stammered.

"Are you ready to order?" he asked hopefully.

She pushed the menu under his nose and pointed. "Do you recognize this?"

He read the card and shrugged. "No, ma'am, but it's supposed to say that our special is Dijon chicken with potatoes Lyonnaise for $11.95 and includes soup or salad, hot rolls and a beverage." He recited this too quickly for Kaitlin to stop him.

The waiter couldn't possibly be hiding anything; he was too fresh-faced. And anyway, it wasn't he who'd given her the menu. It was that little sourpuss of a maître d'.

She thought a moment, then asked the waiter, "Do you, by any chance, know who I am?" It wasn't an entirely inane question, even though Moon Lady, both in pictures and in person, was always veiled, her makeup infinitely more dramatic than Kaitlin's light blush and mascara.

The waiter was looking intensely uncomfortable. "No, ma'am."

"Have you ever heard of Moon Lady?"

His eyes lit up with pleasure. "Oh, yeah, I listen to her all the time; she's all right." Then he knotted his brows. "Come to think of it, you kinda sound like her—"

Kaitlin waved her hand. "I'm not Moon Lady, but people sometimes mistake me for her. You know, I don't think I'm as hungry as I thought." She tore the card off the menu, dropped some change on the table and got up. "Thank you for your trouble."

The maître d' was, at the moment, gushing over newly arrived patrons who positively dropped with affluence. Kaitlin waited until they were seated, then she cornered him. "What do you know about this?" she demanded.

Deprecatingly, he lowered his eyes to the paper in her hand. "I have no idea what madame is referring to. What *is* a Moon Lady?"

"Never mind. I want to know who put it in my menu."

He looked at her as if she were quite mad. "I beg your pardon?"

"It was in my menu instead of the daily special."

"Oh, dear, how unfortunate. Well, the chef's special is Dijon chi—"

"I don't want to know the special!" Kaitlin's voice was just a notch below a shriek. "I want to know where this came from. Did someone pay you to give it to me?"

"Most assuredly not, madame!"

Kaitlin threw up her hands in exasperation. "Then how did it get here? Did you see anybody fiddling with the menus when I came?"

Heaven forbid anyone should dare to fiddle with his menus, the maître d's expression seemed to say. "I saw no one. However, as you can see, we are extremely busy. It is possible I might have been escorting a patron to his table when the, er, offense was committed. Perhaps you would like to take it up with the manager?"

"No, there's no point." She looked around again for some likely culprit. It made her feel disturbingly vulnerable to know that a person with such a bizarre sense of the dramatic would recognize her on the street as Moon Lady. "Thank you, anyway."

She slipped the card into her purse and quickly left the café, carefully scanning the streets as she hurried home. In less than fifteen minutes, she reached the safety of her apartment building. No one had tried to follow her.

THE CONSOLE in the control room flashed shortly after midnight, and Kaitlin was expecting the call to be an answer to her trivia question on Australian rock groups. Instead, she heard the same harsh, rasping whisper of a few nights earlier.

"Moon Lady, I thought it was time we talked again."

She gripped the receiver and reminded herself that she was safe. "Who are you? What do you want?"

"I thought you'd know by now. I want to feel that yellow dress beneath my fingers. I've touched your skin already, but I want more."

Whoever it was had seen her today, before she'd changed into her working attire. Horrified, her flesh crawling, she had to struggle to stifle a scream. If only she could force herself to listen, perhaps she could recognize something in the caller's voice. Besides, if she hung up, the person would probably call back, and somehow that thought was even more terrifying than staying on the line.

"You don't frighten me," she said, nearly convinced the caller would hear her hammering heart and know she was lying. "You're sick and you're disgusting, but you don't frighten me." Then, as an afterthought, "We have a tap on this phone, by the way."

The caller made a sound of derision. "Now, now, we both know better. Let's not change the subject—"

"I'm going to hang up." She couldn't take it any longer. "But first, answer one question. Did you send flowers?"

There was a pause, a sharp intake of breath and then a cackle of laughter. "Why, my sweet . . . what could I possibly know about a dozen, long-stemmed ivory roses?"

Chapter Four

She felt as though a pair of icy hands were slowly squeezing her throat, a pair of unseen eyes taking their fill of her even though she knew, logically, that she was alone. "What do you want from me?" she managed to gasp.

"I want you to leave."

"Leave what? This is my job; my home is here."

"No!" the voice protested, though still in a whisper, an awful shrieking whisper. "There's no room for you in this city. Go somewhere else to find your fame and fortune."

To allow herself to become frightened would be playing right into the caller's hands. She couldn't let it get to her. "What have I ever done to you?" she asked in a deceptively calm voice.

"You already know what you've done, Moon Lady. You've become too big, too self-important for the rest of us."

The rest of us? Kaitlin strained to catch some nuance of familiarity in the voice. "Who are you?"

The question seemed to strike the caller as highly amusing. "Who am I? I'm everyone, everywhere—I'm anyone you want me to be. Look around at those closest to you. Don't listen to their words, but to how they say them, and you'll soon discover that not everyone loves Moon Lady, my dear. In fact, some of us loathe the very sound of your voice.'' Before she could reply, the caller had hung up, and only the dial tone buzzed in her ear.

The rest of the night was a disaster. She cued up the wrong commercials and forgot what she was going to say. She announced a song by Gino Vanelli and played Liza Minelli instead. She jumped at every noise and quailed at every phone call. Though the whisperer didn't bother her again, the damage had been done.

AT HOME, Kaitlin tried to make herself relax. She orchestrated a regal breakfast—or whatever one called the first meal after a night's work—of bacon, eggs, toast and fruit, but all she could manage to eat was a few nibbles of bacon. She wrapped up the fruit for later and tossed out the cold eggs and toast, with silent apologies to her mother for wasting good food.

It was unthinkable to let this situation go on. No sniveling, grudge-bearing coward had the right to turn her new life upside down like this, no right at all. It was just a matter of putting herself in control again.

Having abandoned the notion of food, Kaitlin filled the bathtub with hot water and added a generous dollop of the most expensive bath oil she owned. Then she climbed in, stayed all of two minutes and climbed back out again. It was no use. Lolling in warm water was not conducive to cold, calculating thought, and she simply could not go to sleep until she'd formulated some plan for routing out this menace.

She dressed in a short satin kimono and padded to the living room for her purse. She hadn't looked at the card since she'd left the restaurant the day before, but here in her apartment with the dazzling morning sun bouncing off the white walls, she felt quite safe.

The note was typewritten on a plain three-by-five-inch card and, as far as Kaitlin could tell, there was nothing unusual about it. The type was standard manual pica, a relic from someone's high school essay days. If there had been a crooked letter or a chopped-off capital . . . Oh, sure, she chided herself, it would be an elementary matter of checking the card against millions of typewriters in the city to discover whose machine bore the telltale flaw. Nancy Drew might have been able to pull it off, but this was a far cry from fictional sleuthing.

"Did you enjoy the roses, Moon Lady?"

They were harmless enough words, with nothing overtly threatening, nothing inherently evil in their meaning. But that did not prevent the shiver of fear from crawling along her spine. Someone, the caller, had been watching her, had been close enough to slip a note to her, unseen. She'd been part of a crowd, but what if she'd been alone on some deserted side street? What if he'd had a gun, or—

No, this was stupid! She was doing it to herself now, whipping up images of danger where none existed. Whoever it was didn't even have the guts to face her, and she was not about to be intimidated by fear tactics. These kinds of things happened to people in the public eye all the time. It was a simple case of jealousy, of warped adulation. If she stayed cool and refused to let it bother her, the thrill would eventually wear off and the creep would find some new idol to torment. Unless . . .

Kaitlin shoved the card back into her purse and tried, with limited success, to keep herself from completing the thought. She was going to say, unless it really was someone she worked with. After all, she hardly knew them; she knew nothing about their backgrounds, their ambitions. What if one of them actually saw her as a threat? How far would that person be willing to go to eliminate perceived competition?

Despite her good intentions to think this through, her mind was becoming foggy from lack of sleep. She decided that grapefruit juice was what she needed to clear her head. She got up and went into the kitchen. As she poured herself some juice, she forced herself to go over everything she'd said or done to her co-workers, trying to pinpoint a time when she might have offended someone. The results of her survey were less than conclusive.

With Charlie Carr, at least, there had been no problems. He'd been her first contact with CSKY; he'd heard her early-evening information show in Sandusky and had come around to offer her a position with the station. At the time she'd been somewhat put off by his checkered pants and matching sports coat, but she'd got on well with him and respected CSKY's reputation. If the ratings of Moon Lady's show were any indication, she hadn't let Charlie down.

Mike, at times, was a bit overwhelming and there were a few too many business dinners for her liking, but she hoped the novelty of having the sponsors meet her would soon wear off. And while she suspected that Mike relished the idea of an attractive woman at his side, Kaitlin preferred to view the matter philosophically. It saved her a fortune in groceries, and she was becoming familiar with Toronto's best restaurants. There were worse perquisites in the world.

The only time she and the station owner had ever had words was when he'd called her in and said she wasn't sexy enough on the air. Come on to them a little more, he had said; make the listener feel you're whispering words just for him. When Kaitlin reminded him that a good many of her listeners were women, he brushed it off, insisting that females would appreciate advice on the dying art of seduction. That had been the wrong thing to say. Kaitlin declared most emphatically that she had not been hired as a call girl or a spy and had no more expertise in seduction than any other modern professional woman. If he had any objections to her format, he could discuss it with Elliot. At the mere mention of her program director's name, Mike had backed off and ever since made a point of praising her with irritating frequency.

Then there was the Duke. Basically, she liked him. The fellow was outrageously witty and a consummate master of flamboyance. She wished they could get along better, but the unvarnished truth was that he resented her success, and it showed. She could see his upper lip curl, his eyes flash during production meetings when Mike lavished needless praise on her, ignoring the announcer who, for all intents and purposes, had put CSKY FM on the map. For years, the Duke had been the city's reigning disk jockey and the supremacy of his realm had never been threatened—until now.

Perhaps if she'd gone out with him that time, she might have convinced him his resentment was groundless. She had a long way to go before she could ever pose a threat to the Duke's genius. But after a moment's reflection, she dismissed the idea. When one reached the ripe old age of twenty-seven, one learned to avoid sympathy dates. Experience had taught her that they invariably led to hours of wasted time, as well as unpleasant scenes and wounded egos when the entanglement was ended. A simple rejection was both easier and more honest, she'd found.

The only other people she had regular contact with were Lorna and Elliot. There was certainly no doubt that the receptionist hauled around a very large chip, and though it had bothered Kaitlin at the beginning, she was caring less and less. If the woman wanted to be a sourpuss, it was her affair; besides, it got tiresome bending over backward to be nice to someone without getting anything in return. As for Kaitlin's being a threat to Lorna, that was ridiculous. After umpteen years at CSKY, she was as firmly entrenched as the foundation of the building itself.

That left only Elliot, her puzzling, quiet-spoken and, oh, so perceptive program director. He had warned her something like this might happen, but that didn't mean he was the... No, absolutely not. If Elliot Jacobs were the last person on earth, she would never suspect him of terrorizing her. Never!

THE NEXT DAY, Kaitlin decided it was time she told Elliot exactly what had been going on. She went to his office and found him on the phone, working out the details of a rock concert.

"I don't care what your usual ticket prices are for the pavilion!" he said, scowling at the receiver. "Kids can't afford to pay that much. You'll double your take if you cut the price by ten dollars. I guarantee it...no, I won't sign in blood, but I have a couple of Blue Jay tickets that say I'm right...course they're good seats...okay,

Ted, sounds good. I'll get back to you." He put down the phone with a sigh.

"Promoter?" Kaitlin asked.

"Bloodsucker's more like it." The intercom rang again, and Elliot pounced on the receiver. "Who is it this time, Lorna? Take a message and hold my calls, would you? Kaitlin's here with me now, and I don't want to hold her up any longer than I have to."

"Thanks a lot," she said when he'd put down the phone once again. "Am I that hard on the eyes in the light of day?"

An endearingly boyish grin crossed his face. "Sorry, I didn't mean it that way. If it weren't for those purple half-moons under your eyes, you'd look great. What's wrong?"

And so she told him about the calls and the roses and the veiled threats. He didn't interrupt but sat back and listened, fingers steepled, his expression thoughtful. Only when Kaitlin concluded her diatribe with "I'm pretty sure there *is* someone in the station who has a grudge against me" did his expression change.

"That's an idiotic accusation," he said in curt dismissal.

"What's so idiotic about it?" she tossed back.

"I've worked with these people for years, and I'd trust any one of them with my life."

Kaitlin crossed her legs with a huff. "Maybe you would, but I wouldn't trust half of them with my house key at the moment."

"Of course not—you've already convicted us in your mind."

"That's not quite true—" she began.

"Isn't it?" His eyes were blazing with accusation.

She should never have brought up her suspicions; she knew that now. "It's just a feeling I have," she tried to tell him.

"Feeling, hell! Why don't you come right out and start naming names? We can probably come up with plenty of motives."

Nice going, Kaitlin, upsetting the one person who might have been sympathetic. "Look, I'm sorry, I—"

"Don't apologize!" He stood up and leaned across the desk. "Maybe one of us really does have something buried deep in our past. One of us might have been locked in a closet until the age of twelve. They say such things can warp a person's life forever—"

Kaitlin covered her ears. "Stop it, just stop it, would you?"

Elliot fell silent and waited until Kaitlin lowered her hands. "I'm sorry, Kaitlin." The bitterness was gone from his voice, and his tone had become gentler. "But you have to be aware of how easy it is to lose perspective when things like this happen. The first thing a person wants to do is lash out at everyone around him when something goes wrong. You have to look at things rationally and not let your imagination run away with you." He came around the desk to her chair, his fingers reaching out to play with a curl near her ear. "No one wants to hurt you. You have to trust us, Kaitlin. At the very least, you have to trust me."

She looked into the deep dark refuge of his eyes and felt her panic recede. "What can I do, Elliot?"

He stood there for a moment, the warmth of his gaze like a tonic. She could almost feel the subtle undercurrents of his desire, perhaps because it so closely mirrored her own. If only he'd take her in his arms, she'd feel better. If only he'd kiss her, she might even forget why she'd come. But he didn't do either. He moved away and sat down across from her.

"I don't know if there's anything you can do," he said. "You've gotten two phone calls and flowers. The police aren't going to consider the case life-threatening, and the phone company doesn't have any iron-clad preventive measures, either. We can't very well take out an unlisted number for the station, and changing the number won't help. Let's face it, if this person wants to call again, we can't stop him."

Deep down, Kaitlin knew he was right, but it wasn't what she so desperately needed to hear right now. "You don't sound too encouraging," she said.

Elliot seemed to have abandoned her for thoughts of his own. Suddenly he slammed his fist on the armrest. "Dammit, I knew something like this was going to happen, but nobody would listen." He looked angrily at Kaitlin. "Maybe if you hadn't been so blasted quick to go along with every harebrained scheme of Mike's, you wouldn't be in this mess."

"Wait a minute. Don't go giving me the old line about asking for it!"

"Weren't you?"

"No! I did not ask for it!" She leaped to her feet, aware that her neck felt stiff and sore. "A fat lot of help you turned out to be! I come all the way down here because you told me I could come to you with my problems. And what happens? You tell me there's nothing you can do, and it's all my fault!"

She swept past him so quickly that when Elliot caught her arm, she spun around. "Let go of me!" she cried.

"Not until we've finished this discussion." His fingers did not loosen their grip and although the pressure was almost painful, there was something reassuring about their strength.

"What discussion?" she asked in guarded tones. "Discussion implies the exchange of ideas, and as far as I can gather, you haven't come up with any."

He drew in a sharp breath. "What the hell do you want from me? Armed guards and twenty-four hour surveillance? I don't own this station."

She locked her eyes with his steely gaze. "Maybe that's exactly what I need," she said, knowing how childish she sounded, but caring little at this point. "I'll go and see Mike about it."

"Don't waste your breath. Why don't you go in and tell Mike you're finished with Moon Lady instead? Tell him you'll only do a regular night show from now on."

A tiny inner voice was hinting that Elliot's suggestion made sense, but she knew that it wasn't his suggestion she'd be acting on. Dropping her Moon Lady image would be nothing but a reaction to the threats of a whispering psychopath. What if another crazy took a sudden dislike to her new show? Would she have to jump again? When would it all end?

"I'm not going to change the show," she insisted quietly.

His fingers fell away from her arm, and she felt like a boat cast suddenly adrift. But that was to be expected. When it came to Elliot, Moon Lady had always been on her own. Kaitlin was prepared to abide by the consequences of her decision even if it drove a permanent wedge between her and a man who was beginning to matter very much. She turned and walked to the door without another word. Elliot didn't try to stop her.

"You're a fool," he muttered to her back.

"I can live with it," she said and left the office.

Lorna was buried deep in a book on astral projections and didn't look up when Kaitlin came into the reception area. "Have you had coffee yet this morning?" she asked the older woman.

Lorna continued to read. "No."

"Are you going to?"

"Hadn't thought about it."

Stifling a sigh, Kaitlin pressed on. "Do you think you could spare a few minutes? I need to talk to you."

Finally Lorna looked up, and after a moment, she said, "Yes, I have a few minutes to spare. Hold on, and I'll call my relief."

They went to the bakery next door. Kaitlin bought the coffee and brought it to the small table where Lorna was sitting.

"Tell me," Kaitlin said, "have you ever heard my show?"

"A few times, but I have trouble staying up past midnight. My fiancé tunes in all the time."

"What do you think of Moon Lady...honestly?"

Lorna sipped her coffee and pondered the question in her usual expressionless way. "She's okay. I like her, or rather, your sense of humor and the music you pick out. There's nothing like the oldies, but...well, I don't know how to say this exactly."

"Go ahead. I asked for an honest opinion."

"All right. I think Moon Lady's appeal is going to wear thin after a while. People are going to get tired of your extraterrestrial fantasies, and you'll fizzle out like an old star."

"Oh." She had asked for it. There was no reason to feel that she'd just been dealt a brutally low blow. "What do you think will happen when I... wear thin? What will Mike do?"

Lorna didn't even have to pause. "That's easy. He'll replace you."

IT SEEMED LIKE AGES since Kaitlin had been on a real date. She'd had no shortage of them in Ohio, but since she'd come to Toronto, her whole life had revolved around her career. The situation hadn't bothered her until one particular Saturday. She'd had a blissfully quiet week at work and the following night she'd be hosting the premiere at the Royal Alex, but that night she wanted to do something special on her own. She could not abide the idea of staying home or sleeping or reading or watching television.

For one thing, it had finally dawned on her after all this time that the apartment still didn't feel like home. It was undeniably a charming place. The breakfast nook was separated from the large living-dining room by a screen of white lattice. All her favorite pictures hung in brass frames, the simplicity of the watercolor florals exquisite against white walls. There were lace doilies she'd crocheted herself and bouquets of baby's breath and bluebells she had dried and arranged in delicate ceramic vases. All the elements of a home were there, but she still did not feel welcome when she walked in the door. Right now, she craved the feeling of being welcome. Trouble was, she had no takers.

Rummaging through a kitchen drawer in search of a can opener for her vegetable cocktail, Kaitlin came across Larry O'Neill's card. The taxi driver who'd issued a standing invitation to take her out. Now there was an idea.

She called the dispatcher first, who told her Larry wasn't working that day. Then she tried his home number and got him on the third ring.

"Hi, Larry? It's Kaitlin Harper."

"Kaitlin! How ya doin'?"

"Not too bad, thanks." For a few minutes, they exchanged the usual pleasantries. "Are you busy tonight?" Kaitlin finally asked.

"Not especially. I'm studying lines, but I'm starting to see double. Don't tell me you actually have an evening with nothing planned."

"I do."

"Unbelievable. What do you want to do?"

"Anything. You decide...oh, except for hanging around my apartment. I'd go bananas."

"Okay, then leave it to me. Pick you up at six?"

"Six is fine. Bye, Larry."

The evening was cool and pleasant as Larry and Kaitlin strolled along the streets of Chinatown. "Do you like Szechuan?" he asked after he'd examined the menu hanging in every restaurant window for three city blocks. If he didn't make a decision soon, Kaitlin was sure she'd pass out from starvation.

"Szechuan's the hot stuff, right?" she said. "I once bit into one of those little peppers and thought I'd die. I don't think I have the nerve to repeat the experience."

"Then we'll go for Hunan. It's spicy, but not lethal." Larry led her to a small informal restaurant with an upstairs dining room holding no more than a dozen tables. They were the only non-Orientals in the place.

"Would you like me to order for us?"

Kaitlin was busy looking around at the tasteful jade-green and black decor. It was a distinct change from red dragons and lanterns.

"Kaitlin?"

She turned to him. "Yes?"

"I asked if you wanted me to order for us."

"Oh, I'm sorry, I didn't hear you; I was too busy gawking. Yes, please, I trust your judgment implicitly."

Dinner was delicious, Larry's company pleasant. Kaitlin felt her sense of loneliness vanish as she listened to his endless store of anecdotes and local tales.

"I hope you won't mind if I quote you on my show now and again," said Kaitlin.

Larry carefully poured Chinese tea for each of them. "Quote me? On what?"

"Your stories; they're marvelous, especially the one about the shipwreck near Centre Island. It's just the kind of incident that would entrance Moon Lady."

"Then go ahead and use it. None of it's a secret."

"Too bad I don't host a talk show so you could come on the air and relate them yourself. You have a nice way of expressing yourself."

He laughed. "Tell that to my agent; I'm expecting him to put in an unlisted number any day."

Kaitlin reached out and patted Larry's hand. "Roles are still scarce, are they?"

"So-so. I got the part at the dinner theater, but ticket sales were so bad they closed us after three performances. Now they're doing a tacky Vegas-style revue, and it's sold out every night."

The waiter brought the check on a tray and placed it in front of Larry. When her friend picked it up, Kaitlin nimbly lifted it from his fingers. "I'll get that. After all, I asked you out."

Larry grinned and held up his hands. "I won't argue. We starving actors learn to swallow our pride."

They were walking along Spadina Avenue to Larry's taxi when Kaitlin brought up the subject of the phone calls. It would feel good, just once, to talk to someone sympathetic, and Larry didn't disappoint her.

"Hey, that's rough," he said when she'd finished her story. "Wouldn't something like that start affecting your work after a while?"

"Probably, if it kept up, but nothing happened last week, so I'm starting to put it out of my mind."

"Do you think the caller has lost interest?"

"Either that or they're waiting to find out if I'm going to leave town like they wanted me to."

"Are you?"

Kaitlin glanced at him in surprise. "Going to leave? Of course not. I love my job, and I love Toronto. No heavy breather is going to scare me away."

"Glad to hear it," Larry said. "I always knew you were made of tough stuff. But doesn't it bother you to think the caller might be someone you work with?"

She nodded. "It does, but there's not much I can do. If I went around and accused everyone, I'd only be hurting myself."

"You have a point." He was silent for a moment. "From what you've told me about your colleagues, it's pretty obvious who's got it in for you."

Kaitlin stopped in her tracks. "Who?"

"That fellow you've got the hots for—what's his name—Elliot."

"Impossible!" she protested immediately. "He may be quiet and hard to read, but he'd never hurt anyone."

"How can you be so sure? A lot of times guys who have trouble expressing their feelings are harboring some deep-seated problems."

"Uh-huh," she teased. "Armchair psychologist, are we?"

Larry grinned in his usual affable way. "Between fares, you might say."

THE TELEPHONE WAS RINGING in Kaitlin's apartment when she opened the door shortly after midnight. She dashed across the dark living room, stubbed her toe against the coffee table and bit back an oath as she grabbed the receiver. Too late. The caller had hung up.

"Damn!" She flopped onto the sofa and rubbed her foot. Perhaps it had been someone from her family in Ohio, but if so and if it was important, they'd call back. Meanwhile, she was going to bed.

Sliding beneath the covers, she thought about her evening with Larry. It would probably classify as one of those rare perfect dates idealized in vintage Emily Post: nice dinner, drinks and pleasant conversation with a perfect gentleman, topped off by a chaste good-night kiss at the door. Too bad the whole experience couldn't come close to one single misbegotten kiss from Elliot Jacobs.

ELLIOT SLAMMED the receiver down after he'd let it ring twelve times. If Kaitlin was still out at this hour, he'd be the last person she'd want to hear from when she came in to fix a nightcap for her date. She might get the mistaken impression that he'd been worried about her, when all he wanted to do was apologize. After she'd stormed out of his office, he'd gone looking for her only to find that she was having coffee with Lorna. Then he'd had to take an important call and temporarily put the matter out of his mind. Now, as he thought about it, it struck him that the alliance between Kaitlin and Lorna was an odd one. Lorna had never been known to trust a woman within a hundred miles of CSKY. What could she possibly want from Kaitlin, he wondered.

Elliot tapped the end of a pen against the desk in his study. Where was she tonight? Kaitlin never spoke about a social life or having friends outside the station, although that in itself wasn't so difficult for him to understand. The deliberate pursuit of the opposite sex was something he rarely wasted his time on these days. Despite the undeniable drawbacks of celibacy, there were always too many other things that were higher on his list of priorities than women. Unfortunately, if he weren't careful, Kaitlin would move up the list very quickly, and he was going to have to work like the devil to make sure she didn't.

IT WAS TIME to reconnect with the blank pages, fill them with thoughts and ideas and creative conclusions about life. Someday this journal could become famous, like Virginia Woolf's diaries. Woolf had been slightly mad herself, but brilliant, and when one is brilliant, one can be forgiven many aberrations. And so, inspired, the pen was once again put to paper.

My plan is proceeding according to schedule. Moon Lady isn't feeling safe orbiting in her heaven, so it won't be much longer now. If I work hard, if I don't become discouraged or give up, I'll be exactly where I want to be . . . and Moon Lady will be gone.

Chapter Five

She reminded him of a mermaid. Her floor-length gown was covered with emerald-green sequins and clung to the sensual curves of her body, the neckline plunging provocatively. Her sun-streaked hair was pulled to the top of her head in a loose knot, the trademark veil interwoven with green satin ribbon. As the hostess of *Deceptions*, Moon Lady was magnificent. When she had walked onto the stage before the performance, the audience had roared its approval. Then they applauded as she praised Toronto for its cultural excellence and the Royal Alexandra for its elegance and old-world charm. She introduced the play with wit and aplomb and an artist's impeccable sense of timing. By the time the curtain rose on act one, the audience was breathless with anticipation.

Elliot waited for her in the wings, catching his breath at the sight of her approach. She lifted the veil to reveal green eyes as brilliant as her dress. If she was beautiful as Kaitlin, she was positively bewitching as Moon Lady. He had to keep reminding himself that she really was one and the same person, that it was entirely within the bounds of reason to be attracted—perhaps even obsessed—with both Kaitlin and her phantasmic counterimage.

When she reached him, he took her gently by the shoulders and kissed her. "You were wonderful out there."

"Was I?" She smiled with the guilelessness of a child needing reassurance. "I was absolutely terrified. There isn't a single empty seat in the entire theater."

"I know, and I'm willing to bet most of them bought tickets to the premiere just to see you." He linked her arm with his and led her to the greenroom, where performers relaxed.

"Of course," she answered. "It has nothing to do with the stellar cast or the seven awards the play has won so far."

Elliot laughed. "Nothing whatever."

Kaitlin could hardly believe that a few hours earlier, she had been bone weary, almost without the energy to get herself dressed for this evening. There had been severe thunderstorms the previous night; between cracks of thunder and flashes of lightning, it had been impossible to fall asleep. Finally, she had dozed off twenty minutes before her alarm was set to ring, its angry buzz jarring her out of sleep. No matter how persistently she tried to assume a normal waking schedule on the weekends, her body rebelled. She'd forced herself to stay awake all day, wishing vehemently that she had a nice, normal weekday job, something more congenial to a Saturday evening out.

But now, as she watched Elliot pouring coffee for the two of them, resplendent in a black suit and tie, she knew there was nowhere else she'd rather be, nothing else she'd rather be doing. Every cell of her body was alive with gentle pleasure at the mere sight of him. He turned around and smiled at her as if he knew precisely what she was thinking and was not at all disturbed by what he read in her eyes.

It didn't seem to matter that they lived their lives on entirely different planes, or that they spent half their time sparring. When the dust settled and there were just the two of them, face-to-face, it was impossible to be unaware of their growing attraction for each other.

It was impossible because every time she saw him, Kaitlin was reminded that they had kissed twice. Then, invariably, her eyes would drop to his mouth, and she would recall how it had felt, how his lips had pulled gently on hers, how his tongue had caressed her, evoking sensations of desire deep within her. Any other man, at that point, would have pursued things to their natural conclusion by asking her out, hoping to end up in her bed. Elliot, however, hadn't even tried.

They were together, here, only for professional reasons, and in a few hours she was due in the control room, so there was little chance of events taking their course tonight. Yet as frustrating as it was at times, there was something intrinsically appealing about Elliot's reticence. His sense of self-discipline fascinated her. He was like a Spartan warrior or a crusading knight, a man who held back not because he wanted to, but because obligations dictated that he must. It was, admittedly, a bizarre analogy, and Kaitlin hadn't the foggiest notion of the forces that drove him, but for some reason the image of a stoic seemed to suit him. She liked the idea of being attracted to a man who'd somehow been born a thousand years too late.

"Where were you Friday night?" he asked, handing her a coffee.

She took it from him, their fingers brushing lightly. Was it he who had called then, she wondered in surprise. "I was out. Why?"

"No reason. It's just that I tried calling you and didn't get an answer."

"Oh, I see." She was trying desperately to convince herself that it was none of his business where she'd been on Friday. "I was in Chinatown having the best Chinese meal I've ever had in my life."

"Until midnight?" His eyes were searching, but his expression was carefully restrained.

Smiling secretly, she fought to keep exhilaration out of her voice. "We were talking and the time flew by. Next thing we knew, it was midnight." Are you going to ask me who I was with?

He didn't.

"That's good," he said, moving away from her to sit down. "I'm glad to hear you're making friends and getting out once in a while."

"Are you?" Now that had been an infantile retort, she told herself. He'd sounded quite sincere, and she might only have imagined a flicker in his dark eyes when he turned away. But if she was supposed to wait until Elliot got around to asking her out, she could die of old age. Kaitlin sat down at the opposite end of the sofa and took a sip of her coffee.

"I think it's healthy," Elliot went on to say, "that you're seeing people who aren't associated with radio. Otherwise, you may get too...oh, I don't know, submerged."

She turned to study his profile. "What makes you think that would happen?"

"It's happened to me." He turned, and their eyes met. This time, it wasn't only desire she saw in their depths; there was warning, as well.

After a long moment, she asked, "Why did you call?"

"To say I'm sorry."

If he had told her he'd called to propose, she couldn't have been more astonished. "Sorry for what?"

"For taking your fears so lightly the other day. I realized later how frightening these incidents must have been for you. At the time, I didn't react well."

Kaitlin looked down and found herself compulsively twisting the rings on her fingers. "Your reaction was quite normal, given your well-known disapproval of Moon Lady."

He reached across the expanse between them, lifted her hand from her lap and brought it to rest on the sofa. His thumb grazed her knuckles, and his grip infused her with an overpowering sense of sexual urgency. *Dear God,* she thought, *if he pulls his hand away now, I don't think I could bear it.*

"We seem to keep going over the same arguments, you and I," he said. "Perhaps we're both refusing to listen, in case we hear something that threatens our own opinions."

Kaitlin lifted her eyes to him. He was too far away, but at least they were touching. "It's entirely possible," she admitted. "I have been known on occasion to balk against bullheadedness." A smile teased the corners of her mouth and it was reflected at once in Elliot's eyes. "Are you willing to admit I was entirely right and you were wrong?"

His smile spread to the rest of his face. "Not quite; don't push your luck. But I realize now—or maybe I've always suspected—that you're a strong, independent woman, a survivor. You aren't the type who runs screeching to the nearest man at the sight of a mouse. I told you to come to me whenever you had a problem, but when you did, I let you down. I shouldn't have, and it won't happen again . . . I promise.''

He wasn't exactly offering her the world on a platter, but it was a start. In this, their silly contest of wills, he'd staged the first retreat. She owed him at least as much.

''For all the harm those phone calls did, it might as well have been a mouse I came running to you about,'' Kaitlin said. ''But thank you for reaffirming your support; it means a great deal to me. Things are fine now though—no goblins following me, no heavy breathers tormenting me at night. Moon Lady has been good to me, so I'm going to stick by her, but it would make me feel a hundred percent better if I knew you were behind . . . both of us.''

He slid across the couch and took her face in his hands. ''I'm behind you all the way, Moon Lady...and you, too, Kaitlin.'' Then, softly and tantalizingly, he brushed his lips against hers. ''Mmm,'' he murmured. ''Strawberries.''

Kaitlin felt as though a window had opened just a crack and that finally she might catch a glimpse of the inner Elliot. Later she'd think about everything that had happened, but right now all she wanted was to luxuriate in this rare, exquisite attentiveness. ''You like it?'' she asked, her head tipped back lazily, as she basked in his slow, deliberate sampling of her lip gloss.

''It's sumptuous.'' He paused long enough to answer, then ran his tongue along the outline of her mouth and plucked her lips gently with his own. ''To think...the audience has no idea...of how delicious Moon Lady tastes...an edible delight.''

His kiss deepened and Kaitlin responded with eagerness, more than willing to risk the ravages to her makeup. There would be plenty of time to make repairs before the second act. In order to emphasize her wholehearted approval of his actions, she brought her hands up to clasp the back of his head. He responded the way she had hoped he would, by crushing her close to him.

''I don't know what you've done to me, Kaitlin...'' Elliot mouthed the words against the soft flesh of her throat, and she felt his breath, warm and redolent of coffee, ''but I've...oh, hell...'' Giving up the effort of speech, he yielded instead to the dizzying sensations of her nearness. With one hand pressed against her back, the other stroking her shoulder lightly, he took in her subtle, heady fragrance. It reminded him of northern wildflowers whose season is brief but unforgettable. He studied the curve of her long dark lashes resting against the delicate cheekbones. He kissed her earlobe and traced the shape of her ear with his tongue. When she moaned and shifted closer, he felt the respondent flame deep in his own body.

He thought he would not be able to hold back any longer. He was only human, and there were some feats of endurance beyond even the most determined of men. He had to have her...soon. He had to know the sweet release of making love with this woman, or he'd die from wanting her. At a moment like this, he could even declare with reckless certainty that there was nothing in the world he wanted more than Kaitlin Harper; but of course once he'd had her, it would be a simple matter of getting himself back on course and concentrating on the things that were really important.

ELLIOT DROPPED HER OFF in front of the station at twenty minutes to twelve. Kaitlin had never wanted to go to work less than she did tonight. The cast party was just beginning to liven up, and she and Elliot had been having a good time. The change in his attitude was remarkable. He was suddenly so attuned to the currents that flowed between them. The heated looks, the incendiary touches, the softly spoken words told her that he'd finally come to terms with what she'd been acutely aware of for weeks: they wanted each other—desperately. And if Elliot's behavior this evening was any indication, the opportunity was going to present itself very soon.

Kaitlin unfastened her seat belt and slid across the front seat of Elliot's vintage Olds Toronado. "Are you going back to the party?" she asked.

He took her into his arms; with one hand, he pulled the pins from her hair, letting the chestnut curls fall loose to her shoulders. "Of course not," he said. "Without you, it wouldn't be a party." Cupping her face in his hands, he kissed her, releasing her own unbridled longing and returning it twofold.

When they parted, Kaitlin was slightly breathless. "I wish I was going back there with you."

He smiled indulgently and stroked her hair. "If you were free tonight, the last place in the world we would go is somewhere with a hundred other people. I want you all to myself, Moon Lady." He spoke the name as if it were a term of affection, as lyrical as a line of poetry.

"You've never called me Moon Lady before to-night," she whispered, awestruck by the rush of new feelings flowing through her so quickly that she couldn't identify them.

"I have," he murmured, "but at times and places you wouldn't know about. Believe it or not, my dear, even I have been cast under your spell." He kissed her again, then abruptly released her. As if a page had suddenly been turned, he was once more Elliot Jacobs, program director. "Mike wants to see you in the morning in his office."

"Why?" Kaitlin tried not to notice how hurt she felt by his startling change of mood. They were, after all, still co-workers; business still needed to be discussed.

"He's going to implement additional security measures."

"Really? Did you have a talk with him?"

He allowed himself the small luxury of touching her cheek, but it was a brief gesture and not meant to be followed up. "It was the least I could do."

There was no point in reminding him that things were quiet now and she didn't need any security measures, especially since he'd already gone to the trouble. "What time does he want to see me?" she asked.

"As soon as he comes in. When you've finished your show, why don't you go into my office, lock the door and get some sleep? I'll wake you when I get in."

Kaitlin suddenly felt better for no reason other than that Elliot would be waking her up in the morning. "See you then," she said and stepped out of the car.

Once she was inside the station, she popped her head into the control room. "I'm here, Duke, and I'll be right back after I change."

The Duke of Rock looked up from the latest issue of *Rolling Stone*. "Hold on there a minute. Let me look at you first."

Embarrassed, Kaitlin stepped inside and thrust out her arms. "Campy enough for you?"

"Turn around," he said. To avoid a fuss, she obeyed. "All together too damned much, Harper," he remarked, shaking his head.

"Am I supposed to take that as a compliment, or slap your face?"

"It's praise; take it when you can get it. I've never seen anyone light up in that color the way you do, and you're going to have to give me the name of your makeup man."

Kaitlin wrinkled her brow. "Why? There's nothing special about my makeup."

"No? Then how do you manage to make yourself look like you just climbed out of bed?"

Feeling her cheeks begin to color, Kaitlin lifted her hands to her hair. "Is that how I look? I know my hair's a little messy—"

"No, no, you misunderstand. When I speak of a bed, I'm not talking camp cot. I'm talking the kingsize, satin-sheeted water bed variety shared by at least one other person. No wonder you have the entire city panting after you, looking hot and bothered like that."

"Duke, cut it out!" The pink tinge on her face was rapidly deepening to crimson. It wouldn't surprise her in the least to discover Elliot's name flashing in neon letters on her forehead. "You are positively salacious," she retorted. "I'm sure you could find something suggestive in a rutabaga."

"Nah." He shrugged in false modesty. "Rutabagas give me hives, but a parsnip, on the other hand—"

Kaitlin dismissed him with a wave. "Get on with your show, you beast. I have got to get out of these sequins before I scream." And out of this room before I give anything else away, she added silently.

"THAT WAS 'RUBY TUESDAY' by the Rolling Stones, of course, as we continue with the myths and magic of weekdays." Kaitlin was nearly halfway through her program and surprisingly, still bursting with energy. It was amazing the effect a pair of sapphire eyes and a dazzling smile could have on one's libido. She flipped to the next page of the looseleaf binder propped up in front of the microphone. "I'm going to be taking your calls now to give away a couple of free tickets to *Deceptions*, the fabulous new play at the Royal Alexandra. I saw many of you there last night, as enchanted with the production as I was. It is one terrific play, and if you don't win the free tickets tonight, call the box office first thing tomorrow to reserve your seats. You'll be glad you did. I'll be talking to the third caller, hoping you'll be able to come up with a song in honor of Odin, supreme Norse god who rules over Wednesdays. How odd that he was given such an insignificant day. At least Monday, when the moon rules supreme, is a day we all love to hate. Now, the Moody Blues..."

In less than a minute, the console was flashing. All three lines lit up at once, so Kaitlin started at the top and depressed the button. "You're the first caller, thank you." Then the next. "You're the second caller, thank you." She pushed the last button. "Congratulations. You're the third caller. Can you think of a Wednesday song?"

The first thing she heard was the intake of breath, and then she heard the whisper, as harsh and as ugly and as memorable as if she'd heard it only moments ago. "Moon Lady...hello. It's been a long time since we chatted on the phone."

It would have been easy to panic, to drop the receiver and run from the room. But there was nothing to run from, except her own fear. She couldn't play into the caller's hands; she had to kill whoever it was with boredom. Using all the radio training she possessed to keep her voice sounding calm and natural, Kaitlin said, "It has been a while. Where have you been?"

There was a heartbeat or two of silence, which obviously meant her feigned nonchalance was working. "I—I've been around, watching you."

"Watching me? Isn't it kind of silly to be lurking around when we could meet face-to-face, get to know each other?" God, this charade was enough to make her sick to her stomach, but she had to go through with it. She was a professional.

"There's no need to meet face-to-face," replied the voice silkily. "We know each other well enough as it is."

Was it true? Did she know the caller, or was it a ruse to confuse her? She strained to listen. "If we know each other so well, why do you insist on talking in that ridiculous whisper?"

The caller chuckled, the sound of it sending ripples of fear along her spine. This was absurd, being spooked by a laugh. She'd seen too many horror movies, that was all.

"It's much more enticing this way, don't you think?" the caller said. "It's a pleasant diversion, my knowing you, and you wishing you knew me. By the way, did I mention how stunning you were tonight in your emerald sequins?"

Kaitlin nearly dropped the phone. "You . . . you saw me tonight?"

"Of course. I'm one of your greatest fans, despite what you may think. I especially enjoyed your coy reference to Toronto's cultural excellence. Are you speaking from Moon Lady's vast experience as a time traveler and connoiseur of the arts, or was that just a line you tossed out to impress the audience?"

Now it was getting insulting. "The song is nearly over; I have to go."

"Don't lie to me, Moon Lady. 'Tuesday Afternoon' is a long song. Besides, you could always let the rest of the album play."

"No, I can't. It doesn't fit in with the show, and anyway, I have to take the next call since you haven't been able to come up with a song about Wednesday—"

"Not yet! We still haven't discussed the matter of your farewell."

"I'm not going anywhere," she replied between clenched teeth.

The caller made a clucking sound. "You ought to start taking me more seriously. I don't particularly like having to stay up this late just to keep warning you to get the hell out. I have better things to do with my time."

"Well, go do them!" she shouted, ready to hang up. Then she heard something the caller had never said before, and the very sound of it turned her blood to ice.

"Kait . . . lin." Her name was dragged out in a mocking singsong. The caller knew what effect her name would have, for she heard the cackling laugh.

"H-How did you know my name?" she gasped.

"My, my, we are slow to catch on, aren't we? How many times must I tell you we know each other?"

She had to struggle to control her voice. "Then tell me who you are! I don't want to offend anyone by being here, but if we don't meet face-to-face and have a reasonable discussion, how do you expect me to understand why you want me to leave?"

"Very well. Perhaps we can arrange something more suitable." There was a pause and the slow deep breath, almost an asthmatic sound. "If you want to know who I am...pay close heed to the very next person who touches you. Goodnight, Moon Lady."

Seconds after the caller had hung up, "Tuesday Afternoon" reached its climax. Kaitlin needed all her willpower to put on her headset and continue the show.

"Uh...I...I'm back. I took three calls, and... unfortunately no one could come up with a Wednesday song. We're going to meet Thor, the god of thunder and of Thursdays, in a minute, but first, this message from the Canadian Lung Association." She switched on the cassette player and let her head drop onto her arm.

She couldn't take much more of this. It had been bad enough the first time, but it was ten times worse now after a week's lapse. She had felt her peace of mind return by degrees, felt her confidence build as she began to trust her colleagues—and now this. She had even started to relax in her role as Moon Lady, to enjoy the harmless glitter and the hype—especially last night, with Elliot by her side.

Perhaps she ought to call him now, let him know what had just happened. He had insisted she call him anytime, but it was nearly three. He'd be asleep, and his workdays were always so busy. No, it wouldn't be right to disturb him now. There wasn't anything he could do, anyway. Maybe she could ask him to stay with her for a night or two; the sound of an authoritative male voice might be enough to shut the caller up permanently. She'd have to remember to suggest it to him in the morning.

When the early-morning announcer relieved Kaitlin at the board, she went down the hall and let herself into Elliot's office with the key he had given her. Because she hadn't slept much during the weekend, she was at the point of total exhaustion. She flicked on the overhead lights but found their fluorescent brilliance too painful and flicked them off again, finding her way to the plaid sofa by memory. Slipping off her sneakers, she lay down and covered herself with the blanket. Within seconds, she was asleep and dreaming.

She was on a stage with a huge audience applauding her from tiered seats. The place was something like the Royal Alex but much grander, like the Viennese opera house. The orchestra was in the pit playing something with timpani and violins, but the kettle drums were too loud and the violins were screeching. She wanted them to stop because it was time for her to announce the second act. But the words got stuck in her throat; she couldn't make a sound. The music kept growing louder and more discordant and the audience's applause more frenetic. They weren't only clapping, they were laughing at her, taunting her to leave the stage. She wanted to leave, desperately, but her feet seemed to be glued to the floor. She turned toward the wing of the stage and saw Elliot.

"Elliot!" she cried, but there was no sound. She tried again. "Help me! Help me!" She still had no voice, but she held out her arms and he understood. Slowly, he came toward her across the stage, smiling, his arms outstretched.

But something was wrong with his face. He looked smug, triumphant, as if he had some deep dark secret that Kaitlin wouldn't like. But he was coming to save her from the music and the audience. Everything would be all right.

When he reached her side, he bent down toward her ear. "It's all over now, Moon Lady. Come with me." It wasn't Elliot's voice. It was that awful whisper. She tried to scream...

"Kaitlin! Kaitlin, wake up! You're having a nightmare. It's Elliot!"

Her eyes flew open to find him bending over her in the semidarkness of morning, his hand on her shoulder. Wide-eyed, she shrank away from him, deep into the corner of the sofa. "You...you touched me!" she gasped.

Chapter Six

Elliot pulled his hand away and looked at her strangely. "Sorry, but you were screaming in your sleep."

Half-awake and still not entirely convinced it had been a dream, Kaitlin stared at him. After a time, her racing heart began to slow and her tightly coiled nerves gradually eased. Of course, his touching her had been a natural gesture of concern. She only had to look into those deep dark eyes of his to know that. The fact that he had been the first to touch her since the phone call was coincidence, a tactic by the caller to heighten her paranoia. After all, how could a person possibly plan such an encounter?

Suddenly, with heart-numbing clarity, Elliot's words resurfaced in her mind. *"Why don't you go into my office, lock the door and get some sleep? I'll wake you when I get in."* Nobody else could have touched her when she was locked away in his office.

But, surely, he was incapable of such stark duplicity. He couldn't be kneeling beside her as he was now, his eyes brimming with worry, if he were the one making the calls. The possibility was too monstrous to consider, and emphatically she pushed the thought away.

"What was I saying?" she asked in a voice still thick with sleep.

"You were shouting for help. We could hear you halfway down the hall."

Kaitlin covered her face with her hands and moaned. "Great. Who do you mean by we?"

He smiled at her discomfiture. "Lorna, Mike and I. But don't worry, we've all learned to expect anything from announcers."

She pulled herself into a sitting position. Her mouth felt so dry that she could barely swallow, and her nerve endings were rippling like a wheatfield. "I don't often get nightmares, and I don't think I've ever talked in my sleep before."

"What brought it on?" he asked. "Did you have a bad night?"

Kaitlin nodded. "I got another call." She watched for a reaction, some small sign of culpability, but Elliot gave nothing away. His eyes hardened, and his jaw tensed, but they were signals of solicitude, not guilt. Or so she fervently wanted to believe.

"What did he say this time?"

"Not much. The same old thing about wanting me to leave."

Elliot took her hands in his, and this time she didn't flinch at his touch. "You're not telling me everything," he said.

"You're right," she admitted. "Now they know my name."

"Oh, God, no." He stroked his lower lip with his thumb and forefinger as he grappled with this latest development. "Are you sure? Did they actually call you Kaitlin?"

"Of course I'm sure, and he or she insists we know each other."

He looked at her curiously. "Why do you say he or she?"

"Because I'm not sure if it's a man or a woman. The voice is so strange, such an exaggerated whisper, I honestly couldn't tell you the caller's age or sex."

Elliot stood up and moved toward the window. "You're still convinced it's one of us, aren't you?"

"I don't honestly know what to think," she answered. "I know what the caller wants me to believe, but a part of me resists the obvious. Can't we just call the police and let them handle it?"

He turned around, and his eyes were strangely distant. "We'll get to the bottom of this, I promise, but it's too soon for the police. All they'd do is put a tracer on the phone, and Mike would never agree to it. I wish I could be more reassuring," he said sadly.

Instinctively, she went to him and wrapped her arms around his waist. She rested her head on his chest and closed her eyes, warm in the refuge of his nearness.

The act of tilting back her head for his kiss was effortless, and their embrace moved naturally and inevitably from simple reassurance to intimacy. His mouth offered her more than solace; his arms gave more than comfort.

"We have to spend some time together, you and I," he said when their kisses drew to a close. "There's so much about you I want to know."

Kaitlin looked up at him and smiled. "I feel the same way."

He stroked her hair away from her face. "How about Saturday? We'll spend the day together."

"Saturday sounds perfect," she replied softly.

MIKE WAS ENTHRONED behind his large desk, beaming, when Kaitlin walked in. "Hi there, sweetie!" he said.

"Good morning, Mike."

He picked up a newspaper from his desk and waved it in the air. "Have you seen this?"

"This morning's paper? No."

"The *Globe and Mail* did a full-page spread of you on the front page of the entertainment section. You can now consider yourself a bona fide star."

She walked across the office and took the paper from him. "Full page—I can't believe it. When they interviewed me last week, they didn't give me any indication it would be such a long article." There were two photographs: the one of her at the castle window, which had been made into a poster, and another of her onstage at the Royal Alexandra. The headline read "Moon Lady Bewitches Metro." She quickly scanned the laudatory article. "They seem to have done a nice job."

"Nice?" Mike echoed. "It's dynamite. I expect our phones are gonna ring off the hook today from advertisers begging for commercial space."

Kaitlin sat down in front of the desk and crossed her legs. "That's good." She waited for Mike to finish gushing and then said, "What about the phone calls I've been getting?"

His face hardened, as if he resented the change of topic. "Yeah, from what Elliot tells me, some nut case has been hassling you, eh?" There was an underlying tone of condescension in his voice and, on reflection, Kaitlin realized that shouldn't have surprised her. Men who called women sweetie, expecting them to like it, were usually the first to blame women for the deviant behavior of men.

Instinctively, Kaitlin bristled. Moon Lady had been Mike's brainchild and the cause of her present troubles. There was no earthly reason for him to look at her as if to say, "You made your bed; now lie in it."

"It is getting a little difficult to carry on with my job," she said as evenly as she could manage.

"Hmm. Have any idea who it might be?"

"No. If I did I'd know how to handle it."

Mike leaned back and folded his hands over his paunch. "Would you now? And tell me, what exactly would you do?"

His patronizing tone was as irritating as the sound of fingernails scraped along a blackboard. "I'd call the police," she answered in her sweetest female voice, even raising the pitch slightly to sound convincingly vulnerable.

This made her boss lunge forward in his chair. "Oh, no, you don't. Nobody calls the police into this station without my say-so. We don't need any bad publicity around here."

"I appreciate your position, but when someone starts following me around my own neighborhood, it's not a station affair anymore. I live alone in this city, and I have the right to protect myself."

Mike chuckled nervously. "Okay, no need to get testy now. I know just how you feel. It's not easy being a little lady in a big city without a man to look after her. Hell, you read about it every day, all those perverts out there waiting to get their hands on some fresh young thing."

"Then what do you suggest?" Kaitlin asked between clenched teeth.

"Well, I'll tell you." He sat back with a look of smug satisfaction on his face. "I stayed up most of the weekend thinking, and this is what I came up with. This nut only knows you as Moon Lady, right?''

"So I thought until last night, but he does know my name, and I'm not so sure it's a guy."

Her remark seemed to throw him for a minute. "Yeah, well, a lotta people in this city know your real name. There's the photographers at the studio down the street, most of our sponsors . . . plenty of guys. It's no big deal."

For some reason, that realization had never occurred to her before now, and her sense of insecurity doubled. It could be anyone or anyone's cousin or anyone's friend. Refusing to give in to such musings, she also realized there would be no point in pursuing the matter of the caller's sex with Mike. He simply wasn't capable of believing that a woman could commit this type of aggression.

"Has anyone ever followed you home?" he asked.

"Not that I've noticed."

That seemed to please him enormously. "Good. Then he probably doesn't know where you live or he'd have followed you by now."

"What does that have to do with anything?"

"It's likely the guy saw you at the restaurant by sheer coincidence and slipped you that little note for a laugh."

Kaitlin hoped her silence was ample proof of her doubts.

"Now, of course," he went on to say, "the fellow knows where you work. That's no secret, but you're perfectly safe once you're in this building since we've got all the latest in locks and security devices."

"So I understand," she conceded. As long as the caller's last name wasn't Houdini.

"So the time you're most vulnerable is coming and going from work, right?" Mike laid this before her as if it were nothing less than a brilliant conclusion.

"Presumably," said Kaitlin, "though it could be just a matter of time before he decides to find out where I live by following me home."

"We'll get to that in a minute. What we're gonna deal with first is how you get into the station. The front doors are brightly lit at night, as you know, and Yonge Street's so busy there's no way we can monitor who's passing by or lurking in doorways."

Kaitlin nodded and let him continue.

"I've talked to my good friend, Luigi Santini from the bakery next door. I've known the guy for forty years—we went to school together—and he's agreed to help us out."

"How is he going to do that?"

"See, our two buildings are joined together by a corridor in the basement, linking up the old boiler system. From what Luigi tells me, this was all one building at one time. Anyway, he's agreed to let you use the back entrance of the bakery when you come in and go out every night. That way, he can make sure you're safe."

Mike was looking quite pleased with himself, and well he should. He had managed to secure a pseudosecurity guard at no cost to himself.

"What about the two-block walk from the subway?" she asked. "And not only that, if I use the back entrance, I have to get off Yonge Street. At least on a main thoroughfare, the lights are better."

Her employer assumed a look of overt exasperation. "Look, sweetie, I appreciate your problem, I really do, but you're not the only broad—lady—who has to work after dark. You ever hear about any employers providing escorts to walk their employees to the subway? As much as I'd like to protect our Moon Lady door-to-door, we're on a tight budget around here." He rubbed his nose before delivering the final salvo. "Course you could always buy yourself a car and park it right behind the station like everyone else does. Then you wouldn't have a two-block walk."

"I can't afford it quite yet," Kaitlin mumbled, amazed at how blithely Mike could suggest ways to spend her money but not his. It didn't look as though he were going to offer any other magnanimous safety measures, so she said, "When can I start using the back entrance?"

He grinned widely. "That's my girl. The corridor hasn't been used in a lot of years, so I hired a couple of guys to clean out the cobwebs and make sure there aren't any exposed wires or mice to scare you."

"Mice don't scare me," she couldn't resist saying.

Mike grimaced. "No, of course they don't. We should have the system working by next week. Do you think you can hang in until then?"

Her jaw ached with the effort of a smile. "I'll try," she said.

IT COULDN'T HAVE BEEN a more perfect day to take the ferry to Toronto Island Park. Saturdays like this came only rarely in the short Canadian summer. The sky was a flawless, haze-free azure, the air a perfect blend of the sun's warmth and the breeze from Lake Ontario. The docks near the Hilton were teeming with people. There were families with grandparents and young children, teenagers with ghetto blasters, lovers arm in arm.

Elliot held Kaitlin's hand as they crossed the ramp to board the ferry and climb the stairs to the open deck above. The gesture thrilled her even though it might have been construed as one of caution, as simply a way to avoid losing each other in the crowd. At one point, the stairway became so congested that she had to walk ahead, so he released her hand and lightly touched the small of her back instead. That felt just as nice, she thought, leading him to a vacant spot along the brass rail encircling the deck.

She had never seen him so relaxed. His dark hair had been allowed to fall into its natural ruffled style, and he was dressed in an open-necked rugby shirt and faded corduroys. This morning there was little about him that called to mind the intense, driven program director who, in many ways, was still a stranger to her. But if there was such a thing as Elliot Jacobs at play, she suspected this might be it.

They had spoken hardly at all on the drive to the ferry docks, but the silence had been oddly comfortable. They were two people who felt right together without knowing why, who were intrigued with each other yet unsure of how to begin a deeper acquaintance. It was not something Kaitlin really understood. But small talk seemed frivolous when all she wanted to do was enjoy the experience of being with Elliot.

As the boat slowly made its way from the harbor, he turned to her. "It's funny, I can't remember the last time I went to Toronto Island. I'm sure it's been years."

Kaitlin looked up at him as she leaned against the rail, relishing the feel of the breeze against her skin. "When was the last time you actually relaxed?"

"Are you suggesting I don't know how?" he asked, his mouth lifting in a grin.

"All I've ever seen you do is work, and I know you keep longer hours than anyone else in the station."

"I have my reasons, but I guess it's habit as much as anything else. What about you? If you counted all your business dinners and benefit appearances, your hours would be as long as mine."

"You're probably right." Kaitlin was intensely aware that they were standing very close to each other. Granted, the deck was crammed with passengers, but that wasn't the only reason. One of the few things Kaitlin had determined about Elliot with any certainty was his shyness with her, and shyness in others was something that invariably brought out the more gregarious elements in her own nature. If he had been a flashy, outgoing sort of man, she wouldn't have edged so close to him that their hips touched. But since he wasn't, she had. And it was patently obvious that he had no desire to back away.

"I like my work," she went on to explain. "When I had my show in Ohio, I used to put in fourteen-hour days for weeks at a time and not even notice it."

He looked surprised. "You enjoy the business that much?"

"Of course. Don't you?"

Looking away from her, he ran his fingers through his hair. "More than anything else, I suppose, though I don't intend to be a program director for Mike Andretti for the rest of my life."

His tone implied it was all he was going to say on the subject, which was fine with Kaitlin. The less said today about work, the better.

"Oh, look, Elliot—the skyline. Isn't it beautiful?" she asked, her voice alive with enthusiasm. Surging into the sky were towers of smoky glass and gold. The waterfront was bordered by old warehouses converted to luxury condominiums. Most spectacular of all was the lofty CN Tower, gleaming white and silver, reminding her of a flying saucer impaled on a giant needle.

"It is impressive," he agreed, his eyes scanning the lakeshore. Then he turned and lowered his eyes to hers. "Are you always like this?"

There were rare moments when the mere act of looking into each other's eyes was searing, like two sources of heat fusing together. This was such a moment. But it never lasted long—only until one of them spoke. "Am I always like what?" she asked reluctantly.

"Enthusiastic...buoyant. It seems no matter what happens, you don't stay down for long."

She smiled. "My father used to call me Pollyanna, and for years I thought it was because of my blond ringlets. But I did learn a long time ago that optimism takes a lot less energy than negative emotions do. The ringlets darkened, but my attitude hasn't."

"It sounds like you had a happy childhood." There was no mistaking the wistful tone in Elliot's voice.

"It was, now that I think about it, even though at the time I considered myself the most unfortunate person in the whole world."

"Why?" he asked.

"When I was very young—maybe about four—my older sister told me during a squabble that my parents had wanted four children, two girls and two boys. I was old enough to figure out, even then, that my two sisters were older, my twin brothers were younger—by only ten months—and that left me sandwiched in the middle. I was convinced from then on that I'd been a mistake, which probably accounts for every outrageous thing I've ever done in my life. I was the class clown in school, wormed my way into being Daddy's pet and tormented my younger brothers no end by playing with their toys instead of my sister's castoffs."

"But your parents loved you, anyway, didn't they?"

"I bent over backward to make sure of it," she said with a chuckle. "Every time one of the others got into trouble, I'd whip out a painting or some little home-made trinket to impress my parents. It's disgusting when I think about it, my relentless need to be accepted."

Elliot propped his elbow on the railing, shifting slightly so that their hips were no longer touching. His fingers, however, grazed the cotton fabric of her T-shirt near her waist. He might not have been aware of it; then again, it might have been quite deliberate. Either way, Kaitlin continued to be grateful for the ferry's crowded conditions.

"Something about your compulsion confuses me," he said, his expression amused but thoughtful.

"What's that?"

"Why get into radio? I realize announcers are fa-mous for well-developed egos, but you could have got-ten a lot more adulation in television or films, looking the way you do."

Unconsciously, Kaitlin brought her arms around her midriff, at the same time brushing against Elliot's hand. His fingers curved around her forearm and held there; it was a subtle gesture but all the more igniting for its subtlety.

"This will probably sound like I'm fishing for com-pliments, but I never wanted to look this way. I used to love playing baseball with the boys and skinny-dipping in the creek, and then puberty came along. All of a sudden, my buddies started treating me differently, and I was expected to dress like a lady. It took me a long time, but I finally discovered a career where appear-

ances were irrelevant, where I could dress how I liked
and still earn a certain respect.''

It occurred to her suddenly that she had never before
put into words what made her choose to become a radio announcer. And no wonder. The reason bordered
on wackiness, and it wouldn't surprise her if Elliot told
her as much.

"You should never harbor regrets for having turned
out so complete a woman," he said instead, to her de-
lighted surprise. His midnight eyes were roaming over
her in frank appreciation, and for once, Kaitlin was
grateful for nature's endowment. She was fairly sure
Elliot respected her as a person, and now she was nearly
ready for him to desire her as a woman. Nearly, because so far she had refused to consider the consequences or think about the future. She knew beyond a
doubt that their relationship was still at a low simmer
and that, as in all relationships, there would be either
retreat or growth. She hoped fervently for the latter.

They were almost the last to get off at the Centre
Island ferry dock, content to let the crowd surge ahead
of them. They had all day; there was no hurry. In fact,
Kaitlin was almost sorry the journey was over, as if on
the water, time was somehow suspended, reality an un-
charted shore to be carefully avoided.

Now, as they walked, Elliot had his arm around her
shoulders, and Kaitlin felt as though she were walking
on air. She slipped her arm around his waist, linking her
finger through the belt loops of his cords, acutely aware
of the rhythmic movement of his hips as he walked.

A comfortable silence settled on them both as they
strolled through the amusement park with the minia-
ture railroad and swan-shaped pedal boats. They
crossed the causeway between islands, past brilliant

displays of impatiens and marigolds and pansies. From a wooden pier that bridged the rocky shore, they could see for miles. The sight of the graceful yachts and sailboats on the sparkling lake had the serenity of a watercolor painting.

They ambled along the boardwalk until they came to a secluded spot amidst a stand of willows. "Shall we stop here and have our picnic?" Elliot asked.

"It's perfect," Kaitlin replied, stepping off the walkway. He helped her spread the blanket and zipped open the vinyl satchel he'd carried on one shoulder. Soon they were munching contentedly on smoked meat sandwiches and watching people go by on foot, on bicycles and in rented surries with fringes on top.

Kaitlin wasn't one to cast judgment on others, especially without a sound basis, but this time she couldn't help it. Elliot had just poured her some coffee from a thermos when she noticed a couple on the walkway. The woman was heavily pregnant; her ankles were swollen and her face was florid. Walking was obviously an effort for her, a fact that went totally unnoticed by her husband some six feet ahead of her. He was sauntering along in his loud plaid shorts and sandals with socks, trying his best to look like an unattached man-about-town. The child they were expecting probably wasn't their first, judging from the couple's age and their tired expressions, but that was no excuse for the man's dismal neglect of his wife.

"See that?" Kaitlin remarked when the pair was out of earshot. "They ought to have photographs of people like them hanging up in marriage license bureaus. It would make couples think twice."

Elliot was leaning back on his hands, and he chuckled. "Is that why you've avoided marriage all this time, aside from the fact that puberty dealt you such a blow?''

She joined in his laughter. ''I'm not sure, although my attitude probably contributed to a marked lack of offers over the years.'' She took a sip of her coffee and glanced at Elliot. ''You know what really rankles me about marriage?''

The devilish light in his eyes suggested that his thoughts had gone in a direction quite different from hers. ''Why don't you go ahead and tell me?''

''Okay. Let's say, for example, that I had been married when Charlie showed up in Sandusky. He comes and offers me this plum position with CSKY FM, but my husband owns a sporting goods store. How likely do you think it would be that I could come home and say 'Guess what, dear? I've been offered a job in Canada. How about you sell your business and come with me?' And even if that impossibility were to happen, how many husbands would put up with a woman who works all night and has to dress like Mae West for her business functions?''

''Probably none that you'd want to be married to,'' Elliot admitted.

''Exactly,'' Kaitlin said. ''And anyway, who wants a Caspar Milquetoast who'd agree to such a thing?'' She stabbed the air to emphasize the point. ''Now on the other hand, if my hypothetical husband were offered the job, I, the humble missus, would be expected to sell my business and trot dutifully along behind him. As far as marriage goes, there's no more equality now than there was in the Stone Age.''

''I agree with you one hundred percent,'' Elliot stated.

She looked at him in surprise. ''You do?''

"Of course. If I were married, I would never expect my wife to make a sacrifice I wouldn't be willing to make myself."

"That is a wonderfully refreshing attitude coming from a man," she said, nodding in approval. This day was definitely turning out to be more pleasurable than she had hoped. Not only could she spill the silly secrets of her childhood to Elliot, but she could even play street-corner philosopher without fear of having her ideas scoffed at. She would never have expected him to be so open-minded. "How have you managed to escape the clutches of matrimony?" she asked, wondering why some marriage-bent feminist hadn't snapped him up years ago.

He was looking at her, but suddenly his eyes seemed to become distant, as though he had withdrawn to some deeply private inner thought. He wasn't seeing Kaitlin anymore, or at least she hoped he wasn't. The expression on his face was one of overt unhappiness.

"Marriage is an obligation," he answered at last, "and it seems that for most of my thirty-four years, I've been trying to get out from under obligations. The last thing in the world I need right now...is a wife to drag me down."

Chapter Seven

His comment shouldn't have made the slightest difference to her. She didn't want a husband any more than he did a wife. And after all, seconds earlier Kaitlin had applauded his attitude and welcomed the notion of a friend as comfortable with his independence as she was with hers. He, too, was a complete person. They were both people who had no need of anyone else to round out their lives, except perhaps in the purely physical sense.

If there was a mutual attraction—and she wasn't so naive as to think there wasn't—she longed to believe it was deeper than mere chemistry. He couldn't have asked her out today only to seduce her. If that had been his intention, it would have made more sense to wait until the traditional evening hours, when he could wine her and dine her and sweep her off her admittedly willing feet. Instead, what they were discovering about each other on a day like today, she told herself firmly, was a bond of shared values, a camaraderie born of highly cherished individuality. They were, in a way, both loners, and the fact that they were a man and a woman was incidental, the sparks between them insignificant when considered against the rest. It was even plausible that a casual tumble or two might dissolve all the tensions, and afterward, they could simply resume their friendship. But if there was a risk that sex might jeopardize a good partnership, then it was out of the question. She would have to learn to ignore the sparks.

Nevertheless, as she studied his strongly defined profile and wished he would come back from wherever his thoughts had taken him, Kaitlin knew she was deluding herself. Right now, at this moment, she wanted Elliot to touch her body, not her mind. She wanted him to desire her, not admire her. She wanted him as a friend, but she craved him as a lover even more. It was a dangerous bridge she was crossing, shaky and treacherous, but—heaven help her—she didn't want to turn back yet.

But no matter what direction things took, it was still early in the day and there would be plenty of time for serious soul-searching later. "Wouldn't it be fun to rent a couple of bicycles to explore the islands?" she asked, deliberately adding a touch of levity to her voice.

It was some time before Elliot could pull himself away from his thoughts, but at last he did, studying her face before he answered. "Sounds fine, but why don't we get a tandem bike so we'll only have to work half as hard?"

"Wonderful," she said, caught up in the sudden brilliance of his smile. So he was even capable of something as banal as fun—a realization almost as disturbing as it was gratifying. Still, it wouldn't do to like him too much. Elliot Jacobs could too easily become a hard habit to break, to easily assume a captivating monopoly of her thoughts. But she knew this was not the right time or place to resist the attraction she felt for him, and she gladly took his hand as he helped her to her feet.

Moments later, they were riding one behind the other on a bicycle built for two. They pedaled the length of Ward's Island and back again, to the tip of Hanlan's Point, beyond the lighthouse and the trout pond. They stopped to watch a sailboat race and chatted with a juggler working his way through medical school. From cotton candy to foot-long hot dogs to tossing balls for teddy bears, the day was a carnival made for two. Kaitlin wished it would never end.

On the trip back to the mainland late that afternoon, Elliot secured seats for them on the lower deck of the ferry. The sky had grown hazy and the breeze across the lake was now damp and chilly. Kaitlin felt ready to drop on her feet and was grateful when Elliot gently pushed her onto the bench and wrapped his arm protectively around her shoulders. She hadn't thought to bring a jacket, but the warmth of the strong silent man beside her seeped through her entire body. She fell into a state of almost dreamlike contentment as she leaned against him, her head resting on his shoulder. She might even have dozed for a minute or two, though never so deeply that she was unaware of where she was. It was unthinkable to waste a single precious moment because, for some strange reason, she suddenly had the uneasy feeling that no matter how spectacularly they got along today, he might not ask her out again.

By the time they reached her apartment, the fresh air and exercise, as well as the departure from her nocturnal schedule, had caught up with Kaitlin. Every fiber of her body was screaming for sleep, but she refused to give in. It was much too soon to let this perfect day come to an end.

"Would you like something cold to drink?" she asked when they had entered the living room.

Elliot immediately went over to examine her record collection—her single most expensive investment. "If you have it, a beer would be nice."

"Coming right up. You can go ahead and pick out some music." She turned into the kitchen, pleased with herself for remembering to buy beer the day before, and put two mugs in the freezer to frost. Moments later, she returned to the living room with a tray. Elliot was standing by the window as the rough-edged but mellow voice of Lionel Ritchie, her favorite singer, came from the speakers.

Kaitlin placed the tray on the coffee table. "Nice choice," she commented. "I always listen to him when I need to unwind."

He looked at her pensively, as if she'd uttered something of great interest. "So do I," he finally said. Joining her on the sofa, he poured the beer into the cold mugs and handed her one. When a few drops of condensation spilled onto the surface of the coffee table, he wiped it up with a napkin. It was a natural reaction and certainly nothing noteworthy, yet watching him filled Kaitlin with a quiet joy.

She realized this was the first time she had ever invited anyone to her place since she had come to Toronto. She had generally attributed the oversight to lack of time, but now the reason seemed so much clearer. She had never invited anyone because until this evening, the place hadn't felt as though it was her home. For weeks on end, she had been rising at unnatural hours to go to work, fixing herself quick meals in the tiny kitchen with no motive other than sustenance, watching TV alone in the bedroom. But none of these things had endeared the place to her. It took something as simple as Elliot's pouring them each a beer and wiping up a spill to make the apartment feel different. She wouldn't describe it as domestic bliss, exactly, but Kaitlin felt a certain, solid comfort in being there with this man, listening to music and sharing the serenity of her home.

She picked up the mug and drank deeply to soothe her parched throat. The amber-colored lager was delicious and reviving—or perhaps that was the effect of their eyes meeting over the tops of the mugs. They set their drinks down together as if on cue, and Elliot came closer, putting his arm around her shoulders, lifting her face with his hand until their mouths were a whisper apart.

"It's no wonder you have this city in a tailspin," he murmured. "You are so unbelievably, indescribably beautiful."

Kaitlin's eyes widened. After a day like today, she felt grubby and sweaty and stiff and drowsy, but he had called her beautiful—her last rational thought before his mouth claimed hers.

The thrill that rose through her body at his touch was no longer a surprise but a sensation she gloriously anticipated whenever Elliot took her in his arms, a sensation that never failed to send her soaring. His fingers were splayed through her hair, and he drew her deeply into the intimate recesses of his mouth. Their bodies fell in slow motion to the couch and it seemed not a deliberate act but a natural, flowing progression of events. She was lying beneath him now, his lean hard body pressing quietly on hers. She wouldn't have changed it for the world.

A line of music emanated from the stereo. "Is it me you're looking for?" The words might have come from Kaitlin's very soul as she locked her arms around Elliot's neck and dug her fingers into his thick hair. Had he caught the lyrics, she wondered. Had fate woven those particular words through this moment for a purpose, or was it mere coincidence? She'd heard the song hundreds of times before, but the lyrics had never seemed so full of portent.

She wasn't looking for anyone, she reminded herself, basking in Elliot's passionate kisses. No, not at all. This yearning that felt like a tickle deep inside was nothing more than a physical response. It didn't mean she was lonely or that she was searching; it didn't mean her life was empty, and that Elliot was the man who could fill it. It meant none of those things, only that Elliot—when he put his mind to it—knew full well what it took to please a woman.

With herculean strength of will, Elliot reminded himself that what he was doing was dangerous. Taking Kaitlin into his arms was more than a calculated risk; it was a gamble he stood a good chance of losing. Kissing her sweet sensuous mouth blurred the edges of his resolve. Sampling her incredibly soft skin was like tasting forbidden fruit; the essence of it surged through his veins, addicting him to its savor.

She trusted him, the foolish girl—no, woman...she was every bit a woman. He could feel the compliance in her body as surely as he heard his own heartbeat. Part of him wanted to warn her, but how could he when his loins were aching for her? Their thighs were linked, their bodies throbbing with mutual want. He tried to keep her from realizing the full state of his arousal, but in his vain effort to back off, he ground himself against her. Kaitlin's response was a soft moan, and she drew him closer still.

Never in his wildest dreams had he imagined that a woman could have this debilitating effect on him. He liked women, he respected them, but when it came to sex, experience had shown him that it was entirely possible to create fireworks for a night and then walk away unscathed in the morning. There was no reason why the same thing shouldn't hold true for Kaitlin, which made the hesitancy he'd been battling with ever since he'd met her that much harder to understand.

It didn't make sense that he should move his hands over her full breasts in passing instead of allowing himself the sensation of holding them, teasing the taut nipples with his fingertips. This same raging inner battle confined him to the safe neutrality of the bare flesh at her waist, when what he longed to do instead was lift the thin cotton shirt over her head.

God, how he wanted her. Perhaps, if he had sensed that she held something in reserve, kept private some sanctum of her heart, he might have trusted himself to make love to her. Afterward, they could get up, brush themselves off and dismiss it as one more pleasant interlude. But he knew, despite her convincing performances as Moon Lady, that Kaitlin wasn't holding back when it came to him. It flattered him; in fact, it thrilled him to the marrow of his bones, but he'd worked too long and too hard to let a woman—even one as stupendous as Kaitlin Harper—get into his life now. Now, of all times.

Placing his hands on the sofa on either side of her face, he forced himself into a sitting position. "I have to go. You need your rest."

His brusque tone of voice had come from nowhere, like a sudden, dark cloud on a clear sunny day. Kaitlin's fingers slid down the length of his arms. "Wh-

what's wrong?'' Her voice was shaky with unassuaged passion.

''Nothing's wrong, but it's been a long day, and I still have some work to do at the office.''

Kaitlin pointed to the mugs of beer, the frost long since melted. ''What about your drink?''

He mussed her hair with his fingers, a brotherly gesture that rankled her. ''You go ahead and finish it,'' he said with a smile that stopped at his mouth. Getting up, he strode to the door, then turned briefly around. ''Take care of yourself'' was all he said.

Not even a goodbye kiss! The man was impossible! A whole day together, the sweet promise of a night to follow, and without warning, without explanation, he'd left her alone. Suddenly, it occurred to Kaitlin that maybe he felt she was chasing him. Heaven knew, her own objections to making love with him were halfhearted at best, but part of them, she assumed, stemmed from the man's damnable shyness. She'd never known a man who didn't do the chasing and had never imagined herself in the role of pursuer until now.

What was he afraid of? It was usually women who worried about how soon to let a relationship become intimate. How had their roles become so confused? Was there really such a thing as making it too easy for a man? The very thought that she might have permanently ruined things between them made her shudder and she drank down both mugs of beer in short order.

ROSA SANTINI WAS WAITING at the back door of her husband's bakery shortly before midnight. An ample woman with a friendly, gold-toothed smile, she spotted Kaitlin coming up the alley and gestured to her.

"Hurry, come in," she urged in a lyrical accent, clutching Kaitlin's arm to pull her into the bakery as if there were bogeymen following at her heels. "My husband is upstairs sleeping; he does not wake up until three to begin the day's baking, and so I am here to greet you."

"That's very kind of you," Kaitlin said, feeling like a child who isn't trusted to look after herself, "but I'm sorry to put you to so much trouble."

Rosa wagged her head from side to side. "What trouble is it to keep a young woman safe from the evil in the streets?"

Kaitlin didn't bother to remark that not all evil originated in the streets. Mike had probably given the Santinis a modified version of events, which was just as well.

The older woman reached deep into the pocket of her flowered dress and drew out a key. "This is for you. Most nights my son Antonio or I will be here, and Luigi will see you safely out in the morning, but if for some reason we cannot wait for you, feel free to let yourself in."

She took the key reluctantly. "Thank you, but I'm sure we'll work out a more convenient, er...system soon."

"Don't worry. We have known Mike Andretti for many, many years. If he says you need protection, you need protection. Come, I will show you the way downstairs."

Kaitlin followed the woman through a gleaming stainless steel kitchen to a side door that opened into the basement. As soon as she entered the dimly lit stairwell, a heavy mustiness assailed her nostrils. This was ridiculous, she thought, sneaking into work like this.

Mrs. Santini led the way down the steep and narrow stairs; at the bottom, she pointed straight ahead. "There is the door you must take. On the other side you will see the old boiler and beyond that a second door. Go through it and follow the corridor. It will take you directly to the stairs leading to the station. There are light switches at either end of the hall. Do you think you can find your way from here?"

"Oh, yes, thank you. I appreciate your help very much, Mrs. Santini."

"Not at all, my dear. Now be careful, and we will see you tomorrow night."

Kaitlin went past the boiler, opened the heavy steel door and felt around for the light switch. The single exposed bulb was barely enough to light her way. The walls were rough stone, dripping with condensation, and the floor was concrete, with splashes of old paint and grease. But thanks to Mike's hired hands, the cobwebs were at least gone. It wasn't spooky; it was just a dank, unappealing basement.

Halfway along, the corridor turned at a right angle, and it was then that Kaitlin heard the humming, the tuneless sound of a person who doesn't know anyone is listening, the sound of someone who thinks he's alone. Because she was wearing running shoes, Kaitlin's approach was silent. She stopped, her heartbeat quickening, and tried to determine the best way to announce her presence. She had no choice but to continue; it would have been just too embarrassing to turn around and go back through the bakery now. But who on earth would be down here at this time of night . . . and why?

A sudden panic flooded her. Had she been set up for this? Would everything quickly come to an inauspicious end here in this dungeon?

She opened her mouth and forced herself to speak. "Who's there?"

The sound of her voice bounced off the damp walls, and the humming stopped. Kaitlin waited, frozen to her spot.

From around the corner the Duke appeared in black denims and a sequined shirt. He looked menacing in the dim light, his eyes glazed, his lips curled in a sneer, but it was probably the gloomy atmosphere exaggerating his features. Kaitlin allowed herself a small sigh of relief.

"Well, if it isn't the Moon Lady herself, resorting to subterranean approaches these days." His speech was slow, his gestures drawn out, and Kaitlin realized the stub of cigarette in his hand was not tobacco. For some reason, she was not at all comfortable with the notion of the Duke stoned.

"Hi." She did her best to sound friendly and casual. "Taking a break?"

Squinting, he dragged deeply on the joint. "Pink Floyd's babysitting the control room. How ya been?"

"Pretty good. Yourself?"

He didn't answer. His bloodshot eyes ran up and down the length of her body, boldly taking in the cotton drawstring pants and gauzy blouse.

"I . . . uh, I should be on my way," she said, taking a small step sideways. "I still have some mosaics to prepare before I go on."

He took a side step to match hers. "What's the rush? You got plenty of time." Holding out the joint, he said, "Care to mellow a little?"

"No, thanks, I don't . . . that is, I'm not interested at the moment." She suspected that the Duke, in his present state, might not be tolerant of nonindulgers. She was right.

"Moon Lady must be beyond earthly vices like cannabis," he said with a sneer, "since you're flying so high all the time as it is."

There was a hard, wheedling edge to his voice that she didn't like. "I suppose I am," she conceded carefully.

He was moving slowly toward her. "I'd be flyin' high too if I could walk through the city and see my face everywhere I went."

Kaitlin clenched her jaw and tried to step back unobtrusively. "Your posters are out there, too, Duke."

"Sure, in the record stores and the jeans stores for all the teenyboppers. Big whoopin' deal." His head jerked forward. "Do you know what happened to me the other day?"

"What?" Honestly, were there no well-adjusted people left anywhere?

"I walked into my favorite Italian restaurant the other day, and right above my table is you, framed in brass." He gave a caustic laugh. "The manager actually thought I'd be flattered, the stupid twit."

"He probably put it up because it's a nice photograph, but that's a credit to the photographers, not me. They could have made anyone look as good."

His eyes fell to her breasts. "Not quite, doll face. There is no mistaking what a sexy woman you are underneath your threads." He took one final drag before dropping the butt to the floor and crushing it out with his boot. Then he came closer. "Did you know people ask me all the time what you're really like? They think that just because I'm the Duke, I must have had my way with you by now. But since I haven't, tell me, are you the quiet, breathy type or the kind that moans a lot?"

Kaitlin stepped backward. "That's enough, Duke. Let me pass."

"I already told you, no hurry. There's plenty of time for us to get better acquainted. You might think you're too good to be seen with me in public, but maybe you wouldn't object to a little private exploration down here." He slid the palms of his hands down his jeans and licked his lips. "Nobody'd have to know but you and me, if that's what's worrying you. You could keep your lily-white reputation unsullied."

"That's not funny," she said, her eyes never leaving his face.

"Who's laughing?"

She tried to dodge him, but despite his altered perception, he was faster. His fingers clamped around her upper arm. "Hold it! Not so fast, gorgeous. We're not finished yet."

"Let me go." The three words were delivered with pure, icy rage, as she glared at the offending hand on her arm.

He brought his face close to hers, and she could smell the musty weed on his breath. "What's the matter? Can't you close your eyes and pretend I'm Elliot? Would that be so tough?"

Kaitlin felt the color drain from her cheeks. "What is that supposed to mean?"

"Hell, it's no secret, baby. You two have been mooning over each other since you got here—pardon the pun." He had both hands on her now and was backing her toward the wall. It was just a matter of waiting until he was off guard, she told herself. "How many times has Elliot been privileged to partake, eh, Moon Lady?" His mouth went to the side of her neck. "How many times has he done this?"

She jerked her head away. "Stop it! There's nothing between Elliot and me. We're just friends!" Her voice, quavering with revulsion, echoed through the clammy hall.

The Duke lifted his face and his eyes bored into hers. "Spare me the hysteria, sweetheart. You are an ambitious young thing, aren't you? It's not enough that Mike has turned you into the radio princess. You still have to cinch the deal by cozying up to the PD. Then, whaddya know, one little whimper from Moon Lady and they dig up this stupid escape route for you. Can't take the heat? Then get out of the radio business. There isn't room for both of us here."

She stared at him, aghast, but some subconscious impulse must have been triggered, for she wrenched free of him and ran down the corridor to the station. He didn't chase her.

"Go ahead and run, sweetheart, but you won't get very far away from me. I still have to sign off." She could hear his demonic laughter all the way up the stairs.

Only when she reached the relative safety of the rest room and locked the door did Kaitlin allow herself to catch her breath and think. Was it the Duke who had been tormenting her, jealous of her popularity? The pieces fitted, the motives were plausible. She knew how delicate his inflated ego really was, and she'd never tried to hide her lack of interest in him as a date.

She went to the sink and splashed cold water on her face. What was she supposed to do now? The Duke was right. She couldn't avoid him. Her show was due to start in less than ten minutes, and the rule was that the on-air announcer did not sign off until the relief was in the room. She was as effectively trapped in this station as if it were a cage, with the Duke holding the key.

Finally composure—or perhaps it was resignation—set in, and Kaitlin made her way to the control room. She couldn't very well hide for the rest of the night, and Duke was enough of a professional not to leave the board for long. No matter how serious he imagined this unsettled score between them to be, he wouldn't do anything to risk the adulation of his fans.

He was leaning into the microphone when Kaitlin came in. "Be sure to catch the new Tears for Fears video," he was saying, "that was produced by some incredible local talent. I wouldn't be surprised if we see a lot more of their work in the future. Now I'll be leaving you with this memory from Santana...'Black Magic Woman.' The woman herself, by the way, has just come in; Moon Lady is standing by to wrap you up in her witchery."

Kaitlin stood on the other side of the counter scarcely breathing, needing all her strength to look the Duke straight in the eye. When the Santana album started playing, she said, "Are you satisfied now? Have you had your bit of fun, or can I expect to be attacked and left for dead beneath the turntables?"

The Duke was wearing the same smug expression of self-love he always did. He moved away from the board and made a broad sweeping gesture with his arm. "It's all yours, Moon Lady."

"Aren't you even going to admit it?"

"Admit what?"

"The roses, the phone calls. You're behind it all, aren't you?"

"Don't be ridiculous. I wouldn't waste my time on useless pranks like that, but it does make for great office gossip."

"Oh, sure," she snapped, "and I suppose you claim no responsibility for what happened in the basement a few minutes ago, either."

"Of course I do, gorgeous." He laughed harshly. "You shouldn't sneak up on a man like that. It can make him very...unpredictable." Leaning over the counter, he flicked her chin with his middle finger, and it was all Kaitlin could do not to flinch.

"Don't change the subject. Did you or did you not place those disgusting calls while I was on the air?"

His smile was totally bereft of humor. "Why would I go to all that trouble when I have you right where I want you five nights a week? I don't know if it's occurred to you, but we're locked in here alone together every night. What could you do if I decided not to leave one night? Would you like some company for a change?"

It was dangerously tempting to slap his face and threaten to go to Mike, but she had already determined that Duke's behavior was far worse when he was antagonized.

"Go ahead and stay if you want," she answered frostily. "You belong here as much as I do—maybe even more if you're counting seniority. But I'm getting tired of your threats, Duke, and I'm tired of looking over my shoulder all the time. So why don't you stay and keep me company? That way, if I do get another call, I'll know I was wrong to accuse you."

"Clever of you to come up with that little ploy," he said with a menacing leer. "So you'd actually condescend to spend the night with me just to rout out your demented admirer. But no thanks, honey. I have better things to do with my time than listen to you seduce the audience with that satiny voice of yours." He went to the door and grabbed hold of the knob. "Then again, who knows? Maybe I'll change my mind and drop in later on. We could pick up where we left off. I have the key, so you won't have to let me in." An instant later, Kaitlin was alone, but she did not feel the slightest bit at ease.

For five interminable hours, she waited. Waited for the light on the telephone console to flash, waited for the door behind her to open, waited for the outcome of the faceless threat. All night, there was a painful knot of tension in her stomach. She got through her show without a hitch, but it was uninspired. When she wasn't dreading each coming moment, she was wondering how and when everything had gone so wrong.

She'd had such high aspirations when she'd come to this city, such exciting plans. She was going to make new friends, gain the respect of her peers, achieve success and security. Of these, she'd attained precious little, except a measure of success, which had turned out to be an empty achievement. She'd gladly give it up for a real friend or two.

It seemed that, right from the start, everyone was determined to misread her intentions. The more she tried to convince people of her goodwill, the more miserably she failed. A microphone in a locked room at night was not a friend; thousands of fans could not make up for the lack of a lover. They thought she had it all, but no one understood the truth. No one except, perhaps, Elliot.

Despite all their differences and altercations, thinking about Elliot still made her feel better. Despite everything, she couldn't forget that he was responsible for the one and only perfect day she'd had since coming to Toronto. She only had to shut her eyes to bring back the feel of the breeze drifting across the lake...

Kaitlin shook her head to free herself of the memories. It wasn't healthy to attach too much importance to a single day, no matter how idyllic it seemed. There was still a barrier between her and her program director, one so vast that it somehow forced them to deny each other. She knew he found her attractive, and he even sympathized with her... or so it had seemed at the time. Perhaps she'd been deluding herself.

He had listened closely when she'd told him what had happened, listened with almost exaggerated patience. But what proof could she offer, other than her word that they'd taken place? None. There was simply no concrete evidence, and she was also in the unfortunate position of being the new kid on the block, still obliged to prove herself. Their physical attraction for each other—let alone any communication on a deeper level— could hardly be expected to grow if Elliot harbored doubts about her state of mind.

Out of nowhere, a more horrifying realization assaulted her. The incident of the female announcer in Seattle, the one Elliot had specifically warned her about. The woman had introduced unorthodox elements into her show, and they'd found her with her throat— No, she wouldn't think about that now. Elliot wouldn't invent such a story just to give himself credibility. Of course he wouldn't; he'd have absolutely nothing to gain by frightening her or driving her away. Kaitlin lifted a trembling hand to her face, suddenly more terrified by her thoughts than by anything that had happened to her so far. How on earth could she possibly know what Elliot Jacobs stood to gain?

THE SUN WAS ALREADY UP, the traffic of the city building to its usual frenzied pace. It was time to jot down a thought or two. Writing in the journal always released tension and made for a better day.

Things ought to be going better for me by now. I'm not getting any younger. Yet every time I think I'm close to achieving my goals, they elude me. Just yesterday I heard people on the street talking about Moon Lady. They were going to enter that silly contest of hers, and I thought how typical of her fans to waste their time on such a fraud. She doesn't deserve her fame, and she certainly can't handle success—not the way I'd be able to.

Don't worry, though. I haven't forgotten my plans. Moon Lady won't be allowed to continue for long, but I'm biding my time for now, waiting for the exact moment to eject her from the limelight.

Come to think of it, the act of eliminating Moon Lady might even further my plans. After all, who could ever forget what John Wilkes Booth did to Abraham Lincoln?

Chapter Eight

The Duke, as usual, barged into Elliot's office without knocking. "You have to get rid of that woman! She's a menace to us all."

Elliot put down the latest issue of *Billboard* and leaned back in his chair with barely concealed irritation. "Is Lorna trying to poison you again with her coffee?"

Uninvited, the red-haired man sprawled on the nearest chair, folding his hands across his narrow chest. "Not her. I'm talking about Moon Lady."

"Her name is Kaitlin."

"Whatever."

Elliot expelled a deep breath. "I hope this isn't another of your tirades about competition. I've already told you we can't have nineteen hours of mediocre programming just to make your show sound better."

"I know, I'm over that now; and I like all the other announcers. We get along great. But this woman..." He shuddered. "She really burns me."

"Why don't you be more specific?" Elliot's tone was as controlled as it always was when he dealt with the Duke. Give the man an inch of sympathy and he'd take a mile.

"Okay, I'll be specific. Take the other day, for instance. I ran into her while she was skulking through her stupid secret tunnel—"

"What were you doing down there?"

Hardly missing a beat, the Duke replied, "Takin' a break."

"Kind of bleak surroundings for a coffee break, isn't it?"

"Yeah, well, it's peaceful down there, and I don't have to worry about clouding up the station with smoke—know what I mean?"

Elliot's eyes flickered. "I know exactly what you mean."

The announcer squirmed in his seat. "So, anyway, as I was saying, along she comes and starts accusing me of making crank calls. I'm trying to calm her down, make her see the light, and—wouldn't you know it—she starts coming on to me."

"You're lying," said Elliot, rising from his chair.

"No, honest to God, she actually accused me of—"

"I'm not talking about that. You said she came on to you." He had both palms planted firmly on the desk, his eyes riveted on the man across from him.

The Duke lifted his hands, palms up. "Is that so hard to believe? You know my phenomenal success with women."

"But you aren't her type," Elliot countered in a low voice.

"Are you trying to say that you are?"

The program director's dark blue eyes were glittering with rage. "That's not the issue here."

"Well, from what I can gather, she's a pretty lonely lady. If you don't take better care of her, she's bound to go looking elsewhere."

It would be so easy—and so satisfying—to pick up the little wimp and hurl him across the room, but an assault charge wasn't exactly in his best interests at the moment. And he was familiar enough with the Duke's type to know he'd probably go out and inflict more injuries on himself just for added effect in the courtroom. As a less gratifying but safer alternative, he counted silently to ten. "Why are you so intent on making Kaitlin look bad?"

"I'm not," he protested.

"Did you make those calls to her?"

The Duke didn't even move a muscle. "Of course not."

"It would make sense," Elliot went on to say. "Kaitlin puts on one hell of a show, and there's never been anyone around here who could dethrone you the way she can. So why not try to frighten her or seduce her into leaving? You'd do just about anything to stay on top."

"Nice play on words, Jacobs, under the circumstances." He was buffing his nails against his shirt and examining them.

Elliot came around the desk to the Duke's chair. "Get up, Luther."

The man bristled at the sound of his real name. "What did you call me?"

"You heard." Elliot was so close that the announcer had to lean back and push himself up from the chair with both arms. Then he had to tilt his head to stare the taller man in the eye. "If I hear anything, even a single rumor that you're bothering Kaitlin again, I'll have you fired so fast your head will spin."

Despite Elliot's physical superiority, the Duke still managed to hold his own. "Are you afraid she'll get tired of you and come to me?'' he sneered. ''Or is it that you're the one who made the calls and you think I might spill the beans?''

His patience exhausted, Elliot grabbed the front of the disc jockey's shirt and yanked it up to his neck, lifting him to his toes. ''You scrawny little bastard. I'd be doing all of us a favor to kick you out of this station right now.''

The Duke's face was turning a tomato red. ''Hell, boss, it's no secret how furious you were when the big man hired Moon Lady. According to Lorna, Mike was all set to give you two weeks' notice 'cause of your attitude. Getting canned sure would have messed up your schemes, wouldn't it?''

Elliot released him as if he'd suddenly become too repulsive to touch. ''That's all in the past, and it had nothing to do with Kaitlin personally. She turned out better than any of us could have imagined.''

''Sure, but it sticks in your craw to admit it, doesn't it?'' He slithered from between Elliot and the chair like an eel. ''Naturally, you're going to be one hundred percent cooperative now; a few words from Mike in the wrong places and your future could be screwed up for good. Maybe that's why you're chasing Moon Lady's skirts. What better way to show Mike that you're still his boy than by bedding the announcer you were ready to quit your job over a few months ago?''

Seething, Elliot fought to suppress the overwhelming urge to ram the man's capped teeth into his head. His self-discipline won out and he turned to pick up the briefcase beside his desk. ''I'm going downtown,'' he said evenly. ''When I get back, I don't want to see your face around here until it's time to do your show.''

''You can't threaten me, Jacobs.''

Lord, the man didn't know when to back off. He stared the Duke straight in the eye. "One more thing. If you do have reason to come into this office—and it better be a damned good reason—be sure to knock. If you don't, you'll be out of this station on your ear. I guarantee it."

SEEING HIS LIGHT BLUE 1966 Toronado in the parking lot always gave Elliot a quiver of possessive pride. The body of the brawny Oldsmobile was immaculate, and he knew every inch of its Rocket V-8 engine by heart. It had been his dream as a boy, this ultimate luxury sports car, all sleekness and muscle. At the age of fourteen he had made the first of two promises to himself—to own a '66 Toronado someday. And though it had taken ten years to find one that had been gutted by fire and destined for the scrapyard—and was therefore affordable—his boyhood dream had eventually come true. Scrounging up the money as he went along, he had refitted and rebuilt the entire vehicle, piece by piece. Today it would be worth triple the original price, and though he could easily afford a more contemporary model now, some dreams died hard. If he were down to his last nickel, he wouldn't sell this car.

Sliding in behind the chrome-tinted dash, he turned the key in the ignition and automatically tuned his ear to the controlled roar of the engine. He depressed the throttle and with a quick twist of the wheel, headed south. Once he was on the road, his thoughts returned to the unpleasant incident in his office.

Insufferable egomaniac though he was, the Duke of Rock hadn't been far off the track. Things had been touch-and-go while they'd been putting together a new night show. Elliot always prided himself on being the

cool and collected one amid a bunch of chronic hot-
heads, but when his good, solid program of upbeat
classical and jazz had been axed by Mike, he'd seen red.
Bad enough that it had meant the waste of months of
hard work and the end of an opportunity that wasn't
likely to come again, but to have his proposal turned
down in favor of Mike's audio-burlesque Moon Lady
had been the final affront. His show could have been his
ticket out, and the fulfillment of the second promise
he'd made to himself as an impoverished Saskatch-
ewan farm boy. Now, as he approached his thirty-fifth
birthday, he feared that it was becoming more and more
unlikely that his plans would come to pass. There
weren't many options at the moment for what he
wanted.

Elliot found a parking spot as close as he could to the
monolithic skyscraper on Bay Street. As he stepped out
of the car, mentally preparing himself for the meeting
with the heads of the investment conglomerate, he reminded himself that real opportunities were self-
initiated. They did not fall into one's lap. His all-night
snow and everything it had entailed was no longer a
reality... period. Therefore, it was simply a matter of
creating a new reality. When the meeting was over—
successful or not—he would call Kaitlin and invite her
to his favorite Mexican restaurant. It was definitely time
they got together again.

FERNANDO'S WAS THE KIND OF PLACE one frequented
for the food, not the ambience. Elliot and Kaitlin were
seated at one of five small tables, beneath a hanging
planter made of coffee cans. The bullfight posters had
seen better days, and the curtains on the windows
looked as though they might disintegrate at a touch.

Once she got over her initial shock, however, Kaitlin allowed herself to be wafted away by the tantalizing aromas of oregano, cumin and hot chili peppers. Someone in the kitchen definitely knew how to do things right.

After they'd placed their orders, the waiter arrived with two frosty bottles of Mexican beer and a pair of mugs. On the house, he said, since Elliot, practically a resident of the place, had graced them with a guest.

"I probably shouldn't drink before my show," Kaitlin said, eyeing the cold drink longingly since air-conditioning wasn't one of the restaurant's charms.

"Still, you ought to go through the motions of enjoying the beer or you'll offend the owner. He still labors under some pretty traditional ideas of machismo," Elliot replied.

She turned and saw the swarthy, mustachioed owner watching them with proprietary pride. Dutifully, she took a sip. One drink couldn't make much difference, especially since she was with Elliot and his presence alone always seemed to stimulate her for hours afterward. "I was pleased," she said, "when you asked me out for dinner, though I'll admit I wasn't expecting a place quite like this."

He laughed good-naturedly. "You may not believe it, but I only share this place with a very select few, people who I think will appreciate the restaurant's subtle fine points." He raised his glass to his lips. "The reason I asked you out is that I didn't want to leave you with a totally negative impression of our day at Toronto Island."

"You didn't," Kaitlin protested. "It was a wonderful day."

"I'm referring more to the evening that followed, actually. I must have come across like a terrified schoolboy, running off like that." Elliot's eyes were downcast, and Kaitlin sensed he was having trouble putting his feelings into words.

She reached out and covered his hand with hers. "It's all right; I understand." She'd been through it herself in the past few days: the doubts, the anger, the confusion, the waves of desire that seemed to wash over her when she least expected it.

"I feel...very strongly about you, Kaitlin. You have to believe that. But I ..." His words trailed off, and he looked away.

"You have trouble accepting your feelings in light of the things I've told you, is that it? The phone calls, the flowers—I could have set it up myself." She found it easy to finish his thoughts for him if only because tonight her feelings were on an upswing. Had it been another occasion, such as the night she was alone and frightened in the control room, it would have been a different story. But theirs seemed to be a familiar and recurring theme: one of them willing to believe while the other doubted, and then the reverse. She wondered if there would ever come a time when they would be of the same mind long enough for happier emotions to take their course.

"I'm grateful that you understand my misgivings," he said. "Deep inside, I know you're not lying, nor do I think you're the kind of person who does things to attract attention, despite what you've told me about your childhood. I'd be more likely to suspect the Duke of staging something to make us sit up and take notice of him."

Kaitlin traced the rim of her glass with one finger. "I don't think even the Duke is capable of it. In fact, I don't know anyone who is. That's the trouble."

Elliot didn't answer right away. His face revealed concern, as well as the intense expression that always made Kaitlin feel like the most desirable woman on earth.

"Next time someone does something to you," he said, "I don't care what it is or when it happens, just call me...right away." He brought Kaitlin's fingers to his mouth and held them there for a moment, his eyes riveted to hers. "What I find hardest to understand is how anyone could want to hurt a woman as exquisite as you."

NO ONE, NOT EVEN THE DUKE of Rock, was capable of ruining her frame of mind that night. It was a refreshingly cool summer evening and Kaitlin breezed into the station like a glider on a tailwind, humming a silly love song as she went.

To her great amazement, she found the Duke sitting at the board in ordinary clothes—plain blue jeans, a regular T-shirt with nothing obscene or glittery about it. Even his hair had been trimmed so that the curls touched his shoulders instead of coiling several inches below. He looked up from the foolscap pad he was writing on. "Hi," he said. No sneers, no innuendos, just a simple friendly greeting. Kaitlin looked heavenward and offered a silent word of thanks. Perhaps normalcy had finally descended on them all, she thought, herself included.

"Hello, Duke. You seem to be hard at work."

"I am," he said, sighing. "It's my résumé."

She perched on a corner of the counter. "Your résumé? What on earth for?"

He moved the sheets of paper aside so she couldn't read them, not that she'd intended to. "I'm just ready for a change, that's all."

"A change to what? You *are* CSKY. We'd wither away without you."

He lowered his head modestly. "Nice of you to say that, but I'm too old to keep up this life-style. Besides, there's an awful lot of new talent coming up behind me and not much I can do to stop it."

Kaitlin waited for the inevitable barb. It didn't come. "Are you feeling all right?" she couldn't help but inquire.

"Sure. Why do you ask?"

"You're being so...nice," she said, for lack of a better word.

His grin was anemic. "It's a shame you and I have had so much trouble...uh, clicking. I'm sorry about what I did the other night...and for all the other things."

All the other things? She was loath to ask exactly what he meant, as if the question might unleash a whole new batch of unpleasantness. Strange, she had never noticed before that one of his eyes didn't focus quite right, and though she was looking straight at him, she had the impression that he was gazing somewhere over her shoulder.

But that didn't mean he wasn't being sincere, and if he had been the one harassing her, at least he'd admitted it, sort of. It would be petty of her not to accept his apology, and besides, what could be more fitting to end a perfect evening? First, dinner with Elliot at a marvelous Mexican restaurant, and now an admission of guilt from the Duke. As Lorna might have put it, her bio-rhythms had to be up.

"It's okay, Duke. We all act a little foolish now and again. Desperate times call for desperate measures, and all that." She held out her hand. "Friends?"

He squeezed her fingers lightly. "Friends. Now, if you'll excuse me." He swiveled his chair to the control board and said good-night. Kaitlin noticed his banter was a little off, but that happened to the best of them, especially when they were down. He got up from the chair. "You're looking great tonight," he said. "Did you get a raise or something?"

Kaitlin smiled. "Not exactly. I had a very nice date."

The Duke punched her gently on the shoulder. "Way to go, kid. Glad to see you're getting out. It wouldn't, by any chance, be Elliot?"

There didn't seem to be much reason for her to keep it a secret, since Elliot had deigned to take her to a res-taurant three doors down from the station. "It was El-liot," she admitted.

The Duke nodded his approval. "You two make an . . . interesting couple. You deserve each other. Well, I gotta go."

"Heavy date?"

He stretched his arms upward and gave a huge yawn. "Not tonight. It's straight home to bed for me." He picked up the résumé, folded it and jammed it into the back pocket of his jeans. "Good night, Kaitlin. Have a good show."

"Thanks, Duke. Good night," she said, incredulous at this sudden change of character. What could possi-bly have come over him?

A few minutes into the show, she spotted an inter-office memo, stapled shut, with her name written on it.

Opening it, she immediately recognized Elliot's handwriting.

> If you get a chance, I have a request—"Midnight Confessions" by the Grass Roots. By the time you play it, I'll be recovering from that third enchilada I never should have had.
>
> Yours, Elliot.

Thoroughly enjoying her show for the first time in weeks, Kaitlin slipped the headphones over her ears. "This next song is a great golden oldie, dedicated to all of you who might be recovering from that last piece of pizza or extra helping of dessert...or, for some of you, that third enchilada."

She was too young to remember the song, but the rock rhythms were as fresh and contemporary as if it were brand-new, and the lyrics told her exactly what she wanted to hear. "In my midnight confessions, when I'm tellin' the world that I love you..." Leaning back in her chair, she let out a whoop of sheer, indefatigable joy.

THE CSKY BARBECUE was an annual tradition hosted by Charlie Carr at his home. His bungalow was small but had a large backyard to entertain the station's staff, their spouses and children. According to Charlie, the event had been rained out only once in twenty-three years, and this year the sun was as accommodating as ever. Kaitlin and Elliot were the last to arrive, since she had needed a chance to catch up on her rest. He ushered her through the gate to the back, where they were greeted by the sight of children splashing happily in the pool and adults, holding tall cool drinks, clustered in lawn chairs beneath the shade of a cedar roof.

Charlie, who was manning the barbecue with long-handled utensils and wearing a silly apron, waved when he saw them. "Hi, folks—glad you could make it. Get enough sleep, Kait?"

"I did, thanks." Kaitlin looked around at the tall cedars bordering the fence and the hedge of climbing roses by the house. "You have a lovely place here, Charlie." She'd grown to like the man since she'd begun working at the station. He came across as a bit overexuberant, but he had a heart of gold that couldn't help but shine through. Next to Elliot, he was her favorite colleague.

"We're happy here, Edith and I," he said. "It's taken us a while to get things the way we like them, but that's what it's all about, isn't it—puttering our lives away together."

"I guess it is," replied Kaitlin with a laugh, almost envying the look of supreme contentment on the little man's face. Not that she wasn't in heaven herself, considering that Elliot had invited her as his date to this event. She knew there were many curious eyes focused on them, and since Elliot's arm was firmly clasped around her waist, no one could mistake that they were a couple.

"Where is that terrific wife of yours, by the way?" asked Elliot, scanning the crowd.

"In the kitchen, putting together her famous hors d'oeuvres. Go on in, say hello. She's been dying to see you."

"We'll do that." Elliot took Kaitlin's hand. "There's something I want to show you first," he said, leading her through the house to a set of French doors. "These are left closed on barbecue days to keep little ones out," he explained as they entered the family room.

She looked around in awe at the extensive collection of radio memorabilia: microphones dating from the twenties, crystal sets, the most primitive of receivers and radio kits from the forties. The walls held collages of industry pioneers, awards and clippings, as well as photos of a much younger Charlie Carr sitting in the news booth of a local station.

"This is absolutely remarkable for a private collection," said Kaitlin. "I haven't seen this much since I was at the Smithsonian."

"Edith is the real aficionada," Elliot said. "She's the one who's collected most of it. Rumor has it that she met Charlie by sending him a fan letter."

"No kidding? Have you noticed how Charlie's eyes light up when he talks about her?"

He lowered his head to give her a quick kiss. "They're the most in-love couple I know. Odds are it has to happen once every generation or so."

Kaitlin wholeheartedly echoed his sentiment as they walked to the kitchen, reminding herself that Elliot's kisses, no matter how tantalizing, were not promises of a lifetime of bliss. At the most, they would brighten up the present—and that was fine, too.

She was expecting a plain woman to match Charlie's somewhat comical, dated appearance. She certainly wasn't expecting the exquisite silver-haired woman with luminous eyes who looked up from her wheelchair as she was preparing tidbits of shrimp, crab and cheese.

"Elliot, you charmer," Charlie's wife exclaimed, "how wonderful to see you. I was so afraid you weren't coming."

He crossed the room and bent to kiss the woman's cheek. "You know I would never miss an opportunity to see you, Edith."

Kaitlin wasn't sure why her eyes suddenly filled with tears. It might have been the warmth in Elliot's voice or the sweet affection that radiated from Mrs. Carr. Whatever it was, she could understand why Charlie was still head over heels in love with his wife, and she felt strangely envious.

The woman's laugh was clear and bell-like. "No need to flatter me; it's the shrimp balls you come for." She turned to greet the younger woman. "So this is who captured my Charlie's heart in Sandusky."

She spoke the words with sheer delight, and Kaitlin liked Edith Carr at once. She introduced herself, saying, "From the way Charlie talks about you, you don't need to worry."

"Oh, he's a pet, all right," Edith replied. "I was lucky to find a man like him. But tell me, Kaitlin, how are you settling into the city? I heard you had some problems with harassing phone calls."

Kaitlin glanced up at Elliot, whose slight nod told her that Charlie shared everything with his wife. "It's all right now," she said. "No one has bothered me for weeks. I'm thoroughly enjoying my job and the city now."

"That is good to hear. I was so worried for you when Charlie told me." Edith glanced from one to the other. "I understand the two of you have become something of an item these days."

It was delightful to see the usually cool Elliot groping for words. Kaitlin would even have sworn that he turned a shade or two darker. She answered for both of them. "We're getting along well ... so far."

Edith clapped her hands. "It couldn't be more perfect. This man here has been alone for much too long, and I've always maintained it's because he would never settle for second-best in a woman."

Elliot folded his arms and looked askance at the women. "Did the two of you rehearse this speech ahead of time?"

"Absolutely not," Edith said. "I've been listening to Kaitlin's show since she started and always knew I'd like her." She wagged her finger. "Now mind, Elliot, you look after her. And the same goes for you, Kaitlin, dear. If I were thirty-five years younger and didn't have my Charlie, I wouldn't let Elliot out of my sight until I knew he was mine."

Kaitlin burst out laughing. "I'll remember what you've said."

"Would you like us to carry these trays out for you?" a bemused Elliot asked.

"Please, would you?" said Edith. "It's time for me to mingle. I do so enjoy this event." She touched each of them lightly on the arm and wheeled herself out of the kitchen. When she was gone, Kaitlin nabbed a cheese puff and brought it to Elliot's mouth.

"Unnerved, are we?" she teased.

He grabbed her fingers and pretended to devour them along with the hors d'oeuvre. "I'm still convinced it's a conspiracy."

Kaitlin's laughter rang out again. "I'll never tell."

FOR MONTHS, SHE HAD INTENDED to take pictures of her co-workers to send home to her parents, but getting people together during working hours was impossible. Today was a perfect opportunity. At Edith's insistence, Kaitlin had stowed her camera in the master bedroom closet, and after they'd finished eating, she went into the bedroom to retrieve it.

She was sitting on the bed advancing the film when the bedroom door flew open, slamming against the wall. Kaitlin's head shot up. "Mike! You startled me."

His nose was bright red, and it wasn't entirely because of sunburn, if the Scotch fumes were any indication. "Hi, sweetie," he said in a telltale slur. "Fancy meetin' you here."

Determined to conceal her revulsion, Kaitlin kept her expression pleasant. The man was still her boss, drunk or not. "I'm getting my camera ready to take some pictures. The lighting outside is perfect right now."

He sat down beside her, making the bedsprings bounce wildly, and Kaitlin slid into the ravine created by his weight. With their sides pressed together as though they were in a hammock, she tried to push herself off the bed, but before she could make her escape, he'd clamped a beefy arm around her shoulders. "Don't go away," he said. "I was gonna come in here for a snooze, but I'd rather talk to somebody."

Not entirely convinced of his motives, Kaitlin tried to take a surreptitious peek. To her surprise, he wasn't ogling her; he wasn't even looking her way. He might have had his arm around her to hold himself up, and maybe he really did want to talk.

"What's the matter?" she asked.

"Everything. Nothing's going right."

Kaitlin thought about the perfect light outside, dwindling by the minute, and hoped he'd settle for a few well-meaning phrases. "We all have days when we feel like that. The best thing to do is get a good night's sleep, and things will look better in the morning."

"Sleep won't help a damned bit this time. I got money problems and health problems and woman problems."

She had to agree that sleep might not be the answer in this case. With the sinking feeling that she would regret this, she asked, "Would it help to tell me about it?"

He jerked his head in her direction, as if he wasn't quite sure who'd asked the question and then, apparently satisfied, commenced his tale of woe. "I was seven years old when I came to this country. My old man had a wife and eight kids, and twenty-seven dollars in his pocket."

His arm had slipped off her shoulder, and he hadn't noticed, so Kaitlin managed to move a few inches away. "That's fascinating," she said.

Mike grunted. "I had my first job when I was nine years old, selling papers on the street corner." He gaped at her. "Didja ever see pictures of snotty-nosed kids dressed in patches, with a stack of dailies under their arm?" She nodded. "Well, that was me. Those rich tycoons from Rosedale would look down their skinny Anglo-Saxon noses and not even bother to check if the coin had dropped into my hand or on the ground. It got so I couldn't stand stooping into the gutter to get my money, and I swore I'd get out of that gutter for good someday. Now I got me a radio station, a TV station, real estate on Queen's Quay, and partnerships in six restaurants. Not bad for an immigrant kid, eh?"

"You've done extremely well for yourself," Kaitlin agreed.

"And I'm not near finished yet. Trouble is, I had to sell some of my stock to pay back taxes on the real estate. A couple of days later, my broker tells me the stock tripled after I sold. I started getting chest pains, and the doctor tells me if I don't quit drinking and smoking and worrying, I won't last five years."

Now what was a person supposed to say to a confession like that? "I'm sure the doctor knows best," she remarked, groaning at the triteness of her response. Why couldn't someone like Edith come in? She'd know the right thing to say.

Mike leaned forward and covered his face with his hands. He was making strange noises with his sinuses; it was entirely possible that he was crying.

Her hand instinctively went out to his shoulder in a gesture of sympathy. "You're going to be all right, Mike. This is just a temporary setback—it happens to all entrepreneurs sometime. Hang in there, and if you do what the doctor tells you, you might even feel better."

"I can't do that," he blubbered. "Mike Andretti's got an image to keep up. I can't go orderin' spring water and give up my cigars. People'd think I'm a pansy."

"No, they wouldn't," she protested.

He sniffled again. "Then there's my woman. She says if I don't marry her in six months, she'll leave me for good."

"So why don't you marry her?"

"I got no time for a wife. I work eighteen hours every day, except for Sundays when I work twelve. What am I gonna do with a wife?"

Kaitlin lifted her hands helplessly. "I don't know. Love her, I guess."

Something she said must have penetrated, because Mike's head lurched up and he tried to focus on her. My goodness, she thought, he certainly was hammered.

"Love her?" he echoed. "I already love her good, every chance I get. Why, just a couple nights ago, three times—"

"Not that kind of love," she cut in hastily, not in the least interested in hearing any details. "I was referring more to the...uh, bonding of two spirits." That euphemistic drivel seemed to float right over his head—understandably, since she wasn't quite sure of its meaning herself.

Changing the subject with drunken abruptness, he asked, "You ever love somebody?"

All set to toss off a blithe affirmative, she stopped herself. Had she ever loved anyone? Her thoughts drifted back through all the years of dating, rife with pleasant infatuations and the occasional broken heart, but she came up empty. Then Elliot's face popped into her head. It was conceivable, she supposed, that she was falling in love with him, but it was just as likely that she was feeling the effects of sexual tension. She hardly knew the man, and one did not fall in love with a stranger. "I'm not sure," she finally answered.

"Well, it ain't worth the trouble," he said, shaking his head from side to side so hard the bed rocked. "Better to stay free than to get tied down to some broad who'll spend all your money and take the best years of your life."

Some innate feminine instinct made her bristle. "That's not always true. Look at Edith and Charlie."

"Yeah, but she don't nag. My woman wants a ring and a promotion and a raise...and kids even!" He shuddered, then shot out his pudgy hand and slapped it onto Kaitlin's knee. Horrified, she stared at the offending appendage and wondered whether she should lift it, leap off the bed or both. For the moment, she froze.

"You wouldn't be so hard on a fellow, would you, sweetie?" he drawled.

"Uh . . . I don't know."

He raised half-crossed, bloodshot eyes to her, no doubt trying to be intense. She tried to edge away, but the sudden movement made Mike lose his balance and topple, his head landing with a thump in her lap. "You'd make a fine wife, Kaitie," he mumbled in her thigh.

At that instant, Lorna appeared in the doorway, her expression murderous with rage. "You conniving bitch!" she screamed. "Get the hell away from my man!"

Chapter Nine

It took Kaitlin a full second to make the connection between Lorna and the man on her lap, but when she did, she leaped off the bed without regard for the fate of Mike Andretti's head. "This is not how it looks!" she blurted in her own defense, hoping the remark didn't sound as clichéd to the others as it did to her.

But it must have, for, if anything, Lorna's expression hardened as she went to the rescue of her barely conscious fiancé. He, by now, had slid off the bed to the floor, like a beached beluga, propped upright only by the paunch wedged between his knees.

"I know what I saw, and I know what I heard," the woman snapped, bending to cradle Mike's head as if he were the injured party.

"Oh, you do, do you? For your information, I happened to come in here to get my camera!" Kaitlin pointed at the bed. "See? There it is, right beside my purse. I had absolutely no idea Mike was going to stagger in here and pour out his life story to me."

Lorna's head spun around. "What did he tell you?"

A white lie was definitely in order here. "He told me about his childhood."

Lorna responded with a vitriolic glare, as if she weren't quite convinced of Kaitlin's truthfulness. Then she resumed her ministrations to Mike. "It's all right, baby. Your sweetheart's here."

The sweetheart might have been there, but the baby certainly wasn't. He was long gone, his head lolling, eyes closed.

"Lorna," Kaitlin said, "why didn't you ever tell me you and Mike were engaged?"

"Would it have made some kind of difference?" the woman tossed back. "Would you have left him alone then?"

"Yes ... I mean, no, but— Oh, for goodness' sake, believe what you want, but I am not interested in Mike and vice versa. Look at the man; he's practically comatose. He'd have poured his heart out to a coatrack if there'd been one handy."

Lorna didn't reply.

"Why the secrecy?" Kaitlin asked again.

She seemed to ponder her answer. "Mike never liked the idea of showing favoritism in the station. People knew we dated once in a while, but he wouldn't let me make any announcement until we set a date."

"How long have you been engaged?"

"Six years." Her admission was so soft that Kaitlin could barely hear it.

No wonder Lorna was so insecure, thought Kaitlin with a twinge of sympathy. There was no accounting for the course of true love, but it was obvious Lorna loved the man, which made the situation that much more pitiable. At the moment, Lorna was doing her best to hoist her lover onto the bed, a challenge akin to moving a 240-pound beanbag.

"Here, let me help," Kaitlin said, taking Mike under the opposite arm. Together, the two of them were able to move him not one single inch, and the only thing Mike did on his own behalf was moan. Finally, after they'd sweated and strained for several fruitless minutes, Elliot showed up.

"There you are, Kaitlin, I've been look—" His eyes fell to his boss on the floor. "What's happened to him?"

"Too much Johnny Walker," Kaitlin muttered, blowing upward to get the strands of hair off her sticky forehead.

"We need your help," Lorna said. "We can't budge him."

Suppressing his disgust, Elliot came into the room. "Okay, the two of you grab his legs. I'll hold him under the arms." When they'd taken their positions, Elliot counted to three, and then, together they swung him crosswise onto the bed. Elliot tried to revive him by slapping his florid cheeks, to no avail.

"What are we going to do with him?" Lorna, apparently finished with her accusations, was directing the plea to Elliot. Kaitlin knew perfectly well that she was being given the silent treatment. But who cared anymore? Trying to make Lorna understand what had actually happened was the ultimate exercise in futility, when one considered the alternating hostility and coolness of the past few months. By Monday, Lorna would probably have forgiven her this incident, and by Wednesday she'd have come up with another.

"Go to the kitchen and get some black coffee," Elliot said. "I'll try to wake him up. Then we have to get him home."

"How?" Lorna wailed. "We came here in Mike's car, and I can't drive."

"Call a cab," he replied.

"I can't do that."

Elliot stared at her. "Why the hell not?"

"What would people say?"

Elliot glanced at Kaitlin, as though hoping she might somehow be able to interpret this woman's chatter. He was also beginning to look extremely annoyed. "What do you mean, Lorna? What people?"

"Well, the cab driver, for one. What if he went around and blabbed to all the other drivers? You know what a celebrity Mike is in this city. If the gossip started spreading about him passing out at his annual barbecue, he'd kill me."

The program director abandoned the effort of reviving his employer for the moment and stood up. "That's the stupidest thing I've ever heard. If the man's dumb enough to drink like this, he's got to be willing to pay the price."

Lorna blanched. "No, Elliot, please. He'll take it out on me for letting him get into this mess. Couldn't we just let him sleep it off right here?"

"So he can throw up on the Carrs' bed? No way. Besides, Edith comes in here to rest partway through the afternoon. She won't take kindly to having this elephant snoring at her feet."

Kaitlin glanced over at Mike to see if Elliot's descriptions were being absorbed. They weren't. "I have a suggestion," she said. Lorna and Elliot turned to look at her. "Why don't we call my friend Larry? He drives a cab, and I've known him since I came to Toronto. I'm sure he'd be discreet, especially if we made a point of explaining the situation to him."

"I don't know..." Lorna said.

"I'll take full responsibility," Kaitlin offered. "I wouldn't bring it up if I didn't trust him implicitly." She looked at Elliot. "Sound reasonable to you?"

He shrugged. "To tell you the truth, I think everyone's acting paranoid, but I suppose it's as good an idea as any."

"I'll get the coffee," Lorna said, sighing, as she left the room.

Eventually, they succeeded in propping Mike up in a sitting position and making him swallow several sips of black coffee which, considering his size, probably accomplished nothing. But it was a way of passing the time until Larry arrived half an hour later. Charlie ushered the cabbie into the bedroom and Kaitlin introduced him.

Larry wasted no time in getting to the task at hand. "How ya doin', big guy?" he asked Mike, helping Elliot pull him to his feet. Mike responded with a lopsided grin and what was supposed to be a comradely gesture.

Larry and Elliot were strong men, but that did not prevent them from staggering under Mike's dead weight. Charlie had to guide them through the halls and doorways while Lorna trailed along behind, fretting.

The taxi was parked right outside the house. Charlie opened the car door while the two younger men heaved Mike into the back seat.

"I hope we're doing the right thing," Lorna muttered.

"Don't worry," Larry assured her in his affable way. "We'll get him home safe and sound. Now which one of you is going to be the big guy's chaperone?"

Kaitlin moved almost defensively to Elliot's side, relieved when his arm came around her. She wondered, with a twinge of guilt, whether she should offer to accompany Larry, as his friend and as the person who had asked the favor. But she didn't want to—she wanted to stay with Elliot.

Lorna sent Kaitlin one final scowl and a petulant toss of her head. "I'm coming with you," she said.

"Okay," Larry said, shaking hands with the men. "Might as well be off."

"Thanks a lot for helping us out," said Charlie. "If you have time when you're finished delivering our boss, why don't you come back for some refreshment? There's plenty of food—can't let it go to waste."

"Yes, please do," echoed Kaitlin, grateful that Larry had proved so cooperative.

"Hey, sounds great," he said. "I think I'll take you up on it." He slid into the driver's seat and drove off with a wave, a morose Lorna and a sluggish Mike in the back seat.

"Thank goodness for Larry," Kaitlin remarked as they returned to the party.

"Yup, he's a nice fella," Charlie said.

Elliot didn't say a word. But later, when they were in the backyard on lawn chairs with Charlie's famous daiquiris to help them recover from the ordeal, Elliot asked, "Where'd you meet this guy, anyway?"

"Who?" As far as Kaitlin could recall, they hadn't been talking about anyone for some time.

"Larry." He practically spat the name out.

Why, Elliot, don't tell me you're jealous. But of course it wouldn't have been gracious to let on that she suspected. "In his taxi, where else? He picked me up at the airport the day I moved here."

"And more than two months later you can still remember his name?"

Kaitlin struggled to keep from smiling. "Sure I do, because we've gone out once or twice since then, and I call him whenever I need a taxi."

"Oh, yeah? Is that all he does, drive cab?"

His remark surprised her. There were a lot of things she'd sometimes suspected Elliot of being, but a snob was not one of them. "As a matter of fact, he happens to be an actor."

"What's he done?" he snarled. As he looked at her, his midnight eyes were glittering with suspicion. She wasn't sure she liked this side of him, come to think of it.

"I don't know," she said. "Some stage work, I think, here and in the States."

"How do you know so much about him?"

"Well, seeing as how *you* insist on knowing so much about him, it's a good thing I do, isn't it? But if it eases your mind any, he and I are just good friends, and I'm lucky to have him. When I was getting those awful calls and everything, he was totally supportive and sympathetic." It wasn't necessary to add *unlike some people I could mention*; the implication was there.

Elliot took an abrupt swallow of his daiquiri. "Damned women's drink," he muttered. "I'm going inside for a beer." Kaitlin watched him go in through the patio doors and could have sworn he was stomping.

Larry arrived an hour later without Mike and Lorna, the job successfully completed. He had even found time to change his clothes and looked even more crisp and immaculate than usual. As he came out from the house, Kaitlin went to greet him, irritated that Elliot remained standing by the barbecue with a couple of sales reps and didn't join her in thanking him.

Knowing that Elliot was watching, Kaitlin linked her arm through Larry's. "Come on," she said. "I'll introduce you to some people."

"Looks like a pretty lively party," Larry said, observing the animated groups of adults and the teens dancing to a ghetto blaster at one end of the patio.

Kaitlin laughed. "It's gotten noticeably livelier in the past few hours."

After she'd introduced him to the other announcers, Larry asked, "Is the Duke of Rock here? I've always wanted to meet him."

She glanced around the yard. "He was here a few minutes ago. Oh, there he is, just coming out of the house." She waved to get the Duke's attention. "Over here."

The Duke, who had been treating her with extreme delicacy ever since the night he apologized, immediately hurried to join Kaitlin and her friend.

"One of your fans would like to meet you," she said, watching the Duke's face light up like a beacon. Adulation meant so much more to him than it did to her. "Duke, this is Larry O'Neill; Larry, you know who this is."

The two men shook hands and exchanged hearty greetings. "Let me get you a drink, Larry. What's your pleasure?"

Larry was beaming. "Uh...I'm an abstainer actually, but a Coke'd be great."

"It's over there." The Duke led him away, and neither of them even gave Kaitlin a second glance. But it didn't matter. The meeting of fan and idol was a sacred thing, she mused, not to be interfered with or interrupted. Suddenly she was aware of Elliot standing beside her with a pair of hamburgers on a paper plate.

"Care for one?" he asked, his voice expressionless.

She looked down and wrinkled her nose. "We just ate a few hours ago."

He lowered himself onto the nearest lawn chair, and Kaitlin followed suit. "I know," he said, "but there didn't seem to be anything else to do." With that, he bit into the first burger.

After a few minutes, they were joined by Larry and the Duke, who by now were getting along famously. Larry sat directly across from Elliot and smiled politely.

"So how's business?" Elliot condescended to ask, albeit sourly.

"Can't complain," Larry answered. "Fares are steady."

"It's all right," Kaitlin told him. "Elliot knows you're an actor; no need to be modest."

Larry chuckled. "Sure, but who am I kidding? I haven't had a part in months, not even a nibble."

"Don't sweat it," the Duke interjected. "You'll get your big break one of these days. Look at me. I used to work in a shoe store and had to look at people's bunions all day long. Hang in there."

Larry grinned at his new buddy. "I'll try."

"I understand you met Kaitlin when she came to Toronto," Elliot said. If the abrupt change of topic was apparent to Larry, he didn't show it. Probably a good acting job, thought Kaitlin, with growing impatience at her program director's behavior.

"That's right," replied the cabbie. "Prettiest fare I've ever had."

"Actually," Kaitlin said, quickly determining that undue flattery on Larry's part was not going to help matters at all, "not only did he rescue me from a lascivious porter, but he hauled twenty tons of luggage up to my apartment for me. From that day on, I've been convinced that chivalry still lives."

Elliot harrumphed, twisting the bottle of beer in his hands. When the Duke was called over to another group and had to excuse himself, a haze of silence descended on the remaining three.

"It turned out to be a nice day for the barbecue." Not one of Kaitlin's most memorable contributions to a conversation, but she was beginning to get desperate. Larry looked at her with something like gratitude and then turned to Elliot.

"Been in radio long?" he asked.

"About fifteen years." Elliot stood up. "Don't mean to be rude, but there's a Frisbee game over there that looks interesting, if you'll excuse me." Then he was gone.

"I see what you mean about the guy," Larry said when they were alone.

Kaitlin watched Elliot walk away. He was dressed in a well-worn pair of khaki shorts and a field shirt. She had never taken the time to observe his legs before and now discovered that unlike a lot of men, he didn't suffer from scrawny calves and knobby knees. In fact, his legs were definitely quite appealing. After a long while, she managed to tear her eyes away. "What did you say, Larry?"

"Your director, Elliot. You told me one time that you had trouble getting along with him. I can see why. Is he always this cranky?"

The mere mention of Elliot's name seemed to draw her eyes his way once again. "No, he's not at all...and we're not having trouble getting along anymore. He's just..." Elliot was picking up the Frisbee and tossing it expertly across the lawn.

"Just what?"

Kaitlin turned at the sound of Larry's voice. "I beg your pardon?"

He sighed and laughed gently. "You were saying something about Elliot. You said 'he's just,' but you didn't finish the sentence." He was looking at her strangely.

"I'm sorry, my mind must be wandering. It's been a long day."

"What's the matter?"

"Nothing." At least, there was nothing the matter that Elliot couldn't cure, if only he'd put his mind to it.

"Is he treating you well?"

"My program director, you mean?" Kaitlin smiled, and her expression softened perceptibly. "Oh, yes...I'd say he's definitely treating me well."

ALTHOUGH IT MIGHT HAVE BEEN ARGUED that he was doing a passable job of tossing and retrieving the red plastic disk, Elliot's attention was continually diverted to Kaitlin and her friend the taxi driver. Even from this distance, there was no mistaking the dreamy look in her eyes, the vague smile playing at the corners of her delectable mouth. He'd never noticed her looking quite that way before, so what the hell had Larry done to merit that kind of emotion from her? And what did she see in him, anyway? The guy didn't even know how to carry on a decent conversation. Some cabbie he was.

For the third time in a row, Elliot threw the Frisbee too high for his teammates to catch. Their complaints were growing more audible.

"Hey, Elliot, cut it out!"

"Come on, watch what you're doing!"

It took quite a while for their adolescent shouts to penetrate his awareness. "Sorry, guys, I wasn't paying attention."

He'd been too busy noticing that the Duke had re-joined Kaitlin and Larry, and that the three of them were yakking it up, having a grand old time. Once in a while, it looked as though Kaitlin was sneaking peeks his way, but then she'd toss that golden-brown mane over her shoulder and laugh uproariously at something. He'd never noticed it before, but when she laughed, her whole body seemed to radiate her good humor. What the hell was she so happy about, anyway? A couple of hours ago, Mike was slobbering all over her and Lorna was screaming at her. Anyone else would have had the good sense to go home after that.

And another thing, if Larry was such a damned prize, why hadn't she invited him to the barbecue in the first place? There was no need for her to act so thrilled when he'd asked her himself, earlier that week, if she'd had this O'Neill guy in mind all along.

The speeding Frisbee he should have caught ended its trajectory right in the middle of his diaphragm, momentarily knocking the wind out of him. "Oomph!" he groaned and doubled over.

The boy who threw it came running toward him. "Gosh, I'm sorry, but I thought for sure you'd catch it."

Elliot rubbed the tender spot and grinned. "It's okay, Scott, it was my fault. You guys go ahead and play without me. My reflexes are getting too old.'' He cut across the lawn past Kaitlin and her entourage, straight into the house. Enough of this hedging. He was going to stake his claim, once and for all. By the time this day was over, Kaitlin would no longer have any doubts as to how Elliot Jacobs felt about her.

A SHORT WHILE LATER, Kaitlin felt rather than saw Elliot approaching her. She turned, and something about him made her stare openly. The set of his broad shoulders was even more compelling than usual, and his eyes were fastened unwaveringly on hers. Whatever Larry was saying to her faded like a mist from her mind, and she was reminded once again of how she'd felt the day she and Elliot had met. Everything and everyone else were relegated to the background as he approached her; this man who seemed to belong to another time, another place. Without quite knowing why, she stood up.

''We're going home,'' he said, capturing her hands in his.

''All right,'' she answered without hesitation.

''What for? It's still early,'' Larry said.

The Duke guzzled the rest of his beer. ''You don't know the program director. He always leaves early.'' Casting a distasteful glance around the thinning crowd, he added, ''Come to think of it, leaving's not a bad idea. Hey, Larry, want to go downtown and catch some action?''

Larry shook his head. ''I have to work this evening; in fact, I really shouldn't have stayed this long.'' He stood up beside Kaitlin. ''Can I give the two of you a lift anywhere?''

Virtually oblivious to what was going on around them, Elliot muttered, ''No, thanks, I have a car.''

"Wait here," Kaitlin said in a voice barely above a whisper. "I have to get my purse."

"I'll wait," Elliot said, aware of a growing sense of contentment. He nodded his goodbyes to the other two men, who left without further ado, then shoved his hands into his pockets to await Kaitlin's return.

The delicious prospect of leaving with Elliot added a lightness to her step that Kaitlin would have thought was obvious to the whole world. Perhaps it was the way he had said, "We're going home." It wasn't like an order, but an invitation she'd been anticipating with delight all day. Her place, his place, it didn't matter where as long as they were alone together.

She went into the Carrs' bedroom, where she had left her purse earlier that afternoon. The bed had been straightened since the fiasco with Mike, but her purse was no longer there. Perhaps some kind soul had put it in the closet for safekeeping, she reasoned. Opening the closet doors, she found her camera at once, but no purse anywhere in sight. How odd, she thought, picking up the camera. Had she taken her purse outside with her? It seemed unlikely because she clearly remembered thinking the white canvas duck would end up ruined by grass stains or a spilled drink. Just to be sure she wasn't overlooking any possibilities, she searched under the bed and on all the tables but found nothing.

Surely no one would have stolen it; this was such an intimate party. She pushed the possibility from her mind as she went to check in the kitchen. She found two men talking shop and eating chips, but no purse. With a slightly sick feeling; she realized she might have to replace all her recently acquired Canadian identification as well as her credit cards. She hadn't been carrying much money in her purse, but there were a number of irreplaceable photographs. On an off chance, she checked the bathroom; it wasn't there, either. Kaitlin thought hard. Where else could she have left it?

The family room! The first room she'd been in, and she'd definitely had the purse with her then. Though it was unlikely she'd have put it down among such valuable antiques, it was worth checking nonetheless.

She found the French doors slightly ajar, a fact she would not have noticed if Elliot had specifically mentioned that they were kept closed on barbecue days. Pushing the doors open, she stepped inside. It took her a moment to recognize the room and to register what had happened. She gasped aloud, the horror of it slowly sinking in.

Chairs were overturned, lamps knocked over. The delicate antique microphones had been strewn across the floor with their cords ripped, fabric shredded. The crystal sets and the photographs were defaced with slashes of red lipstick, and across the once spotless white walls were scrawled the words, "MOON LADY WAS HERE!"

Her eyes fell to a credenza and there was her purse, in the midst of all the devastation, its contents scattered. She stepped over a receiver, as if in a daze, to take a closer look. The lipstick she'd bought only the week before was lying there with the cap off. She picked up the tube with a trembling hand; there was nothing left but a crimson stump.

Hearing a small noise, a whimper, she turned and saw Edith at the door. Her face was ashen, her eyes large and shocked, like those of a wounded doe. Kaitlin didn't know what to say, and for an interminable moment, neither of them said anything. Finally Edith looked up from her wheelchair, first at Kaitlin's face, then to the evidence in her hand. The woman's voice was stricken as she murmured, "I've never misjudged anyone so badly in my life."

Chapter Ten

If Kaitlin could have done anything to take this moment away, she would have. She'd have fallen to her knees on the floor and pleaded her innocence; she'd have turned herself inside out to reveal her lack of malice—anything, if only she could take away the anguish from Edith Carr's lovely face. It was the second time Kaitlin had been unjustly accused that day, first of philandering with Mike, and now this—an offense so much more ghastly, the victim so much less deserving of cruelty. She was beginning to feel cursed, like a scourge that affected everyone she met and touched.

"I—I swear to God, Edith, I didn't—" was all she managed to stammer before the tears flooded her eyes. Dropping the defiled lipstick as if it were a hot brand, she fled the room, nearly stumbling over the wheel of Edith's chair as she ran past her. She couldn't bear to stand amid the destruction of that room one moment longer, to feel that poor woman's horror and grief. Even now, she would feel Edith's eyes following her as she ran down the hall and out the back door.

"Elliot! Elliot!" It didn't matter that she was screaming or that people were gaping at her as the mascara-stained tears poured freely down her face. She

IT'S A JACKPOT
OF A GREAT OFFER!

- 4 exciting Harlequin novels—Free!
- an LCD digital quartz watch with leather strap—Free!
- a stylish ballpoint pen—Free!
- a surprise mystery bonus that will delight you

But wait...there's even more!

Special Extras—Free!

You'll also get our monthly newsletter, packed with news on your favorite writers, upcoming books, and more. Four times a year, you'll receive our members' magazine, *Romance Digest.* Best of all, you'll receive periodically our special-edition *Harlequin Bestsellers* to preview for ten days without charge.

Money-saving home delivery!

Join Harlequin Reader Service and enjoy the convenience of previewing new, hot-off-the-press books every month, delivered right to your home. Each book is yours for only $1.99—26¢ less per book than what you pay in stores! Great Savings plus total convenience add up to a winning combination for you!

YOUR NO-RISK
GUARANTEE

- There's no obligation to buy—and the free books and gifts are yours to keep forever.
- You pay the lowest price possible and receive books before they are to appear in stores.
- You may end your subscription anytime—just write and let us know.

TAKE A CHANCE ON ROMANCE–THEN COMPLETE AND MAIL YOUR SCORECARD TO CLAIM YOUR 7 HEARTWARMING GIFTS.

PLAYER'S SCORECARD

MAIL TODAY

FREE BOOKS
Free Pen & Watch Set

Did you win a mystery gift?

PLACE STICKER HERE

☐ **YES!** I hit the jackpot. I have affixed my 3 hearts. Please send me my 4 Harlequin Temptation novels free, plus my free watch, free pen and free mystery gift. Then send me four books every month as they come off the press, and bill me at just $1.99 per book (26¢ less than retail), with no extra charges for shipping and handling. If I am not completely satisfied, I may return a shipment and cancel at any time. The 7 gifts remain mine to keep.

NAME

ADDRESS   APT.

CITY

PROV./STATE   POSTAL CODE/ZIP

Offer limited to one per household and not valid for present <u>Temptation</u> subscribers.

142-CIX MDJM

Stylish LCD quartz watch—
just one of your 7 gifts!

You'll love the appearance and accuracy of your new LCD quartz digital watch. Genuine leather strap. Replaceable battery. Perfect for daytime...elegant enough for evening. Best of all, it's just one of 7 wonderful prizes you can win— FREE! See inside for exciting details.

needed him to make things right. He could make Edith understand it wasn't Kaitlin who had done this. He had to help her because she didn't have the strength to fight her own battles anymore.

He came to her at once and wrapped her in the shelter of his arms, letting her sob all over his shirt. Only when she started to choke and gasp for breath did he try to calm her. He stroked her back, still holding her tight, and he whispered soothing words over and over until she began to breathe more evenly and her sobs waned to an occasional ragged exhalation. Never had she considered herself a coward, but at this moment, she'd have given her soul to stay there in his arms forever. She didn't want to see anyone, talk to anyone; she only wanted to melt into this broad, strong man and disappear.

The illusion of refuge was short-lived. Kaitlin felt Elliot's head lift and his arms tighten—not in an embrace, but as if they had turned to wood. She felt the rapid cooling of his compassion and wasn't at all surprised when his arms fell away and he released her. Edith Carr had obviously caught up to her.

"Come on," he said brusquely, "we're going inside." He hooked an arm around her shoulders and steered her in the direction of the house. There was no affection in their touching. It was as if he were trying to prevent her escape.

Kaitlin's had to will her legs to keep moving. She thought suddenly that she understood how it might feel to bleed to death on the inside. The pain was so deep that she couldn't reach it, couldn't staunch the wounds. How much more could she take, she wondered, before she died of people's misconceptions?

Charlie had materialized in her absence and was sitting on the couch in the family room, holding his head in disbelief. When he looked up at them, his face registered the same numb shock and dismay as his wife's. Anger, Kaitlin suspected, would come later.

She had learned that Elliot, when faced with an emotional crisis, showed no emotion. He would observe, analyze and consider all with only the bare minimum of external reaction. But Kaitlin read the shocked horror on his face as clearly as if it had been written there. It came out in the way his skin was stretched tautly across his cheekbones, giving him a haunting, chiseled quality. His eyes narrowed, and his lips tightened until his mouth became a grim, hard line. When he read the words on the wall, she could feel him pull inward, his emotional withdrawal complete.

No one was saying a word. Everyone was waiting for Elliot to take charge; he had that way about him. But this time he seemed to be floundering. After a long while, he turned his eyes on Kaitlin, and she saw the raging conflict in their depths. She saw accusation swirling around with doubt. She saw how desperately he longed to believe her incapable of such a thing, yet she saw, too, that he was unable to deny the evidence. She saw that he cared for her and that he didn't really understand why. All these contradictory impulses lent to his indecision and intensified the cobalt blue of his eyes. Or perhaps it was only wishful thinking on her part, for in the space of a blink, his eyes grew as rigid and shuttered as if they were made of marble.

He turned to Edith. "Tell me exactly what you saw."

She was holding a dainty lace hankie at the corner of her eye almost apologetically, as though she felt foolish displaying emotion over her treasures. "I—I was passing by the room, and I noticed that the doors were open. All I intended to do was shut them...and then...then I saw Kaitlin. She was standing there by the wall holding the tube of lipstick in her hand.''

There was no need to say more. Despite the fact that Edith had been perfectly impartial in her version of the story, the implications were clear. The fact that all the evidence was circumstantial meant little in the heat of the moment. Kaitlin squeezed her eyes shut and fought the wave of dizziness that had come over her.

"Charlie," Elliot asked, "did you see or hear anything?"

He shook his head. "First I learned of it was when Edie came and got me."

"Maybe you should see about ushering the other guests out of here," the younger man suggested.

"Good idea. You people do whatever you think is best, and I'll be back in a few minutes."

Kaitlin stepped aside to make room for Charlie to get by and nearly cried when she saw how he flinched and tried to avoid touching her. From Moon Lady to pariah in one fell swoop, she thought with a strange, sad bitterness.

When Charlie was gone, Elliot asked Kaitlin, "Did you do it?"

She didn't know quite what made her say it, but perhaps it was a way to relieve the tension of being simultaneously prime suspect, victim and scapegoat. She answered Elliot in the same detached tone of voice. "Of course not. Did you?"

Her reply caused Edith to gasp. "How dare you accuse him of such a thing? We've known Elliot for years, and he is totally incapable of such wanton destruction."

"That's precisely my point, Mrs. Carr," Kaitlin said, her tone softly defiant. "No one around here has had the opportunity of knowing me for years, which I'm sure you will agree is not my fault. Just because I'm a newcomer does not make me any less decent or honest." Her voice was quavering slightly and getting louder. For a moment, it looked as though Elliot might try to silence her, but he didn't. "Your husband has an intuitive feeling about people, just as you have. He had a feeling about me when he heard me and spoke to me in Ohio, not to mention the credentials he was able to examine. How often have both of you been wrong about the same person?"

The woman's hands fluttered to her face. "Why... I don't know... I can't think of any—"

"Exactly. One of you might have overestimated me, but it's unlikely both of you would have. The truth is, Mrs. Carr, I'm getting very tired of defending my mere existence. I'm getting tired of having to prove my innocence, let alone my sanity. I'm getting tired of having these kinds of sick acts dumped in my lap every time I turn around. Someone around here despises me so much that they're willing to let me pay the price for something as hideous as this. There are no words to describe how badly I feel that you and your husband ended up victims in this cruel game, all because of me. But I intend to stay here and clean this up, and I'll do what I can to get these things restored. Then, I intend to do my damnedest to find out who really did it."

Edith's shoulders slumped with something akin to relief, and there was even a glimmer of her former self. "Do you honestly think these things can be restored?" The quiet desolation in her voice cut right into Kaitlin's heart.

Elliot knelt and picked up a glass tube filled with metal powder, part of a coherer-type receiver. "I think so," he said. "None of the glass was smashed—probably because whoever did it didn't want to be heard by the others. The worst that's been done is a few pulled wires and some torn burlap. Of course, the station will pay for all repairs."

"Wouldn't it be a good idea to call the police?" Kaitlin asked. "There must be prints all over everything."

"You're probably right," Elliot said.

At that moment, Charlie came into the room. "No police! You know how Mike feels about them."

"But this is your home," Elliot protested, with the slight edge of tension that was always present when he mentioned his boss. "Mike has no jurisdiction on what you decide to do here."

"I know that, but it happened during a station function, and Mike doesn't like any kind of adverse publicity. Cops can have big mouths just like anyone else, you know." He nodded firmly as he surveyed the mess. "Mike will take care of everything. He always does."

Kaitlin bent and began to pick up radio bits. "I think I'm just beginning to realize that," she muttered under her breath.

Her remark made Elliot glance at her curiously. Then he turned to the older couple. "Why don't the two of you try to get some rest. It's been a long day. Kaitlin and I will clean this up."

The Carrs looked at each other helplessly, as if reluctant to abandon what was left of their treasures.

"It'll be all right." Elliot could be infinitely reassuring when he wanted to be. "Charlie, maybe you could find me a few boxes to put these things in so I can take them in for repairs. Oh, yeah, and I'll need some paper and pencil to catalog what you have and what needs to be done."

Now that Charlie had been given a specific activity, he appeared to relax somewhat. "Sure thing. I'll just get Edie settled, then I'll be back with the boxes. I got plenty in the basement."

"There are cleaning supplies in the pantry off the kitchen . . . for the walls," said Edith, looking drained and very tired. It occurred to Kaitlin that traumas such as this had to be even more taxing for people whose daily lives were an unending struggle. She admired the woman so much and wished again, futilely, that she could do something to make all this go away.

"Thanks, Edith," she said. "Don't worry about a thing. We'll take care of it."

Their eyes met briefly, but then Mrs. Carr turned beseechingly to Elliot. "Find whoever did this . . . please."

His jaw tensed in barely restrained anger. "I will, Edith . . . I promise I will."

Neither Elliot nor Kaitlin spoke as they began the task of restoring order to the room. The actual damage was not as severe as it had first seemed. Lamps and chairs were overturned but not broken, so the impact of the chaos was mostly visual. The glass over the framed photographs wiped clean with solvent and a rag, and they were able to scrub the writing from the walls without a trace. But it was a shame about the antique radios and microphones. Once they were repaired with new wiring and fabric, their value would decrease substanstially, even though they would look no different to the naked eye.

The atmosphere in the room was stifling, at least to Kaitlin. She could feel Elliot's struggle as clearly as if there were electrodes joining them. She felt his doubts in the controlled evenness of his breathing; she heard his confusion in the casual manner in which he'd comment on some passing item. She knew he was walking a virtual highwire to make sure nothing he said or did was accusatory, but she would have preferred it if the effort weren't such an obvious strain. Still, the very fact that he was trying to give her the benefit of the doubt was better than nothing. At the moment, she could use any allies she could get.

Finally she couldn't keep silent any longer. "I think Lorna did it."

Elliot was replacing the knobs on a 1948 Heinzelmann. "Is that so?" He didn't bother to look up.

Kaitlin had expected an immediate denial and was surprised by how smoothly her comment had flowed past him, which she took as a sign that her suspicions had merit or at least warranted some thought.

"When do you suppose she'd have had an opportunity?" he asked.

"When you sent her out to get coffee for Mike. Don't you remember that she was gone a long time?"

"Not really. How long was she gone?"

"Ten minutes, at least."

Elliot scanned the room and mentally recreated the scene. "I suppose this could have been accomplished in ten minutes, but she'd have come back looking awfully dragged out."

"Not necessarily. We were both already wiped from trying to hoist Mike onto the bed. No one would have noticed a thing."

"Now would she have gotten your purse?"

"I thought of that, too." Kaitlin was beginning to rally with a novel feeling of cleverness. It was much nicer to play detective than villainess. "When we were trying to lift Mike, she was on the same side of the bed as my purse. I remember that distinctly because I had just pointed it out to her a few minutes earlier. She could have picked it up when my attention was elsewhere, slipped it into the waistband of her slacks and gone out for the coffee. As you can see, it's small enough to be tucked underneath a loose blouse like Lorna was wearing today."

"Would this have been her way of getting back at you for allegedly stealing her fiancé?"

Kaitlin rolled her eyes. "I'll say. She's been suspicious of me since I started. You knew about Mike and Lorna's engagement?"

"Everybody does. CSKY's too small for people to keep secrets. We all let on that we don't know anything for Mike's sake, but Lorna can't help herself. She's been dropping hints like megaton bombs for years."

"Do you agree that she might have done this?" Kaitlin asked hopefully.

He shook his head. "I wish I could. The pieces almost fit, but not quite."

"Then who, Elliot? Tell me who!" His indecision hurt; his lingering doubts hurt. They hurt as much as all the awful things that had happened to her. More than anything in the world, she longed for someone to jump up and down enthusiastically in her defense, to shout to everyone that Kaitlin Harper was one terrific, if misunderstood, lady. She used to feel that way about herself once, a long time ago.

He studied her for several moments, and it almost seemed that there was pain to equal hers in those deep blue eyes. Pain and some deeper emotion, the intuitive kind that steadfastly refuses to accept what the mind inflicts upon it, no matter what the evidence. Kaitlin clung to that possibility.

Elliot ran his fingers briefly through his hair, then resumed working. "Don't ask me who, not now. I need time to think."

By nightfall, the room was once again in order. The collage of photographs was back on the wall, and the wall was free of graffiti. With Charlie's assistance, they carried boxes of radio components out to the trunk of Elliot's car. The neighborhood by this time was quiet, and the slam of the trunk door made Kaitlin jump guiltily as if they were cat burglars stealing away in the dead of night. She wrapped her arms around herself, trying to keep her teeth from chattering, while Charlie hopped from one foot to the other in a fit of nervous aftershock. Only Elliot, as always, seemed in perfect control.

He put his hand on Charlie's shoulder. "Don't worry about a thing. I'll see this through to the end myself."

"I know you will," Charlie said out of the corner of his mouth. "We've known each other a long time. You've never let us down yet...no reason for me to think you'd start now."

It was probably Kaitlin's frayed nerves or the eerie Prussian blue of the night that cast the two men into slightly disreputable shadow. There was no rational cause for her to regard the exchange between Elliot and Charlie as anything but standard reassurances between two people who'd shared a crisis.

A tomcat let loose with a lonely screech from somewhere nearby, and Kaitlin's nerves jangled. This was silly. Admittedly the two men were talking in a rather cryptic manner, but it wasn't some secret pact to dump her in the Don River, even if the setting was straight out of Dashiell Hammett.

"I'll be waiting to hear from you, if there's anything I can do," said Charlie. "If not, it's business as usual on Monday."

Kaitlin's rational side was practically screaming at her to calm down. Charlie couldn't help it if he looked like a weasel; beady eyes did not make a person evil. In the light of day, he was no more villainous than her sweet Auntie Pearl from Sandusky.

"You just concentrate on looking after Edith," Elliot said. "This has been harder on her than anyone."

Now Elliot might have been a puzzler, but she trusted him. She always had—or almost always. Aside from passing suspicions, of the kind that she'd directed at everyone at one time or another, there'd never been any hard and fast reason why she shouldn't place her complete confidence in him. For one thing, she was more than a little attracted to him, and normal, sensible people—like her—did not become attracted to someone who might hurt them. That sort of thing only happened in Transylvanian legends...or possibly in hostage situations. She'd be the first to admit that Kaitlin Harper had a lot of insecurities, but a latent death wish was not among them.

With a bluster that blew in from goodness knew where, Kaitlin leaned over and gave Charlie a peck on the cheek. "Thank you for a lovely barbecue." She should have anticipated the look of abject shock on his face. It was, after all, one of the most ludicrous, inappropriate lines she'd ever uttered. And the mere fact that she'd meant well was no excuse for such abysmal tactlessness. "I'm sorry," she muttered as a lame afterthought.

Charlie nodded curtly, but she could tell he was beginning to find her very presence disturbing.

''I think we'd better go,'' Elliot said, steering her rather sharply to the car, as if fearing she might let loose with another non sequitur.

Not likely. At the moment, she was seriously considering never saying another word in her life. To hell with the radio business. She'd get herself a job in the dusty back room of a public library and never be seen or heard from again. A change in careers would be a lot less devastating than going on with this charade. Since everyone was taking such a hell of a lot of trouble to get her out of the way, why not give in?

Most of the way home she sat with her arms folded across her chest, staring straight ahead. Well, not exactly straight ahead. She was watching Elliot out of the corner of her left eye, watching for some sign of suspicious behavior, some chink in his armor that would reveal once and for all what was on his mind. But his actions divulged nothing. He didn't so much as glance her way, even when he looked over his shoulder to change lanes. He was able to swivel his eyes right past her as if she weren't there at all.

The only reason she wasn't quaking with trepidation at the prospect of an imminent demise was that he appeared to be taking her straight home. Murder plots were supposed to involve circuitous routes through back alleys, with blindfolds and gags thrown in for effect. And while the Don Valley Parkway certainly lent the suggestion of peril, that was only because of the maniacal way people drove on freeways. Elliot, unfortunately, was one of the most maniacal. She was, by nature, a nervous passenger, and he was one of those men who insisted on driving consistently in the passing lane, practically attached to the bumper of the car ahead of him. Kaitlin had always harbored a secret dread that if an airplane were to drop from the sky a hundred feet ahead of them, Elliot and drivers of his ilk wouldn't have a prayer of stopping in time. It was a great relief when they finally exited and he confined himself to weaving through the traffic at slower speeds.

Before long, he had pulled up in front of her building with the force of a jet engine. Kaitlin's head slammed back against the headrest, and she thanked her lucky stars that she'd made it safely this far. But now what, she wondered.

Elliot finally broke the silence. "There's one thing I'd like to get straight with you before we do anything else."

"What's that?" she asked, still staring straight ahead but knowing that he was watching her peripherally, just as she was watching him.

"You don't trust me, do you?"

"I want to, but... No, I do trust you. What about you?"

"Basically I feel the same way," replied Elliot.

"I see." It would have made more sense to react with indignation, instead of feeling as though the air had just been cleared between them.

"Do you trust me enough to invite me to your apartment?" he asked.

Kaitlin forgot herself and turned to stare. "Uh, well, I suppose there's a possibility you might ransack the place or slip poison into my drink, but for some reason, I labor under this intrinsic faith in my fellow man." Or in you, to be more specific.

"Good, because you could just as easily put something in my drink, but I don't intend to look over your shoulder to prevent you from doing it. I prefer that we acknowledge our . . . er, mutual mistrust and let it go at that. For tonight, at least.''

"For tonight,'' she echoed, feeling as though they had exchanged a sacred vow. "No midnight confessions expected?'' A smile had come to her lips, a smile that felt like a cool summer rain after a dry spell.

His expression matched hers. "No confessions, at least none of the criminal variety.''

Kaitlin folded her hands in her lap and studied them. "There is still the matter of—''

"I know,'' he said, before she could finish, "but tomorrow will be soon enough to deal with . . . other things.''

She nodded. Elliot might very well have been the one who had smeared her name on the Carrs' wall with lipstick, but the fact that he suspected her made it plausible that he wasn't guilty, either. They were at a standoff, a cautious truce that, with any luck, would survive whatever tonight demanded of them.

She wanted to forget everything except the real, unshakable desire she felt. Tomorrow, some other unspeakable thing could happen, and they would have to try all over again to rebuild their confidence in each other, a confidence that was already tenuous at best. Tonight, she wanted him. And while sex, admittedly, wasn't something to be employed like a lie detector, well, there were exceptions, weren't there? Kaitlin told herself emphatically that if she and Elliot made love tonight, she'd *know* whether or not he was innocent. She'd simply know.

There was something magical about stepping into one's apartment with a prospective lover, she reflected, magical and almost frightening. Suddenly routines be-

came inappropriate, long-accustomed habits were
abandoned and one didn't know quite how to behave.

Everything about her place was familiar: the pictures, the furniture, the faint scent of coconut that came
from a pair of scented candles she kept by the open
window. But had Elliot not been by Kaitlin's side, she'd
have kicked off her shoes as usual at the front door,
dropped her purse on the butler's table and padded
barefoot to the fridge for something light to eat and
cold to drink. Then she'd have flopped unceremon-
iously onto the sofa and figured out what to do next.

It was impossible to think that far ahead now.
Acutely aware of every breath she took, Kaitlin felt as
though she might actually forget to breathe if she didn't
think hard. As she put one sandaled foot in front of the
other to cross her living room, she had to concentrate.
It was so important not to be clumsy or foolish or
overanxious—or rather, to *appear* not be any of these
things.

There was no need to turn on any lights. A combination of the moon and the streetlamps filled the room
with a silver glow. Kaitlin closed her eyes, pivoted
slowly and opened them to look at the man who so ef-
fortlessly altered her perceptions of the true and familiar.

The air was cool, but Kaitlin was hot, hot from the
inside, her body like a caldron, her blood roiling. Elliot's face was transformed into angled planes of illu-
mination and darkness, and his eyes reflected a mixture
of celestial and fluorescent light, making him appear
more like a dream than flesh and blood.

But he was no dream. She felt the red-hot desire of his
body as keenly as she felt her own. But as long as neither of them thought too hard or did anything as reck-

less as speak or turn on a light, they could allow themselves to dream, unscathed, for this one night.

He didn't say a word as he went to the stereo, nor did she as she walked to the terrace doors and slid them open. The night breeze rode in like a phantom stallion, the sheer drapes billowing in rhythmic seduction. She heard him pull a record from the shelf and knew instinctively how the music he picked would sound. It would sound the way the night felt: ethereal, cool, silky. Music that wraps itself around one's body and one's soul, clinging one moment, escaping the next. There, but not quite there; untouchable, like dry ice. When the sounds of Moe Koffman's jazz flute filled the air, Kaitlin tipped back her head and smiled with deep satisfaction. It was exactly the right music.

He came to her, and his hand gently cradled the back of her head. She nestled into the cool strength of his fingers. Then he moved close behind her, and she sucked in her breath at the way their bodies interlocked, back to front. The curve of her derriere against the front of his thighs; her shoulder blades against his broad, solid chest; her cheek at the side of his bristly neck. His hand slid around to touch her throat, pressing ever so gently. She felt the rapid hammering of her heart, the quickening sense of danger as in his embrace. But this was a dream, reality mirrored, and she allowed herself to drink the delirious sense of danger like a slow sweet poison.

He wrapped both arms around her so her breasts rested against the muscled bulge of his forearms. Her whole body shuddered at the intimacy. Thank goodness for the nighttime. The fluttering breeze was all that kept their fire from raging too fast and too hot; the stillness of the full moon tempered the frenzy that threatened combustion at any moment.

Slowly he turned her around as if she were a weightless, celestial being instead of earthbound woman. Their eyes danced over each other's face, seeking the fire that raged within them both. Suddenly their mouths came together and the spark was lit.

Time ceased; places vanished. All that remained was hot, pulsing colors, vivid extremes of touch and taste and smell. The seductive woodwind snaked its way around Elliot's wet kisses. A quick rush of wind wrapped the gauze curtain around them as they surrendered and sank to the plush gray carpet. Kaitlin fumbled with shirt buttons, and his musky male scent assailed her, mingling with her aura of wildflowers as he lifted her T-shirt over her head. He buried his face in the lushness of her breasts, and her body swayed beneath his in time to the music, her back arching when his tongue lapped her nipples like a rising tide.

Clothes were torn off and cast aside, along with whatever remained of inhibition and doubt. Elliot covered Kaitlin with his naked body and hers seemed to melt and flow into his, and when he entered her with a quick, decisive thrust, she rose up and took him fully, both of them gasping with the sheer intensity of it. Their climb was swift and steady. Their cries of passion were lost as light and sound fused with the liquid melding of their bodies. Then, together, they touched it. That rare otherworld that defies existence, that far-distant universe too explosive and too violent for anything beyond a brief encounter. They touched it, and they fell back to earth exhilarated, sodden, sated.

To Kaitlin, the best part of making love was afterward, when the urgency of passion was over. The consummate lover was a man who didn't want to let go when it was over, a man who was as eager to kiss and caress and stay close after he'd taken his fill as before. She had always sensed that Elliot would be such a man. He was.

They lingered in each other's arms until the night breeze dried their bodies and they began to shiver unconsciously and draw closer. When the sharing of their body heat was no longer sufficient to warm them, Elliot whispered, "Let's go to bed."

Kaitlin nodded but before she could react, he had scooped her into his arms and carried her into the bedroom as if she weighed nothing at all. Gently letting her down to her feet, he turned back the light cotton spread. Then he took her in his arms again as they stood there, and desire rose between them with the same intensity as before.

"This time we won't hurry," he murmured.

She nuzzled deep into his chest. "There is something to be said for hurrying now and again."

His response was a contented laugh. "My beautiful Kaitlin, you are wanton, aren't you?"

She was beginning to suspect with great delight that there would be nothing mundane about Elliot as a lover. He proved her right, by sitting at the edge of the bed, his arousal more than evident, and opening his arms to her. "Have you ever made love like this?"

"How...what do you mean?" she asked.

"Like this, sitting up so we can look at each other. I promise I'll be gentle."

He took her by the waist and lowered her onto himself, anchoring her body to his. Making love this second time was more deeply satisfying than it had ever been before. He seared himself into her heart and her mind and her soul, and she knew—knew with every atom of her body—that she loved this man... completely, utterly, unconditionally.

THERE WAS NOTHING BETTER after spending the night away from home than a cup of freshly ground coffee. When the canister was inspected, however, it was found to be empty. Damn. Instant was going to have to suffice. Because this was Sunday, it would be impossible to buy any of the gourmet variety.

Oh, well, at least it was a day off, and after a day like yesterday, relaxation was a welcome change. Rearranging the Carrs' furniture had proved to be more work than anticipated, not to mention the sleepless night that had followed. A body couldn't be expected to keep up with those kinds of demands for long. Tired eyes fell to the journal. Why not? There had certainly been enough momentous events in the past twenty-four hours to warrant an entry.

I have finally scored my first real coup with Moon Lady. No more guesswork, no more random fright tactics. I have her exactly where I want her, and I'm getting to know all her deepest, darkest secrets. I've already made impressive inroads—everything from the perfume she wears to the color of the curtains by her big brass bed. It won't be long now, Moon Lady; I'll be kissing you farewell.

Chapter Eleven

Monday nights along this stretch of Yonge Street were quiet. There were no bars, no all-night restaurants, no glitzy storefronts to appeal to nocturnal window-shoppers. The cars that traveled this part of the city's longest street were generally bound for someplace more interesting.

Kaitlin could never quite make up her mind whether she would have preferred more pedestrian traffic around her when she came to work. There were times when she missed commuting in the rush of normal daylight hours, jostling for space among business suits and silk dresses and skintight jeans. To say there was safety in numbers was probably inaccurate when it came to strangers, but the vitality and bustle of a crowd certainly made life more interesting.

She was no longer nervous walking alone at night. She'd adopted survival techniques that, if not invincible, at least gave her a sense of being street smart. On the subway train she always sat as close as possible to the conductor's compartment and avoided eye contact with the other passengers. The latter was particularly difficult for someone who had grown up in a small friendly town without underground transit; one never quite got the Midwest out of one's system. However, she'd learned to compromise by sitting behind a paperback and peering surreptitiously over the cover at the varied and colorful assortment of humanity.

Leaving the subway station wasn't always pleasant. Though the corridors leading to the exits were well lit, they were long and cavernous, and she occasionally encountered bums and winos and junkies loitering on the stairs. None of them had ever actually approached her, but in the event that they did, she had decided she could scream loudly enough to bring the transit authorities running, if only to squelch the ruckus.

Once she was on the street, it was another matter. She was on her own then, no uniformed official conveniently nearby to come to her rescue. Still, she had convinced herself over time that fear of the dark was little more than a holdover from childhood and that people who were afraid were their own worst enemies. She had walked these blocks often enough to observe a certain sameness about the movements of those who were out late at night. It could almost be described as a regression to primeval habits. Oddly apelike, they would walk with their shoulders hunched inward, heads lowered and eyes peering from beneath hooded lids as if every passerby was a potential aggressor. Kaitlin had read somewhere that a defensive posture was the most likely to attract trouble, and this she definitely categorized as defensive. So after much experimentation, she had developed a confident, if not jaunty, walk with head held high, arms swinging, as if she hadn't a care in the world. So far, her method had worked.

The Monday night after the weekend barbecue seemed even quieter than usual. The subway car was empty, as were the corridors and the stairs. Outside, there wasn't a single other pedestrian in sight. For the first time ever, she experienced the eerie feeling of being completely alone.

There was no apparent reason for her to clutch her purse more tightly to her chest, no reason to walk faster than usual, but she did. Just as needlessly, she pulled the cotton hat lower over her face, even though the effect was about as productive as an ostrich hiding its head in the sand.

When she heard footsteps behind her, she should have been able to ignore them, but she glanced over her shoulder anyway, seeing no one. Perhaps it had been an echo of her own steps, but no— Though they matched her stride perfectly, they were a fraction of a second too soon to be an echo.

Kaitlin quickened her pace; the footsteps did the same. She slowed down; they slowed down. Dear Lord, she was being followed! Determined not to panic, she stayed as close to the street as she could, away from alley entrances and darkened storefronts. It sounded as though the person behind her was doing exactly the opposite, walking along the darkest part of the sidewalk so as not to be seen. Twice she tossed quick peeks behind her and still saw nothing. Then, an instant before she reached the intersection, the amber light turned red. Damn!

She looked up and down the street. There was no traffic, no reason she couldn't cross on the red and get away with it. She might even be lucky enough to attract the attention of a policeman, who would throw her into the cruiser and drive her to work. She stepped off the curb, and that's when she heard the all-too-familiar whisper.

"Don't cross the street, Moon Lady. You'd be breaking the law."

The hairs on the nape of Kaitlin's neck sprang straight up, and though her first instinct was to run, her feet seemed to be frozen to the spot. One's worst nightmare come true.

"Get away from me!" she cried, not brave enough to turn around, yet morbidly curious to see the person's face. "You won't get away with anything!"

"I only want to talk. They can't arrest me for that."

The light turned green. Kaitlin began to walk across the street in steady, deliberate steps. She heard the footsteps behind her, following her rhythm precisely. Somehow it seemed wiser not to run. Her follower had had ample opportunity to overtake her by now; as long as they maintained this distance, she was safe. Or so she hoped.

"Who are you, and what do you want?" she asked, staring straight ahead until her neck ached with the effort.

"I'll show you who I am in a minute—"

Kaitlin whirled around, but not fast enough. The figure had ducked into a store entrance before she could catch a glimpse.

"Nice try, my sweet," came the hoarse, exaggerated whisper, "but I'm faster than you. Be patient; you will learn everything in good time. Right now, I only want to reminisce."

Forcing herself to continue walking on legs that felt like rubber, Kaitlin retorted, "What could you and I possibly have to reminisce about?"

"Many, many things," the stalker said and laughed, the awful spine-chilling cackle that had turned her blood to ice on the phone.

Get a grip on yourself, she chided inwardly. Laughs weren't fatal; neither were whispers. Damn, why were these city blocks so long?

"Let's start with Saturday's barbecue."

"Oh?" Her voice was little more than a squeak.

"We did such a fine job of cleaning up the mess you made, didn't we?"

At first, she was confused. "We? My mess?"

"Of course. You know, the whole world thinks you were responsible; I only helped you clean up to make myself look good. It's important that I have everyone's respect, you see."

Elliot? It couldn't be. It simply couldn't be! Panic, fear and desperation rose in her throat, and she could barely catch her breath, let alone talk.

"Shall I go on?" he taunted.

Kaitlin shook her head, stumbling blindly now as her eyes blurred with tears.

"I will, anyway. They're such pleasant memories we share, you and I. Remember the gift I gave you, the picture of the lighthouse and the moon? So perfect for the occasion, I thought."

Dear God, how could she have been so wrong about a man? She wanted to scream out for him to stop, but as in a nightmare, the words wouldn't come.

"And then your cozy little apartment. The thought of rolling around naked on that plush gray carpet is so delectable. I remember the curtains in your bedroom with the tiny violets, fluttering beside your big brass bed. So delicate...so feminine, just like you are... Kaitlin. Tell me, when are you going to invite me back again?"

"Damn you!" Rage at last billowed up and pushed terror aside, overcoming even her revulsion at the sick words she was hearing. She spun around and stopped where she was. "If it is you, Elliot, have the decency to show yourself. Come out where I can see you."

For a long time as she stood there waiting, she heard nothing. For a fleeting moment, she wondered if this was all a dream. It would almost account for the deserted streets, her feet that wouldn't walk, her mute throat. But finally she heard the harsh whisper, "Very well," and he stepped out from the entrance of an antique store.

What kept her from fainting, she'd never know. It wasn't Elliot, or if it was, he was more grotesque than she could ever have imagined. The person who stood twenty feet away was wearing a long, white lace dress, long-sleeved, high-collared, a gay-nineties style. Hands were encased in white gloves, and his head was covered with a wide-brimmed white garden hat. The face was a plastic mask of Mae West, made hideous by the night shadows.

"Tacky, isn't it?" the figure jeered from behind the mask. "Now you know how you look prancing around as Moon Lady. It doesn't take much ability to pass oneself off as a cheap tart, does it?"

If she'd had the nerve, she'd have gone up and ripped the mask off Elliot's face, but she couldn't bring herself to move one step closer. She'd had all she could take. Turning around again, Kaitlin began to run as fast as she could. She had no idea whether he was chasing her; the blood was thrumming in her ears too loudly for her to hear. She couldn't even scream; her throat was constricted tight with horror. If she could just make it to the station without doing something stupid like tripping . . .

She reached the front doors safely, by now almost hyperventilating. Squandering a few precious seconds to look down the street, she saw no sign of Elliot. She fumbled through her purse for the keys. Where the hell were they? Oh, no, she thought. They were at home! They were on a separate ring from her house keys, and she'd changed purses during the weekend, not bothering to put in the station keys since she hadn't needed them.

Normally she'd have gone in the back way, but in her terror she'd ended up here, stranded outside. Kaitlin glanced at her watch. It was ten minutes to twelve. The Duke would be getting edgy, and soon Rosa would come looking for her. She had no choice but to walk around to the back of the station.

There was still no sign of Elliot, but that didn't mean he wasn't lurking somewhere. In fact, the chances were pretty good that he was, waiting to pounce again. In all honesty, she didn't think she had the stamina to withstand another fright. She decided to take the offensive and try to draw him out of the darkness first.

"Where are you?" she called out.

There was no answer.

"I know you're out there. You wouldn't just disappear. *No matter how much I might wish you would*.

More silence. This was getting ridiculous, horribly ridiculous. "Look, you know as well as I do that Rosa Santini is expecting me this minute. If I don't show, she'll come out looking for me!" Kaitlin glanced around. She was shouting to an empty street. No, there was one person bustling along on the other side—a cleaning lady, probably—who looked quite terror-stricken by Kaitlin's solo pronouncements. She couldn't blame the woman. Was this what insanity was like? To see phantom visions and hear voices that others didn't? Merely entertaining such a thought was almost enough to bring on real madness.

Nevertheless, figment or not, she was not going to head into that alley until she knew where...Mae West had gone. And time was running out. "Listen to me," she shouted to the night air. "I'm going around to the back now. If you're going to pounce or whatever, this is your chance. But I won't be frightened by you anymore. If I know you're out there, you can't scare me."

With wooden legs, she took one step, then another and another. Each movement was an effort; her body and mind screamed in protest as she advanced toward the unprotected darkness of the laneway. To get there, she had to backtrack, which meant each step brought her closer to the apparition. It was a struggle to keep moving, a struggle unlike any she'd ever faced, and it didn't come easily.

She was halfway around the building now, in the darkest part of the journey. In a moment, when she turned the corner, she would see the hundred-watt bug light Luigi had hung above his door. It didn't do a thing to light the street, but the sight would be welcome nonetheless. It would have been logical to run, now that she was so close to safety, but something prevented her. Some long-ago Girl Scout training about getting away from a wild animal—no sudden moves, don't let it smell your fear.

Not too much farther now. Twenty, thirty more steps. She began to relax. Rosa would be there, and she was one tough lady who wouldn't tolerate any non—

"I'll be waiting for you, Moon Lady..." The whisper came from directly behind her ear, so close that she felt its hot breath. She screamed at the top of her lungs and tore the rest of the way to the bakery, practically falling in when Luigi, not Rosa, opened the door.

He dragged her limp body into the warm room that smelled of rising bread and sat her down in a chair. Peering into her face with concerned button-eyes, he said, "I heard you screaming when I opened the door. What happened?"

She couldn't catch her breath and pointed outside, gasping. "Out there . . . in a white dress . . . Mae West!"

He gave her a brief curious look then grabbed his hat. "Stay here. I'll be right back."

There was no time to tell him she didn't want to be left alone. By now, it wouldn't have surprised her to see the figure—Elliot—pop out from behind the ovens or from beneath her chair. Maybe she really was going mad.

She thought about bolting the door and watching from the window for Luigi to come back. But it was too much effort to get up, and besides, what protection could a locked door offer? The whisperer probably had a key of his own to the station.

After a few minutes, the baker returned, hat in hand. "I could not see anyone, certainly not this . . ." He gestured for the name.

"Mae West," Kaitlin said resignedly. "She's a dead actress."

Now he was looking at her strangely, but who wouldn't have? Explaining that it was Elliot in the white dress certainly wouldn't have made things any easier. People had high opinions of the man, but they probably considered her sanity rather questionable, if Luigi's expression was any indication.

"I'm sure whoever it was won't bother you again," he said with kindly patience as he patted her shoulder.

Her nerves had begun to settle to a semidormant, if not quite tranquil, state, and her legs hardly wobbled at all when she managed to stand up. "Thank you for being here, Luigi, and for going out there, too. It was very courageous of you."

He gave her a thin smile. "It was not courageous at all, I assure you. Do you want me to walk you through the tunnel?"

Kaitlin tried to return his smile, but the best she could do was produce a halfhearted grin. "No, thanks. I'll be fine. See you at five."

As soon as she entered the control room, she knew the Duke wasn't pleased at her showing up ten minutes late. Even the heavy percussion piece he'd chosen sounded angry. "I hope you realize you're cutting into my love life," he snarled.

Kaitlin looked at him through eyes that were red-rimmed and swollen with fatigue. "I'm truly sorry, Duke, and I'll make it up to you, I promise. But right now I'm too beat to explain."

He donned a full-length cape and adjusted it in front of the mirror. "How are you going to make it up to me—in cash or services?"

Her head dropped onto her arms. "I don't care. You work it out."

Her unexpected answer was enough to render even the Duke speechless. "Take it easy, kid," he said and swooped out the door.

By 2:00 A.M., anger had set in. Fear, frustration, abject disbelief—each had reigned, but now Kaitlin was furious. She was furious for having been deceived so cruelly and so long and for having denied the truth to herself when all the evidence was there. Elliot had always seemed a man apart, reserved, sharing his thoughts and his dreams with no one. It shouldn't have required any great feat of imagination to picture him on the fringe, marching to a different, twisted drummer. She should have been feeling thoroughly revolted at the thought of making love with such a man two nights earlier; her flesh should have been crawling at the thought of his touching her. But it wasn't. And *that* was making her furious.

There was something wrong with her, too. There had to be. How else could she look back on the night they'd made delirious love and feel a rise of excitement at the thought? The memory of his mouth on her breast, his hand on the inside of her thigh—she'd give anything to repeat the experience again and again. But one fleeting thought of the figure in the white dress and she positively recoiled. No matter how hard she tried, the two images refused to coincide.

She repeated the words he had whispered to her on the street; their nakedness on the gray carpet, curtains with violets, the brass bed. He was the only person who'd even been in her apartment and he was certainly the only one who'd been in her bedroom. No one else could have known unless he'd told them.

Unless he'd told them . . . Of course. Why hadn't she thought of it sooner? No wonder she'd been jumping from one suspect to another each time some new trick was played. They were all involved. A conspiracy . . . the Duke, Lorna, Elliot. And what had Charlie said the other night? "You've never let us down yet . . ." She had had a strange feeling even then and dismissed it as groundless paranoia.

Then there was the whole nasty business with the Carrs' family room. It could all have been carefully planned, starting with Mike's coming in drunk, setting the stage for a jealous Lorna to enter. The ransacking was so meticulous—no furniture destroyed, no glass broken, only the precisely constructed appearance of Moon Lady gone mad. They were clever—she had to say that for them.

But why? Were they some bizarre cult banding together in the guise of a radio station to practice their twisted ideologies? Radio attracted odd types, anyway; no reason that CSKY couldn't be odder than the rest. Come to think of it, Moon Lady herself could have been some pseudogoddess spawned in the mind of their ringleader Mike. Good heavens, what had she got herself into? What did they want with her? Did they intend to offer her up as a sacrifice? Or did they just want to push her over the edge?

She slammed her fist on the counter, grateful an instant later that the tapedeck had been playing and not the turntable. Moon Lady was far from beaten yet! She didn't care who it was or how many of them there were, she was going to expose the whole lot of them. If she was careful, played her cards right, they wouldn't dare hurt her. Besides, she really didn't think they were out to kill her, just drive her mad. And they were succeeding. She was beginning to sound downright hysterical, even to her own ears. What she needed was a plan. That was it—a plan. What she had to do was stay sane, catch them in the act and then bring in the police.

The call she'd been half expecting came around three. Strange how it wasn't nearly so frightening, now that she could put a face—or a mask—to the voice.

"Good morning, Moon Lady," came the whisper.

"What took you so long to call?" Kaitlin was rather proud of the newfound brashness in her voice. She caught the hesitation at the other end.

"I've . . . been busy."

"So what do you want from me now?"

"I want to meet you to discuss the arrangements of your departure."

"My departure. Oh, you mean my quitting." If she'd suspected the caller meant something more permanent, she'd have been shaking in her sandals.

"I think it may be too late for that." The rasping whisper was almost petulant this time. "You should have implemented that option sooner. Now we'll have to make alternative arrangements."

No amount of reasoning could totally banish the chills that voice gave her. She'd never heard a death rattle, but this was how she imagined one would sound, and she shivered. "You said you want to meet me face-to-face. I want to see you without the mask."

"Agreed."

His prompt reply surprised her. "All right—when?"

"After you finish your show, at five."

So soon? Kaitlin held her breath. She hadn't prepared herself for another encounter quite yet, and at five o'clock it was still dark outside. "Where do you propose we meet?" she asked lamely. "Your place?"

He cackled. "Not exactly. We'll meet right by the front doors of the station. Symbolically appropriate, don't you think?"

"How will I know you?"

"Don't be silly. You'll know me."

Intimidated though she was, Kaitlin was growing weary of always going by the caller's rules. "Why the melodrama? Why can't we just arrange for a normal get-together during the day?"

"Because this way is much more fun, Moon Lady. Don't you find it so? Even just a little?"

Oh, Elliot, she wondered, *now can you do this after all we shared the other night?* Sighing deeply, she reminded herself that no real harm had been done, and of course she would never tell another living soul that she had slept with a psychopath . . . or that she'd fallen in love with one.

"Are you still there, Moon Lady?"

"Yes, I'm still here," she answered without emotion.

"Five o'clock in front of the station?"

"Sure, I'll be there." Kaitlin paused as though the thought had just occurred to her. "One more thing . . ."

"Yes?" He drew out the word, almost as if he had anticipated the question.

"You can appreciate, I think, that this isn't the most pleasant experience for me, this prospect of meeting alone on a dark street."

"Go on."

"Would it be all right if I brought a friend for moral support?"

"You're not talking about the friendly neighborhood policeman, I hope."

"Oh, no, not at all. Just a friend." The police could come later.

Unexpectedly, the caller let out another chilling laugh, and the sound sent shivers down Kaitlin's spine. "Bring a friend. The more, the merrier." Then he hung up.

As soon as the dial tone began, she called Elliot's home number. It rang once before he answered.

"Hullo?" His response was grumpy and thick with sleep; as though he'd answered the phone before he'd had time to wake up.

Kaitlin hung up without saying a word. Of course he would make a point of answering that way. What had she expected: that he'd use that awful whisper? He was obviously just as capable of sounding sleepy as sinister.

But right now, she had to get back to her show. "That was the title track from Sheena Easton's latest album, and before that, Joe Jackson to tie in with Moon Lady's jealousy night. Let's admit it—we've all been there at one time or another. Jealousy's as universal an emotion as love; unfortunately, many people think one can't exist without the other. But it's a destructive emotion, one that preys on the victim as well as the person who harbors the jealousy. Take it from Moon Lady. If someone really loves you, believe it and be happy. It's the surest method I know to keep their eyes on 'Only You'..." Kaitlin switched on the turntable and leaned back, mussing her hair with her fingertips.

Sure, tell them another one from your endless store of sage advice, she thought bitterly. Moon Lady, the celestial expert on love and life. If they only knew what a fine mess her own life was.

But right now she couldn't afford to feel sorry for herself. She had a plan to put into action and not much time to do it. Flipping through the telephone directory, she found the number of Larry's cab company and dialed it.

"Could you tell me if Larry O'Neill is working tonight?" she asked the dispatcher.

"Just a minute...uh, yes he is, ma'am."

"Good. I won't be requiring his services right away, but I would like him later on. Could you give him a message to call Kaitlin at 555-2759 as soon as he can?"

"Sure will."

Kaitlin thanked him and hung up the phone. A witness was what she needed. For once there was going to be someone with her, someone who would see or hear or feel the same things she did. It had taken long enough for her to wise up, but now that she had, Kaitlin was not about to be lured down another blind alley only to be passed off as crazy the next day. That's why she needed Larry with her. The reassuring presence of a male companion was strictly secondary, she told herself for at least the third time.

He called less than five minutes later. "Kaitlin, what's up? Are you in some kind of trouble?"

She let out a long breath of relief at the sound of Larry's voice. "You don't know the half of it."

"More phone calls from the whisperer?"

"I'll explain it all later. I have to be back on the air in a minute. Could you pick me up when I finish work at five?"

"Sure, no problem. Front door?"

"Perfect. See you then."

"I'll be there," he said.

Next, Kaitlin called Santini's Bakery to let Luigi know a friend was picking her up after work and that she wouldn't need to use the back exit. He sounded relieved. Probably because he was worried her emotional malady might be catching, she thought wryly to herself.

For the first time in a long time, she began to feel more positive. It felt good to resume control of her own life after months of being at the mercy of others. She could still stand up for herself. And when this night was over, she'd know with certainty that Kaitlin Harper was still of sound mind and body.

LARRY WAS ALREADY WAITING for her in the cab when the early-morning announcer unlocked the door and let Kaitlin out of the station. She climbed into the back seat. "Hi, Larry. I do appreciate your coming."

He smiled. "You're a welcome sight any time. Where can I take you?"

By now she was already scouting the streets for some sign of her pursuer. "Nowhere."

Larry left the engine idling. "I beg your pardon?"

"I'm waiting for someone to show up. He was supposed to meet me here at five." The cabbie turned off the engine. "You can go ahead and keep the meter running, Larry. I don't expect you to sit here and lose money on my account."

"I wouldn't hear of it. Besides, my shift is nearly over. Correct me if I'm wrong, but I assume you called me more as a friend than a cab driver."

Kaitlin gave him a look of gratitude. "Oh, yes, definitely."

"Then why the heck do you always sit in the back seat?"

She glanced around, as if surprised at where she found herself. "Beats me. Habit, I guess. Next time, I'll sit in front...if you remind me." They both laughed, and it felt good to freely enjoy something as simple as laughter with a friend.

Larry sat sideways on the bench seat, stretching his legs out in front of him. "Now how about you tell my why we're on a stakeout at his hour of the day?"

So she told him everything, starting with the events at the barbecue and ending with the figure in white. She intimated that it could be any one of the people she worked with, but she made no mention of her relationship with Elliot. That would forever remain one of her most carefully guarded secrets.

"Incredible," he said when she'd finished. "You have got one tough constitution to be able to handle things like that without freaking out. I've seen *Psycho* seven times, and I still can't watch it by myself."

Kaitlin chuckled, relieved at being able to look upon things more lightly for a change. "Believe me, I'm the original scaredy-cat myself, but you eventually reach a point where it's impossible to be any more frightened. Then other, more rational reactions begin to take over."

He nodded in understanding. "Are you sure no one else could have seen this figure in white besides you?"

"As far as I know. It's possible that someone driving by might have noticed, but who can say?"

"And who in their right mind is going to stop his car in the middle of the night just because he sees Mae West standing there? It's more likely to make him drive away even faster."

"Precisely."

Both of them were watching out the windows for some sign of…anything. There were people passing by now and again on their way to work, but no one slowed or paid them any attention. Kaitlin saw no one she recognized.

After they'd waited nearly fifteen minutes, Larry asked, "Are you sure he said it would be this morning?"

"I'm positive." She struggled against the sinking feeling that no one was going to show up. The last thing in the world she needed was for Larry, too, to doubt her faculties. She was already beginning to question them herself.

"Something puzzles me," he said. It seemed to her he was starting to sound patronizing, the way so many others had when she'd tried to tell them about the things that had happened to her.

"What is it?" She tried hard not to sound dejected.

"Why didn't you call Elliot to be here with you this morning? The two of you seem to be hitting it off."

She turned her face away and looked out the window. "I thought we were, too, until Mae West started telling me things only Elliot could have known."

"Oh, no." Larry's voice was sympathetic. "Not the old classic about the identifying mole on the left shoulder."

She nodded. "Something like that." It didn't matter any more that she was admitting to what they had shared together. Larry wasn't the type to abuse a confidence. "So it was either him or he told someone else everything."

"I see. I'm beginning to understand why you couldn't have him here with you this morning." He reached over the seat and patted her hand. "Chin up, kiddo. Something will trip him up sooner or later."

How nice it would be to believe that. Half an hour had already gone by; she'd been duped again. She was also beginning to feel very sleepy.

"We might as well forget it, Larry. No one's going to show up. I'd been so sure this time." She looked beseechingly at her friend. "I'm sorry I dragged you into this."

"Hey, what are friends for? Besides, I haven't had this much excitement in ages. Can I buy you breakfast?"

"No, thanks. I appreciate the offer, but I'm really tired. Would you mind taking me straight home?"

"Not at all." He started up the engine, and they rode in silence for a while. "I don't want you to take this the wrong way, but have you ever thought about taking a break for a while?"

She shouldn't have been surprised that he, too, had finally come to the conclusion that her phantoms were all in her mind. But this morning, it was the proverbial straw that broke the camel's back. "You mean like some nice little asylum in upstate New York?" she retorted.

"Come on now, you know better than that. I just mean it might be a good idea if you went away for a while until things settled down. You're entitled to a break like everyone else."

She passed her hand tiredly across her eyes. "To tell you the truth, I'm considering it. Things are really beginning to get to me. But I'm going to hang in a little longer, just until I can catch somebody red-handed. Then I'll either take a long vacation or quit."

"Now that's a healthy attitude," he said as he pulled up at her apartment. "As long as you have a release valve built into your plans somewhere, that's the important thing."

She lifted heavy-lidded eyes and smiled. "Thanks for worrying."

"I'll walk you to your door."

"There's no need—" she began, but he was already halfway around the car to help her out.

"I'll feel better seeing you safely inside, just in case your friend in white got his directions mixed up and is waiting in the hall."

Kaitlin shuddered. She'd never even considered that possibility, but it was certainly a reasonable one. Gladly she took the arm that Larry offered and walked up to the building. When they were at her door, he took her in his arms and kissed her, a light and pleasant brush on the lips.

"What's that for?" she teased gently. "We weren't exactly on a date."

"I know that. I did it because I wanted to. Elliot's not the only man to recognize a terrific lady when he sees one. I care about you, Kaitlin. I want you always to remember that."

"I do remember, Larry, time and time again. You're a good friend."

He doffed an imaginary hat. "I do what I can. Call me if you need me; I'll be there."

"Okay." She touched his cheek lightly and said goodbye, sighing as she closed the door behind her. *Oh, Larry, why couldn't I have fallen in love with you instead of Elliot? Life would have been so much simpler.*

THE JOURNAL KEEPER sat with fingers laced together, staring at the blank pages. It was hard not to grow conceited over that last marvelous bit of artistry. Mae West—such a nonthreatening character in her films, but a veritable phantom after dark on a quiet street, especially for a woman who's losing her grip. This was getting to be such fun that it seemed a shame to end it. But of course the end was inevitable and promised to be better than all the rest. And so the writer began a new page.

I expect it won't be much longer before Moon Lady comes pounding on my very door, begging me to help her save her scrawny neck. Won't she be in for a lovely surprise? I can hardly wait.

Chapter Twelve

Kaitlin had intended to sleep for several hours before confronting Elliot at his office, but the adrenaline that kept her alert during the early-morning vigil had yet to leave her system. The nervous energy combined with her righteous indignation at being played for a fool once again, made her feel as jittery and wide awake as if she'd drunk a gallon of coffee. She paced her apartment from one end to the other, ignoring her body's screaming need for sleep. Her shoulders were stiff and sore, her eyes would have looked better on a bloodhound and there was a bunched knot of pain at the base of her neck. But it was the only thing she could do; tossing and turning in bed only made things worse. She preferred to wait and think.

At twenty minutes to seven, she couldn't wait any longer. Picking up the directory of CSKY's employees, she thumbed through it for Elliot's home number. Calling him there couldn't begin to rival the inconvenience he'd put her through in the past twelve hours. It would also save having to hear Lorna's nasal drone on the switchboard—worth the effort in itself.

Elliot answered the phone as gruffly as when she'd called him in the middle of the night. No wonder, she thought; he was probably still suffering from a lack of sleep, as she herself was.

"It's Kaitlin," she announced. "I believe you and I have something to discuss."

There was a pause. She could almost feel the tension through the wires. Her call shouldn't have surprised him, though. How long did he expect her to tolerate this abuse?

"If you say so" was his answer. "How about right now?"

Kaitlin fumbled for a response. She had actually intended to set up a mutually convenient time later in the day, but perhaps it was a mistake to put off the unavoidable. Better to get it over with now. "All right, I guess so."

"Your place or mine?"

She glanced around in momentary panic. Could she actually bear to have him come here after— No, she most definitely could not! "Your place," she replied, then wondered if the decision had been too hasty.

"How soon can you be here?"

"Let me think. You live near the station...twenty minutes."

"Do you know how to get here?"

"I have a map." She was suddenly anxious to be off the phone to weigh the consequences of meeting him right now, and on his territory. "So I'll see you in twenty minutes," she concluded.

"Fine. Goodbye," he said and hung up.

At first thought, it did seem foolhardy to go to Elliot's apartment on her own, all things considered, but she wasn't really any safer at the station. If her theory was correct, they were all his henchmen, anyway. At least at Elliot's place, there would be only the two of them, one on one. And they did have a certain rapport, so to speak. Surely he couldn't disregard everything they'd shared together.

As she rode the subway, Kaitlin reminded herself to adopt the same steely indifference her program director seemed to employ, no matter how difficult that might be. To rant and carry on, to burst into tears would be a victory for his side; it would prove only that he'd succeeded in getting to her. So this morning, she would, above all, be cool, and she'd force him to admit fully to everything he'd done. What she intended to do after that, she didn't know. It was simply too soon to say. One step at a time was enough.

She arrived at his door eighteen minutes after she'd called him. His apartment was on the first floor of an older two-story brick house. She noticed that the neighborhood was well looked after, but by no means affluent.

He was buttoning his shirt as he opened the door, which meant that Kaitlin couldn't possibly miss the sight of his naked chest with its sprinkling of black hair. How well she remembered the feel of it on her palm, a perfect combination of coarse and smooth. She drew in a sharp breath and forced herself to look into his eyes.

"Good morning," she said in a voice gone slightly hoarse. "Sorry to bother you like this before work—" Now what had made her utter an apology, for heaven's sake? The more she inconvenienced the man, the better she would feel.

"It's okay." Was that a smirk she saw on his face or was he trying to disguise his pleasure at seeing her? "I don't have anything special going on at the office." He stepped back and gestured her inside, and she could feel the probing questions in his dark eyes. But she'd be damned if she was going to give anything away a moment sooner than necessary.

Curiosity was an infuriating thing, at times, a reflexive and almost involuntary reaction that made it impossible to walk into a strange place without looking around. She'd have preferred to sit down and look nowhere in particular, to remain cool and aloof instead of allowing her eyes to wander and take in the decor, the personal touches, the state of cleanliness. The place reflected the man, with nothing of the swinging bachelor about it. The living room looked warm and lived in. There were brick-and-plank bookshelves, inexpensive but practical, and as crammed with books as the shelves in his office. The furniture was in dark earth tones and well worn, and the closest thing to high tech she could see was a small black-and-white television. On the coffee table in front of her were the latest issues of *Car and Driver*, *Motor Trend* and *Road and Track*, the only departure from a life-style that apparently bordered on the monastic. What on earth did he do with his salary, she wondered. He obviously didn't spend it on himself.

On a low table beside her was a chess game in progress. Because she couldn't think of any other way to begin, she asked, "Who are you playing with?"

"An old buddy of mine in Winnipeg. We play by mail; it helps pass the time."

Until what, she felt like asking. The way he'd said it suggested he was waiting with barely controlled patience for something important to happen.

"Would you like some coffee?" he asked.

Kaitlin had smelled the rich, freshly perked aroma when she came in. "Yes, pl— I mean, no thank you. What I've come here to say won't take long."

He had obviously sensed the coolness in her voice on the phone, since he made no attempt to resume their intimacy of a few days earlier. He sat down at the far end of the sofa, opposite the chair she had chosen. "Go ahead," he said, "I'm listening."

This was it—her chance to get everything out in the open. *So stay calm,* she told herself. *Pretend you're on the air, and keep your voice low.* "As of last night," she began, "I've reached the limit of my tolerance." Elliot's only reaction was a polite look of expectation. But what else did she suppose he'd do? So far, she hadn't exactly presented him with a forceful ultimatum, or made any explicit accusations. She pressed on. "I don't know whether you were the one who actually followed me to work last night or whether you're just coaching someone else like Lorna, but it doesn't matter. I refuse to be intimidated anymore and I will not be made a fool of. That was a cute little ploy, getting me to wait outside at five in the morning for nothing, but I won't do it again. Even Larry is beginning to suspect I'm seeing things."

Elliot reacted for the first time. "Larry was with you this morning?"

Kaitlin let out a graceless snort of laughter. "You don't honestly think I'd have shown up for our mask-less rendezvous by myself, do you? I may be stupid, but I'm not suicidal."

"Probably not," he remarked dryly. "What's this business about a mask?"

"Oh, please, give me a break." Kaitlin rolled her eyes. "I suppose you're going to deny any knowledge of the white lace dress as well."

His reaction, a sharp burst of laughter, was not what she'd expected. "White lace—is that what you said? You don't think I'd be caught dead in lace, do you?"

Her eyes glittered with fury. "Come on now, enough with the routine denials. I've put up with calls, flowers, being followed in Yorkville, the barbecue fiasco, and now this. It's getting tiresome."

He stroked his lower lip. "I couldn't agree more."

Dammit! Couldn't he flinch just a little? Did he have to go on looking at her like that?

"All right, forget it," she said. "I don't have to hear your confession to put all the pieces together. I understand now why I was unable to pin down a single culprit. You were all involved, every last one of you, playing your parts at the right time and bowing out to let the next one in. No wonder I could never quite point a finger in the right place." She sat farther forward in her chair. "It was all quite brilliantly masterminded, I must say, the way one of you would be off consoling me while another was busy implicating me in something else. Most businesses aren't operated as efficiently as your little cult. I haven't quite determined which of you is the true ringleader, but I suspect it's you. Mike is sort of a puppet leader. He has the money and the connections, but you have the brains."

He was watching her as though she had suddenly begun speaking a foreign language. "I suppose I ought to take that as a compliment."

Kaitlin ignored him. "So much as I enjoyed my job, I'm here to tell you I won't take any more of your garbage. Find yourself another Moon Lady to worship or sacrifice or whatever. Find yourself somebody else to drive crazy."

"You're quitting?" Now he did look genuinely surprised.

"Uh...well," she stammered, not intending to have gone this far so soon, "if you don't cease and desist from further practical jokes, that's exactly what I'll do."

"Where would you go?"

The man was too much. He was actually looking at her as though he'd miss her. "As if I'd tell you," she said. "What do you take me for?"

He shook his head. "I don't know offhand, but I could hazard a guess." He didn't sound sarcastic; he sounded...concerned.

Suddenly the distance between them seemed much too close for comfort. Kaitlin leaped up from the chair and crossed the room to the fireplace. "Go ahead and call me a raving lunatic, but it won't make the slightest difference. I'm aware of how well adjusted I've managed to stay, and I don't intend to change."

"Pity," he remarked, more to himself.

She whirled around, her eyes blazing. "How dare you sit there and patronize me after all you've done!"

"Is that what I'm doing?" He stood up and began to come toward her, slowly, deliberately, offering ample opportunity to get out of his way. So why didn't she? Why was she standing there as if to invite him nearer? What if he curled both hands around her throat this time, instead of only one the way he had that night at her place?

No, she told herself firmly, there was no similarity between then and now. Saturday night his plan had been to seduce her; this morning, he was probably ready to...

"Don't come any closer," she snapped, suddenly afraid.

"Why not? What do you think I would do?" he asked, still walking straight toward her.

Effective, Elliot, very effective; a voice like warm brandy, liquid sapphire eyes. He could've been an announcer, his delivery was so smooth. "I'm not afraid of you, if that's what you think," she lied.

"On the contrary, I think you're very frightened."

"What else is new?" she countered sarcastically. "I haven't felt anything else for some time now." She thrust her hands out on either side. Any minute now she was going to back right into the fireplace. How had she managed to get herself cornered like this? Had she no sense of self-preservation when it came to Elliot?

"How odd," he said. "We still don't trust each other, even after Saturday night." His eyes moved over her body like a lingering caress, and she could feel the response inside herself—a lick of flame, a burst of ill-timed desire. "Doesn't that strike you as odd?"

"How can I trust you when all you do is lie?" she asked.

He bent his head. "I feel the same way, but I prefer to call your lies hallucinations. You have the most colorful imagination I've ever known, and while it's endlessly fascinating, it's also beginning to hurt innocent people. Accuse me all you want, but keep the others out of it."

"Accuse you?" Her voice was sharp. "Does that amount to a confession?"

He threw out his arms and took another step. "Look at me. Do I strike you as the kind of man who would dress in white lace and follow you to work?"

"N-no," she admitted, "but that doesn't mean anything."

"I suppose it doesn't, since you don't seem like the kind of woman who makes up tales for attention, yet apparently you are."

Forgetting all her resolutions to stay calm and controlled, she shrieked, "I didn't make them up! They're all true—every word! I swear it!" Then her voice broke, and there was nothing she could do to keep from crying.

He reached her in two strides and pulled her roughly to him. "Shh, Kaitlin, I know, I know. You believe them to be true. That's the important thing."

"No, it's not the important thing! What's important is for *you* to believe me!" The words were out before she realized what she was saying. Whether or not he believed her was hardly the issue here. He was, after all, her prime suspect. She struggled to break free of his embrace by pounding with her fists, but she had no strength in her hands, and Elliot's chest was like stone. "It's not in my head!" she cried. "Someone did follow me in a white lace dress and knew all about my bedroom and the color of my carpet. You're the only one who knows those things. It had to be you!" She'd abandoned any hope of intimidating the man with her cool dispassion. The only thing she wanted to do now was let it all out, release all the terror and the fears and, yes, the treachery she'd endured.

It was totally illogical to be wrapped in the arms of her tormentor and yet feel safe; it wasn't right to feel relieved by his lies when what she wanted was a confession. And it was sheer unmitigated folly to look into his eyes for some sign of guilt and allow herself to be kissed instead.

Their mouths sought each other hungrily, dipping and tasting, recapturing the essence of desire that always simmered just below the surface. She heard the low moan that escaped his throat; she felt his heartbeat answering her own. She gripped his hair tightly in her fingers as he lifted her to her toes, his hand pressed to the small of her back. But when he pulled her urgently toward him, forcing their bodies even closer together, Kaitlin abruptly returned to her senses. With a fury directed mostly at herself for letting this happen, she wrenched away. "How dare you?" she rasped. "How dare you kiss me now, of all times?"

Contrition seemed to be the farthest thing from his mind. "You wanted it."

"I did not!"

"Women generally don't return the kiss if they disapprove."

"But it's totally irrelevant to what I came here for," she insisted, abandoning the fruitless argument for what she really wanted.

He moved away from her to the chessboard, studying the pieces absently. "I suppose it is." He thought awhile and looked up. "I have a suggestion."

"What?" She wasn't about to let down her guard again, she told herself nervously running her tongue along her lips. She could still taste the essence of Elliot's coffee on them.

"I'm as interested as you are in getting to the bottom of this, so why don't you let me spend the next three nights in the control room with you?"

Kaitlin folded her arms defiantly across her chest. "You propose to subject us both to a sham like that for three nights, instead of just coming clean?"

"I have no choice. I am clean." The careful tone of his voice suggested that Elliot, too, was reaching the limits of his endurance. "You can take my offer or leave it. But if you refuse it and walk out of here with your ridiculous conspiracy theory intact, then I suggest you seriously consider tendering your resignation. We do not require the services of an announcer with a persecution complex."

Kaitlin's mouth dropped open. "You're threatening to fire me."

"I'm offering you a way out, that's all. The decision is up to you."

She thought hard. "Three nights in the control room, you said. What is that supposed to accomplish?"

"I don't know exactly; we'll have to play it by ear. But if you do get a call, I might be able to identify the person."

"And thereby let you off the hook," she added cynically.

"That's right."

Kaitlin shook her head. "Not good enough. Whoever the person is could be acting on your orders. Your being there or even identifying him wouldn't mean a thing."

Elliot sighed deeply. "I suppose you're right, but wouldn't it at least prove my good intentions if I managed to stay there with you all night and not harm you?"

"I doubt it. You could still sit there and drive me crazy by degrees, which seems to be the ultimate plan, anyway." After more deliberation, she said, "Why don't you tell whoever it is—assuming it's not you—not to call for three nights? It'll give me an idea of how much influence you wield in this escapade."

He was quick to understand her insinuation. "No deal. If for some reason no one bothered you, it would amount to my admission of guilt."

"Something like that," she admitted softly.

"Forget it. But let's reverse the situation. If you get no calls, my dear woman, that indicates to me that there never really were any." He didn't so much as flinch at Kaitlin's expression of shock. "For your own peace of mind, you had better hope something does happen while I'm there."

It didn't take her long to realize the tables had been swiftly and effectively turned. He was right. His being there wouldn't prove or disprove a thing regarding his own involvement, but it could destroy her credibility. That in itself made it worth the risk to her. As for spending three nights alone with Elliot—well, frankly, it didn't frighten her. She only found it easy to suspect him when she was by herself, brooding on everything that had happened, not when they were together. Here she'd been in his apartment all this time, and the only thing he'd done was kiss her.

"Very well," she agreed at last. "Three nights in the control room, and we'll take it from there."

"YOU'RE ACTUALLY going to stay alone for three nights with your program director?" Larry deposited his third can of Coke on the sand beside him. "You must be crazy."

"Please don't call me crazy." Kaitlin looked out at Lake Ontario from Kew Beach and watched the heat waves rising from the sand.

"I'm sorry," he said more gently. "You know what I mean."

"I know it sounds risky," she admitted, "but I don't think it is. Despite everything that's happened, I've never actually been harmed, and CSKY is a legitimate, well-respected station. They're not going to risk their reputation by doing anything on the premises. Let's face it, Elliot can't very well bop me on the head during my show. Half of my listening audience are cops, and they'd be down there in a flash if I were to suddenly drop off the air."

"Guess you have a point." He took another sip of his soft drink and wiped his damp forehead. "It sure is a scorcher, isn't it?"

Kaitlin turned to him, and even the slight movement was an effort in the sweltering, airless heat of the afternoon. "It sure is." He was lying back with his eyes closed. She studied his slim body. Larry's chest was glossy and hairless like a boy's, his legs long and a trifle too slim. He was a nice-looking man, and they had spent a pleasant few hours on the beach, but she was already bored. Was there actually such a thing as being overexposed to danger so that normal life became monotonous? Or was it just that every time she looked at Larry, she was reminded of how much more attracted she was to Elliot? What a shame if it were true.

"He warned me from the start that something like this could happen," she mused more to herself than to her friend. No matter how hard she tried, the same tired questions kept circling in her head.

Larry sat up. "Who are you talking about?"

"Elliot. He told me about a female announcer who was murdered because of some advice she gave on her show." Kaitlin made a gesture of dismissal. "Not that I put any credence in a theory like that. I mean, the two situations aren't even remotely related."

Her friend seemed to consider this a moment. "Probably not," he said and lay back once again. "Although you've got to admit it is some strange co-incidence that your boss would tell you that story not long before weird things start happening to you. Almost like he set it up that way."

"No, I don't believe that," said Kaitlin, shaking her head as if to drive the very idea from her mind. It wasn't an original conjecture, anyway; she'd entertained it once or twice herself. "The only reason he even brought up the subject was to explain why he was against the concept of Moon Lady."

"Why was he against it?"

"I don't know exactly; perhaps just the possibility that somebody might misinterpret my show and...cause problems. He does tend to be overly cautious about things."

"How did Elliot's boss feel about the Moon Lady concept?"

"Mike? Oh, he loved the idea. He and Charlie thought it was the cleverest format they'd ever dreamed up. Of course the more enthusiastic they became, the more Elliot resisted."

"Well, that certainly clears things up," Larry announced.

Kaitlin turned and gave him a quizzical look. "What are you talking about?"

"Your program director. He wanted to prove to his boss that Moon Lady was no good. What better way to make his point than to conjure up some warped creep? You'll eventually go off the deep end and quit; then Mike will see the light and cancel the show. Voilà. Elliot is vindicated."

Kaitlin was doing her best to listen with an open mind. "I don't think so, Larry... well, I suppose it's possible. He's such a private person... Oh, dammit, I don't know what to think anymore. Elliot's ambitious—I know that much—but I can't believe he'd stoop so low for the sake of his pride. There has to be some other explanation." Her shoulders were beginning to feel sunburned; she wished she'd thought to bring an umbrella. "Would you mind if we changed the subject? I was hoping to get away from my problems for a while."

"Sure," Larry said with a nonchalant shrug. "Where do you think you'll go when you leave CSKY?"

"Hey, you were supposed to change the subject!" Kaitlin tossed a handful of sand onto his back, then sighed and gazed wistfully at the barely rippling water. "I don't know. I haven't allowed myself to think about it yet. This job was supposed to be the answer to all my dreams."

They sat in silence for a while; it was Kaitlin who spoke first. "It's hard when a dream dies, isn't it, Larry?"

He nodded, his gaze as distant as hers. "Sure is...one of the hardest things going, I suppose."

His dejected tone made Kaitlin realize she'd been dwelling on herself too long. She touched his arm lightly. "You ought to know, if anyone should. I'm sorry you've had such lousy luck getting auditions lately, but it's a bad time of year. Maybe you ought to ease up for a while and concentrate on other things to regain your enthusiasm."

His mouth lifted in a wry grin. "So now it's your turn to counsel me, huh?"

"Fair's fair."

"Yeah, you may be right, actually. I have pretty much abandoned acting for the time being, while I formulate a new direction for my life. Actually, I think my biggest problem was not aiming high enough. I just didn't realize it for a long time. That can be a problem, too, being so close to things that you can't analyze them critically. Know what I mean?"

"Most definitely," Kaitlin said. And it can be applied equally to people.

They fell silent, and both of them seemed to sense that the day was over. Once they'd caught up on the latest current events, there never seemed to be anything left to say. Kaitlin brushed the sand off her legs and stood up, vaguely aware that Larry was assessing her body. Strange how a different set of eyes doing the same thing made all the difference in the world. With Larry, she didn't feel even the slightest twinge of excitement.

"When is Elliot's first night in the control room?" he asked.

"Tonight."

Together they folded up the blanket. "I'm going to be keeping in touch with you at the station to make sure you're all right."

"In the middle of the night? You don't have to do that."

"I'm driving nights this week, anyway. It's no trouble, and I'd feel better knowing you're okay."

Kaitlin realized it would be reassuring to touch base with someone who cared about her. "Thanks, Larry. I'll look forward to hearing from you."

LORNA WAS SEATED at a downtown bar nursing a manhattan. The Duke was sitting across from her, looking decidedly uncomfortable.

"You'll never believe what prissy little Miss Harper is up to now," Lorna said.

"I hadn't heard." The Duke sighed. "What is it this time?"

"She's managed to finagle Elliot into spending three nights with her in the control room."

"Sounds cozy. What for?"

"To play nursemaid, of course, to hold her simpy little hand in case the bogeyman calls again."

The Duke drew his brows together. "How'd you find all this out?"

"I have my ways. Anyhow, I called Kaitlin a while ago to see how she was, and she confirmed it for me."

"I can't quite figure this out. Are the two of you friends or not?"

The woman shrugged. "My horoscope tells me I should stay close to an Aquarian to realize my professional ambitions, so I'm doing what the stars say."

"What benefit does Kaitlin derive from your... friendship?"

"Beats me, but who cares?" Lorna peered at him curiously. "How come all of a sudden you're so worried about her? A few weeks ago, you were ready to throttle her."

He swallowed the rest of his beer and signaled for another. "I know. Funny, isn't it? I used to get real paranoid about having her around, but I'm over that now. Tell you the truth, I've kinda grown to like the woman. There's something about her; she's got guts. Too bad I figured it out too late."

Lorna's face wrinkled into a look of disgust. "You're darned right it's too late, and don't you go getting dewy-eyed about her Duke. You've got plans for your life, and there's no room for Moon Lady in them."

He chewed his lower lip and wished he hadn't ordered another beer. He had better things to do than sit here with this overbleached sourpuss who'd lured him in with the promise of a free drink. "You're right, Lorna. Aside from the concert we're hosting together this Saturday, there's no place for Moon Lady in my life."

"That's my Duke," she said and laughed harshly. "She's got no place in mine, neither."

WAS THIS HEAT WAVE never going to let up? For five days now the temperature and humidity had been nudging toward three figures. The cleaners would never be able to get the sweat stains out of that white lace dress. This was Canada, for goodness' sake, not Ecuador. North Americans were not built to take this kind of oppressiveness.

Dog days were dangerous. They sucked the lifeblood out of people, made them lazy and lethargic. Sometimes excessive heat even drove people to do criminal things like rape and murder on the spur of the moment. Of course it helped when one had one's plans mapped out well in advance. Dog days or not, one did what had to be done.

The next three nights would be long and tedious, but the result was going to be worth the wait. You could almost see the headlines now. "Moon Lady found dead after hosting rock concert: suicide suspected." It would be great sport to let them mourn her supposedly self-inflicted demise for a while. Then, when the real details were carefully leaked out, people would be so impressed by the perpetrator's genius. The Boston Strangler would seem crass in comparison. Mmm, yes,

indeed . . . a simple matter of three nights on good behavior, and then the concert. Such excellent timing.

The journal lay waiting in its usual spot near the bed.
How many days had it been since the last entry? Quite
a few, actually; not good at all. If one expected to be
famous—no immortal—one had to be prepared to
faithfully record each day's events or the journal was
useless. But it was so damned hot in this room, and tomorrow might be cooler. Sure, tomorrow was soon
enough. The keeper of the journal picked up a tube of
red lipstick and crossed off the first of three days on the
calendar, while in the center desk drawer a Colt .45 au-
tomatic lay loaded and waiting, ready to do its owner's
bidding.

Chapter Thirteen

Their first night together was easy, bordering on festive, which was ridiculous considering Elliot's reasons for being there. But Kaitlin couldn't help how she felt. It was wonderful to have another warm, breathing body in the control room, and even better when that body was one she'd known so intimately. No matter what happened during these three nights, no one could tarnish the singular memory of the time they'd made love. In fact, Kaitlin thought sadly, there was a good chance no one would ever be able to match that memory, either.

To pass the night hours, they talked of many things. Music, poetry, theater; movies they loved and movies they hated; memories of childhood, traumas of puberty. On occasion, they laughed uproariously, and if the laughter was strained, it was healthful nonetheless. But whenever the light on the console began to flash, levity ceased. Phone calls had become sobering things.

Larry called her three times the first night, and oddly enough, Kaitlin began to find his calls intrusive, though she knew she should have been grateful for his concern. If he hadn't cared enough to check up on her, who would have? Nobody. And it wasn't as if he were intruding on anything intimate—far from it.

Elliot's mood altered noticeably whenever Larry called. His hostility would practically crackle. "How many more times are we going to have to hear from this guy?" he growled after Kaitlin had hung up for the third time.

She clenched her teeth, determined not to undermine her friendship with Larry by agreeing with Elliot. "I think it's thoughtful of him, don't you?" she asked.

Elliot readjusted the magazine on his lap and mumbled something incoherent that sounded like "pansy," but Kaitlin couldn't be sure. She returned her attention to the record-liner bio she'd been reading. Whoever had applied the label of catty to females had been way off base, she decided, shrugging.

The second night was more strained. There was a sense of transition as the hours passed, like sand slipping through an hourglass, grain by grain, each measure of time bringing them closer to some nebulous end. Kaitlin couldn't quite grasp the significance of this changing ambience; she only knew she didn't like it.

Elliot was the same as always, his quiet handsome self, and she wasn't feeling any more threatened by his presence than she'd been the first night. But neither did her erotic fantasies surface as readily at the sight of him as they had before. Something was slipping uncontrollably away from her, and the sensation of waiting was almost palpable. It hung like a haze in the air, muddying their efforts at small talk and all but extinguishing laughter. By the second night, Larry's calls to check up on her had become a virtual irritant; and they disturbed Elliot nearly to the point of rage.

It was increasingly obvious that Elliot was suppressing his emotions with great difficulty, and his apparent loss of control was making Kaitlin nervous. Anything that could disturb the unflappable Elliot Jacobs had to be significant. She was dying to ask what was bothering him, but at the same time, she dreaded knowing. What she feared most, stupidly enough, was that he would reveal his total lack of interest in her and unravel her last strands of hope.

It made no sense, she knew, to cling to the memory of a one-night stand when she'd spent all these hours with the very same man and nothing had happened. Not that she considered his reticence inappropriate. After all, he was ostensibly here to establish her sanity—or insanity—and it would be extremely presumptuous of him to expect intimacy, as well. The night they'd called an emotional truce and made love, each of them had still felt enough trust to allow nature to take its course. But it was too late for that now. Passion hadn't provided them with the answers Kaitlin had hoped for. Passion had only made the answers harder to find, the questions more difficult to ask.

The third night was sheer torture. The show's theme was a whimsical look at first loves, and Kaitlin found it grueling to keep her mood light and chatty. All the silly lyrics with their sappy rhymes—moon, June; mine, pine; miss, kiss; you, blue—made a mockery of her short-lived relationship with Elliot. There he was, sitting an arm's length away from her, not touching her, and she had to reminisce convincingly about holding hands and first kisses. As she babbled on, she wondered how many listeners realized that the inexplicable emotional tailspin of first love happened the same way at age twenty-seven as it did at fifteen. When it came to matters of the heart, things didn't change much with the passing of time. Heartbreak was still heartbreak; love was still love.

The final hours felt like years, and the few phone calls that came reverberated painfully along Kaitlin's nerves. Tonight was decisive, a turning point. Whether something happened or whether nothing did, she would be forced to take some kind of action. Elliot had made it perfectly clear. To him, no phone calls meant there had never been any, and he wasn't interested in retaining an announcer whose emotional stability was questionable. For once, Kaitlin was beginning to wish desperately that the odious whisperer would call; though in the back of her unrelenting mind, she knew he wouldn't...couldn't...because he was already in the room beside her.

When Larry called the last time, shortly before dawn, Elliot blew up. He grabbed the receiver from Kaitlin's hand; she'd never seen him react so explosively.

"What the hell do you think you're doing?" he barked. "Haven't you got anything better to do than harass my announcer? Kaitlin is safe because I'm here, not in spite of it. Your calling only makes things worse."

Kaitlin couldn't hear Larry's response, and she was so astounded by Elliot's rare display of temper that she didn't think of snatching the phone back to rescue Larry.

"I don't give a damn what you think!" her program director shouted. "No, I am not interested in going out for a beer with you. You and I have less than nothing in common!" With one final glare at the receiver, Elliot slammed it down.

"What did you do that for?" Kaitlin asked in disbelief.

He returned his attention to the magazine, even going so far as to move his eyes along the page. "Do what?"

"Insult Larry."

"I didn't insult him."

"You did so," she countered. "I've never heard anything so rude in my life."

Elliot looked up. "I don't like the man and I was merely being honest."

"Well, pardon me!" Kaitlin threw her hands up in the air. "I didn't realize rudeness and honesty were interchangeable. I'm sure Larry is grateful for your truthfulness." Shaking her head, she lowered the volume of the stereo and leaned into the microphone. "How about that one for a nostalgic look at first loves? Abba's 'Our Last Summer.' How many of you out there met your first love while traipsing around Europe? Those were glorious days when you could get three square meals and a place to sleep for five dollars a day. Perhaps you met that special person in a café or on the beach, or maybe on a train while your backpacks shared the same luggage rack overhead." Kaitlin knew she was sounding less than enthusiastic, but she couldn't seem to do anything about it. She took a deep breath and tried hard. "Moon Lady remembers those special days, those simple uncluttered times when you pooled your pesetas or your francs or lire for a bottle of wine and a loaf of bread to last you until you reached the next hostel. They were magic days when we lived for the moment...loved for the night. And now this sizzler from sexy Bryan Ferry and Roxy Music..."

She was lifting off the headphones when Elliot said, "Have you done that?"

Still put out by his unforgivable behavior toward Larry, Kaitlin refused to look at him. "I've never been to Europe."

"I didn't mean that. I meant living for the moment, and loving for the night."

She instantly forgot herself and met his gaze head-on. "Why do you ask?"

His eyes grew warm for the first time in days, and for a moment, they weren't merely program director and announcer, or pshychological adversaries—they were lovers. "You sounded as though you were speaking from experience."

Dammit, I was, you fool, I was. Don't you remember? But Kaitlin didn't express those thoughts. She turned away and replied, "I was merely trying to inject a little romance into the show, that's all."

"I see," he said, and things returned to normal.

When the early-morning announcer relieved them, Kaitlin left the control room with a disturbing sense of finality. Elliot didn't say a word as he followed her out, but he didn't need to. There had been no whispering caller for three nights. She had no witnesses who could attest to anything she had experienced, no long-time friends who could act as character witnesses on her behalf. After a few short months, all she'd strived so hard to achieve was gone. A flicker of success, a brief bittersweet taste of love, and it was over. Why? She longed to scream it out loud. *Why?*

They both stopped when they came to the lobby, as if they knew instinctively that this was the fork in the road. Kaitlin turned to Elliot and saw how admirably he fitted the role of her superior this morning. Haggard and stubbly, he was nonetheless very much in control as he gazed down at her.

"I guess there's not much either of us can say or do right now," she managed to utter in a shaky voice.

"Nothing I can think of, offhand," he agreed.

"There weren't any calls," she said, as if either of them needed reminding.

"I know," he said. Regret, the intense burning kind that reached way down and tore at one's heart, was reflected in his eyes. He didn't like this turn of events any more than she did, but that was small comfort to Kaitlin.

She twisted the ends of her tie belt. "It would be unrealistic of me, I suppose, to stay on and pretend nothing ever happened." Her tone convinced no one, least of all herself, that she'd even be capable of doing such a thing.

She heard Elliot's quick intake of breath. "I don't see how you could . . . all things considered."

Much too hastily, she blurted, "But you only stayed three nights! The caller sometimes went for weeks without . . ." Just as quickly, her voice trailed off. Who was she kidding? If she hoped to leave her job with any of her pride intact—not to mention a possible recommendation—she would have to do it now. Whoever it was—Elliot, Lorna—had no intention of letting anything out. If she stayed, her fear would never abate; a professional rapport with her colleagues would be impossible. And without self-respect, without freedom from harassment, what was left? The flickering memory of one night in Elliot's arms? Here, in the cool dimly lit lobby, the memory was already losing its significance. Whatever there might once have been between them could never continue now. She could see it in his eyes as clearly as if he'd spelled it out in block letters.

"I'll give you my letter of resignation first thing Monday morning, if that's all right," she said in a low toneless voice, trying not to divulge the depths of her misery.

"Monday morning is fine." His expression was grim, and Kaitlin could see the muscles of his jaw working. "I trust you'll be able to handle the concert tonight with Duke?"

"Of course," she answered. "I'll stay as long as . . . you need me."

"Good." He turned to go, then stopped. "I'm going into my office to sleep, but I can give you a ride to the subway if you like."

She shook her head. "Thanks, anyway, but Larry is picking me up. He's probably waiting outside now." She and Elliot parted company without another word.

He went to his office and headed straight for the window, drawing the curtain and stepping back so he couldn't be seen from the street. Elliot watched as Kaitlin got into the taxi with her friend. He watched as they drove away and for a moment he stood where he was, unmoving, his insides churning.

"I'm sorry it had to be this way, Kaitlin," he whispered to the cold empty room, "but I have no other choice." His voice broke when he said, "Forgive me . . . Moon Lady."

WHEN HE AWOKE shortly after nine, Elliot went out to Santini's for his morning coffee. He returned to his office and found Lorna at his desk holding an envelope up to the light. She dropped it when she saw him come in, but not soon enough. They both knew she'd been caught redhanded.

Elliot crossed the room and snatched the envelope from the top of the pile. "Mail's arrived, has it, Lorna?" His voice betrayed nothing but a steely calm.

Mustering an unconvincing look of innocence, Lorna replied, "Uh...good morning, Elliot. I wasn't snooping, if that's what you think. I just recognized the return address. Isn't it from your friend in Winnipeg?"

"I didn't know you knew him." Elliot slid his finger underneath a corner of the envelope, opened it and skimmed the letter briefly.

Lorna shrugged, obviously ill at ease. "I just remember he visited the station a few years ago, and you said the two of you used to work together out west."

"Why would you remember Tom all these years?" Elliot asked absently as he riffled through the rest of his mail. "I would have thought he was a forgettable sort of fellow."

"Oh, I don't know about that. He kind of looks like Larry, don't you think? The way he talks and—"

Elliot's head shot up suddenly at the mention of a man he found totally distasteful. "How do you know Larry?"

Beneath the layers of garish makeup, Lorna's face went white. "I...uh, I met him at the barbecue. Don't you remember? He brought Mike home in his taxi, and I came along..." Her voice trailed off, for no other reason than that Elliot was staring at her with frightening intensity. "What's the matter?" she managed to ask. "Why are you staring at me like that?"

"You do have a remarkable memory, don't you Lorna?" he asked in a low, demanding voice. "For all the little details that other people would put out of their minds."

She giggled nervously, and her hands fluttered limply through the air. "I've been told it's like an elephant's, but I only seem to remember the unimportant things."

Elliot barely heard her and was rapidly tiring of her presence. "Would you excuse me, Lorna? I just thought of an important call I have to make." The receptionist couldn't flee his office fast enough.

Alone, he sat at his desk and pieced his fragmented suspicions together, one by one. It had to be the link he was looking for. It had to be! He looked up the number of Larry's cab company and picked up the phone. "Good morning," he said. "My name is Jacobs, loans officer for the Royal Bank, Sheppard Centre Branch. I've received a loan application from a Mr. Laurence O'Neill. Could you tell me if he's currently employed with your company?"

"Yes, he is," said the voice at the other end. "I can put you through to the manager."

"No need for that, thanks. Someone will be calling you back later to confirm employment details, but right now I'm just going over the basic application and there seems to be an ink smudge across the home address. It looks something like…Gluppington. I tried calling Mr. O'Neill's residence, but there's no answer."

"Hold on a second," said the unsuspecting dispatcher. "Here, I've got it. His home address is 18B Willowbrook, Don Mills. Sorry I don't have a postal code."

"Quite all right. We have directories here at the bank. Thank you for your trouble." Scribbling the address on a scrap of paper, Elliot tucked it into his shirt pocket. Then he picked up the current ratings report and leaned back in his chair. There'd be plenty of time to take care of things later, he thought with intense satisfaction.

LYING ON HER BED was Kaitlin's costume for the gala rock concert beginning in a few hours at Exhibition Stadium. She sat at the vanity and applied a final coat of polish to her nails. Of all the outfits she'd ever been forced to wear for her Moon Lady performances, this one had to be the worst. Unfortunately her own opinions on how she ought to dress for public appearances had always been more or less ignored. Mike, no doubt with Lorna's dubious counsel, collected pictures from old movie magazines and costume books and sent them to the dressmaker with Kaitlin's measurements. There were a few occasions when she had refused outright to wear the outfits he'd chosen, and surprisingly enough, he had complied. Not that he particularly understood the difference between theatrical and lewd, but for the most part, he'd been reasonable. Now, as she looked at this latest creation, Kaitlin couldn't believe she'd let it slip by unnoticed.

The dress was composed of hundreds of tiny silver disks, each one bright enough to serve as a nighttime reflector. Of all the metallic colors, silver was her least favorite. It washed out her complexion and clashed with the highlights in her hair. But she was expected to complement the Duke's attire as his cohost for the night, and his preferences still carried more weight at the station than hers.

It wasn't only the color of the dress that offended her. The bodice was tight and fitted with underwires that pushed up her breasts to almost distorted proportions. By the time she'd tugged the zipper all the way up in the back, she could scarcely breathe. The straps cut into her shoulders, and the skirt was little more than several hundred silver streamers that swished around her legs when she walked, revealing every inch from ankle to thigh.

Looking in the mirror, she sighed. Just as well that tonight would be Moon Lady's final public appearance. She couldn't go through with this nonsense anymore. It had nothing to do with being an announcer; it was a travesty of her profession. Elliot, when he had told her that so long ago, had been right. There were better, more honorable, ways of making one's mark in the industry. Too bad she'd learned too late.

Kaitlin had just finished pulling her hair into a loose chignon and was placing the silver-veiled hat on her head when Larry arrived to pick her up. He looked quite natty in his double-breasted charcoal suit, and Kaitlin wished she could drum up a little more enthusiasm for the evening. All she wanted to do was get it over with.

"You look absolutely...incredible," was Larry's comment as Kaitlin scooped up her evening bag.

She looked at him and grimaced. "Sure, nice dress for a tart, isn't it?"

He chuckled and held out his arm for her. "Hey, what happened to your sense of humor, kid? With all the big-name talent on stage tonight, your glitter's going to get lost in the crowd."

"I sincerely hope so." Out of habit, Kaitlin went to the back door of the taxi.

"Wait a minute," Larry said. "What did I tell you about using the back seat? I'm not your cabbie tonight; I'm your escort." He opened the front door.

Kaitlin grinned sheepishly. "Sorry, I keep forgetting." She slipped into the front seat and wished she had thought to bring a shawl to cover her legs. There was something obscene about wearing tinsel before dark in August. But at least she could be grateful that Larry didn't give her exposed thighs so much as a passing glance when he slid in beside her. He was such a gentleman.

ELLIOT PARKED a few doors away from 18 Willowbrook, close enough to see whoever came out of the B side of the stucco-and-aluminum duplex. Most of the houses in this neighborhood were built in the earliest days of suburbia and were beginning to show signs of dilapidation. Larry's, however, was worse than most. His front lawn was little more than weeds, with a few scruffy flowers along the front of the house. There was little resemblance to the starched, impeccable image he presented to the rest of the world.

At a quarter to six, the sandy-haired man came out the front door of the house, adjusting the lapels of his jacket as he descended the stairs, then climbed into his cab. He glanced briefly into the rearview mirror before pulling out into the street, but if he saw the large blue car, he took no notice of it. So far, so good, Elliot thought as he watched the cab drive away.

Leaving his Toronado where it was, Elliot stepped outside. Here and there a few people were puttering in their front yards, but no one seemed to pay him any mind. He went unnoticed as he followed the sidewalk to Larry's house and made his way up the front steps.

He tried turning the doorknob to make sure he wasn't wasting his efforts breaking in, but of course it was locked, so he brought out a credit card. Though he'd never actually had occasion to try this before, he'd heard it was supposed to work fairly well with old-style locks. Sure enough, after a couple of tries, the card slipped in and pushed the bolt out of the way. As if by command, the door fell open. Elliot glanced quickly around to make sure no one was looking, and then he stepped into the house. The whole operation hadn't taken any longer than it took most people to insert a key into the keyhole.

The cramped entryway led to a small living room furnished with shabby, nondescript armchairs and end tables. Elliot stepped over piles of old newspapers and tried to find anything out of the ordinary, but the place was messy, nothing more.

Beyond the living room was an even tinier kitchen, the counter piled high with chocolate bar wrappers, empty fast food cartons and Coke cans; the sink full of dishes. The backyard was as unkempt as the front, a few spare tires thrown into one corner against a chicken-wire fence.

The only bedroom in the house was at the top of a short flight of stairs. Elliot climbed up, instinctively bracing himself for whatever he might find among Larry's personal effects.

There was such a thing as being too nice, too reliable, too perfect, and Larry had struck him that way from the start. It grated on Elliot the way the man's slacks always held a knifelike crease, his shoes were buffed to a blinding gloss, his button-down shirts were always just so. But it wasn't only his clothes. It was the way Larry looked at a person through those bland blue eyes of his without seeing anything and revealing even less. Oh, he mouthed all the right phrases, exhibited the expected emotions in all the appropriate places, but it was as if he were reciting from a training manual. There was simply no substance to the man. He was either insipidly stupid or he had something to hide. It had taken Elliot one hell of a long time to figure it out, but after those three nights in the control room, he'd finally come to realize that Larry O'Neill was far from stupid.

The first thing he saw when he walked into the bedroom was Kaitlin. Her veiled face appeared on posters that lined the walls, floor to ceiling. One could conceivably have passed it off as harmless hero worship, except for the slashes of red lipstick all over the posters. There were abstract scribbles across her name, arrows and hearts and kisses doodled over her body and obscenities smeared across her exquisite face. Elliot was not easily shocked, but he had never seen anything as repugnant as this manifestation of Larry's twisted malice.

His first instinct was rage. He wanted to tear the pictures off the walls and scrub away the defacement, but he knew that was a waste of energy, and time was precious enough. Nearly retching, he walked across the room to a narrow bed and a table cluttered with writing materials. The window was open and tattered curtains fluttered into the room. From the hodge-podge of papers, Elliot pulled out a thick journal bound in leather and burlap. On the cover, carefully stenciled, was *The Life and Times of Laurence O'Neill*.

The first few pages contained photographs of Larry as an infant, a child, a high school grad. He had always been perfect, a clean-cut, square-jawed boy with a toothpaste smile—president of the students' council, basketball star, voted most likely to succeed. But after graduation, his success appeared to wane.

Entries written in longhand, often meandering and self-pitying, told of his dream of becoming a great actor. There were places where his writing became almost poignant, and Elliot found himself intrigued by the prose. He sat down at the edge of the bed and turned the pages.

There were articles from newspapers, reviews of his plays, even a photo or two of Larry on stage, most of them yellowed with age. The reviews were lukewarm, at best and sometimes censorious. Larry's handwriting grew tighter with the pent-up frustrations of repeated failure. Finally, the articles dwindled away altogether, and it was here that Elliot first found mention of Kaitlin's name. *Everything had been going along so smoothly until Moon Lady arrived...*

So that was it, thought Elliot in sad reflection. Larry was going to punish Kaitlin Harper for everything the world had done to him, for every lost hope and disappointed dream. Gone were the hopeful scraps of Larry's life, and in their place was everything that had ever been printed about Moon Lady. And in the past few months, there had been a great deal. In Larry's warped mind, Kaitlin's success taunted his own flagging career. She was an undeserving satellite that had stolen the light from a greater star. His journal entry the night Kaitlin had hosted the play at the Royal Alex was particularly scathing.

Moon Lady took curtain calls I should have had. They should have been roaring kudos and tossing flowers to me as the star of Deceptions, *not to that primped-up strumpet in green sparkles. I could have stolen that show. I worked for months learning the lines for the lead. I was a natural; I'd have been brilliant. She had no right to step in and lap up the fame when she didn't work for it. You're a fraud, Moon Lady, a she-devil from Hades sent here to torment me. I realize now it's not enough to frighten you out of town. I have to frighten you to death!*

The sick, frenzied words jolted Elliot back to reality and he flipped the pages to the end of the journal. The last entry had been written only a few hours earlier.

Three nights with her hero-protector, and Moon Lady no longer trusts him, as I knew she wouldn't. I played my part so well, I think. She will come to me now with open eager arms, not knowing that tonight her earthly orbit must come to an end. Like asteroids, her life-blood will splatter through the heavens; her moonlight will flow hot and crimson over my body. Oh, yes, your reign was brief and brilliant, but I, the true evening star, will have my way with you in the end. Sweet dreams, Moon Lady...

Elliot closed the book. His eyes fell to a pile of cloth on the floor and when he picked it up, he made a sound of anguish as though his heart were being torn to pieces. The pile of cloth was a white lace dress. "Dear God, Kaitlin," he whispered to the room that was crowded with her images, "how could I have doubted you...my love?" Rising bile threatened to choke him as he stumbled from the room.

THE FINAL SCENE onstage at Exhibition Stadium was one that fans would not soon forget. Five of the greatest rock bands ever assembled were linked arm in arm, with the Duke of Rock and Moon Lady in the middle, leading the audience in a heart-soaring rendition of "Touch the Children." The song was written especially for the event, which was raising money to benefit handicapped youngsters in Third World countries. The song would be sung at the end of each concert in twenty-one cities worldwide, and Toronto was the first stop on the tour.

One of the Duke's friends had written the song. As Kaitlin sang along with the rest of them, she turned to her cohost and saw the tears pouring as freely from his eyes as they were from her own. She'd learned to look past the silver-lined black satin cape, the bare chest and tight silver pants, and to ignore the top hat and the makeup. And she'd discovered that the Duke was really an old softie at heart.

Before they broke into the final chorus, Kaitlin turned impulsively to the Duke and kissed him, and the audience roared its approval. No doubt, tomorrow the headlines in the entertainment section would link their names romantically, since they'd deliberately promoted the image all evening. But that was all right. The more publicity they could muster for a good cause, the better.

As for Kaitlin, she knew she would cherish this moment forever, a brief interlude when pettiness and rivalries were forgotten and people came together for the sake of innocent children. How many more of these special moments might she have experienced in her career, she wondered, if other things hadn't gone so horribly awry?

The postconcert bash was held at a swank neo-Georgian mansion in Toronto's exclusive Bridle Path. Mike was there with Lorna, and Charlie brought Edith. The Duke's date was a stunning blonde who'd flown in for the evening from Los Angeles, and from all appearances, it looked as though the Duke was smitten. Everyone from CSKY was there except for the on-air announcer and Elliot.

Kaitlin couldn't help herself. With a will of their own, her eyes kept wandering over the crowd, trying to catch a glimpse of him. A glimpse was all she really wanted, or perhaps a smile, a nod of recognition. She couldn't understand what would have kept him away, considering the magnitude of the occasion.

Though she danced with Larry and a number of other attractive men, Kaitlin's mind was on another party altogether, the *Deceptions* cast party when she and Elliot had danced together, cheek to cheek, to wonderful old love songs. Things had seemed so different then, a lifetime ago. Her eyes filled with tears at the thought.

Larry caught her wiping away a tear. "What's the matter?" he asked.

She tried to smile. "Nothing. I'm just getting weepy over the occasion."

"It is pretty spectacular," he said, passing her a handkerchief, which she promptly smeared with mascara.

"Oh dear, I'm sorry," she said and stuffed it into her evening clutch. "I'll wash it for you."

He grinned affably. "Not necessary. Keep it as a memento."

Kaitlin nodded, too distraught to talk much.

They stood side by side at the edge of the dance floor and Larry, solicitous as ever, allowed her the luxury of silence. After a while, he asked, "More champagne?"

"No, thanks, it's the last thing in the world I need." She looked up at him. "Would you mind taking me home?"

"Already? It's so early." Larry seemed edgy, but it was probably because he didn't know many people at the party. Kaitlin had done her best to introduce him to some useful contacts, but somehow he'd failed to make much of an impression on any of them. No sooner would she introduce him to someone than the person would beg off and drift away to join some other conversation. Oh, well, thought Kaitlin, maybe it was just an indication of her overall lack of success lately. She was going to have to start studying her biorhythms or something.

"We'll go if you like," Larry finally said, to her relief.

They didn't say much on the way home, but Larry didn't seem to mind. He walked Kaitlin to her door and waited while she fumbled around for her key. It was after two, and she was exhausted. She hoped Larry wasn't too set on prolonging the evening. When she'd opened the door, she turned to him.

"I realize I've used this excuse before, but I'm awfully tired. Would you mind terribly if—"

He silenced her with a quick peck on the lips. "Not at all. I'm bushed myself. It's been a great evening, Kaitlin. Thanks for sharing it with me."

Always the gentleman, she thought and touched him lightly on the arm. "You're welcome, Larry. Keep in touch."

He tapped his fingers to his forehead in mock salute. "Don't worry. I'll be calling you soon. Good night."

Climbing out of her dress was like being released from a straitjacket as the various parts of her body once again resumed their normal positions. Kaitlin dug up the lightest, loosest cotton nightgown she could find and slipped it on, removed her makeup, brushed her teeth and fell headlong into bed.

It seemed as though she had just fallen asleep when the phone rang. She groped her way out of a heavy sleep and fumbled for the receiver.

"Hello?" she muttered.

"Moon Lady...I've missed you," whispered the raspy voice.

"Oh, no," Kaitlin moaned. "Not you again. Why don't you leave me alone?"

"I can't seem to stop myself. Have you ever heard of moonset? It's just like sunset, but the moon goes down instead."

Outrage was waking her up quickly. "Dammit, Elliot! It's you, isn't it? You just stayed away tonight to make this call seem more dramatic!"

"It is I," he whispered. "Who else but the two of us could know about our midnight confessions?"

Midnight confessions? Did he mean the song or what? This further proof of his identity was still no easier to take. "Wh-what are you talking about?" she asked, her heart beginning to hammer.

In his disgusting, breathy voice, he wheezed, "Don't tell me you've forgotten our little hideaway at Fernando's, too many enchiladas—"

"You're sick—"

"I'm coming over, Moon Lady, to finish things off. I know where to find you."

Kaitlin dropped the phone as if it were too hot to touch and, panic-stricken, glanced around the room, deciding what to do. She had to get out of there fast. Elliot could be right around the corner. There was no time to lose.

"Run all you want," the voice said, cackling. "You wont' get away from me..." But Kaitlin didn't hear the caller's final words; she was already halfway to the door.

Reaching the elevator, she pressed the button, realizing in the next instant how foolish it would be to stand there waiting. She ran to the other end of the hall and descended the fire stairs as rapidly as she could, not caring that she was barefoot and clad only in a thin cotton gown. All she could think about was getting out of the building before she was cornered by the demented Elliot Jacobs.

The street at this time of the night was deserted, and the streetlamps did little to relieve the long shadows and dark corners. For a moment, she stood motionless, her hands clenched, trying to determine which direction might lead her to safety.

The corner variety store, a block away! It was open all night and always well lit. She'd be safe there; she could call the police. With a final burst of adrenaline she began to run across the street, only half-aware that a vehicle was careering around the corner. It came to a screeching halt directly in front of her, blocking her way to the store. A taxi. *It was Larry!*

She flung open the door without another thought and practically dived into the back seat. "Thank God, it's you!" Gasping for breath, she tried to explain. "You won't believe...what happened...another phone call..."

"Hey, it's all right. Calm down." Larry's voice was soothing as he depressed the accelerator and began to drive slowly down the quiet street. "At it again, is he?"

"Yes, he...he must have stayed away so he could...plan his final attack."

Larry clicked his tongue like an old mother hen, his eyes riveted to the rearview mirror. "Such a dreadful fellow, so inconsiderate of your need for beauty sleep."

That struck Kaitlin as an odd thing to say, and his voice sounded strange. She looked up, and their eyes met in the mirror. There was something not quite right, a hard glitter in his eyes, a look she'd never seen before. Or was she just getting paranoid?

"Are you all right, Larry?" she asked, her breathing nearly returned to normal.

"Of course, why do you ask?"

His voice *was* different. And why was he driving so slowly? She hadn't asked him to take her anywhere. "I don't know," she said, wondering why the prickling sensation along her spine was growing instead of abating. "I think I'm just overtired."

They were at least a few blocks from her apartment by now, though Kaitlin didn't know precisely where since she hadn't been paying attention. She wished he would stop so they could talk.

"I am rather fatigued myself," said Larry. "I have been working so hard lately..."

"Larry!" Kaitlin wailed, a note of hysteria rising in her voice. "Why are you starting to whisper? That's not funny. Use your normal voice!" The resemblance was too uncanny.

"What normal voice?" No, it wasn't a resemblance; it was a dead ringer. "Perhaps this is it...my other voice might have been part of a role I was playing." Larry laughed, but it wasn't his usual pleasant baritone; it was the horrifying nighttime cackle she'd come to fear and know so well. This was a nightmare. It had to be!

Blindly she groped for the door, but the handle seemed to be missing. She slid across to the other side; it was gone as well. She was trapped! Larry was the whispering voice, and this time she couldn't even get away! "What are you planning to do now?" she stammered, too frantic to think straight yet. "This isn't some kind of joke, is it?"

"Clever of me, eh? Getting you to sit in the front seat earlier tonight so you wouldn't notice the missing handles. I took them out this morning in anticipation of our little nocturnal joy ride.''

It wasn't her friend Larry anymore. She no longer recognized him. Like the transformation of Jekyll to Hyde, his face had taken on a grotesque, inhuman expression.

"Why, Larry, why?" she begged, clutching her knees to her chest, shivering from so much more than cold.

"You ruined things. You destroyed my life, soaring into this city and capturing it without lifting a finger." He was driving erratically now, as his rage threatened to take over.

Think, Kaitlin. There had to be a way out. The man was mad, totally unpredictable. Even now he was humming to himself as if he were alone. If she could catch him off guard... Kaitlin lunged suddenly over the back of the driver's seat to gain control of the wheel, but Larry wasn't as oblivious as she'd hoped. He reacted with surprising speed—Kaitlin now realized that his right hand had hidden a gun. He was pointing it directly at her throat and she slumped in despair against the front seat. "Larry, please..." she moaned quietly.

"That's better, my sweet. Stay right where you are, and we'll all be much happier." He'd moved the gun a few inches away from her, but he was still brandishing it boldly enough that Kaitlin had no doubts he'd use it.

Holding her breath, she waited, daring only to move her eyes to see where he was driving them. She had no sense of direction anymore. It could have been one of the back streets off Davenport, but they all looked alike in the dark.

"How did you know all those things about Elliot and me?" she finally asked, wondering why she felt obliged to fritter away her final moments on things that didn't matter now.

"Convincing, weren't they?" He was speaking in his regular voice again, but there was small comfort in that. "It was quite simple, really. I've had access to the world's most effective grapevine—Lorna—ever since the day of the barbecue."

Kaitlin thought frantically. "But she's never been to my place. How could she know—"

Larry chuckled. "True, but she's blessed with total recall. Everything you told Lorna, she told me. Don't you remember your shopping trip for a bedspread and curtains? You described your bedroom decor to her in vivid detail, and of course every time you didn't invite me into your place, I saw the gray carpet—perfect for making love, I should imagine. Did you ever try?"

Kaitlin ignored his repugnant remark though she couldn't help the shudder that ran through her. "Why would Lorna tell you those things about me? What did I ever do to make her hate me so much?"

"She's always loathed you, couldn't you tell?" he said impatiently. "You came in from nowhere and became everyone's pet overnight—"

"And for that she agreed to conspire with you?" Kaitlin asked, aghast.

"Oh, yes, most eagerly. When I realized how deep her sentiments flowed, I knew I had found the perfect soul mate. Funny, I told her I was the whisperer, and she actually seemed pleased to hear it." He was still driving, but it didn't look as though he had a clear route in mind. "Do you know," he went on to say, "how many miles of pavement I've pounded over the years to get nowhere in my career? Not like you. Poor Lorna, she even had to condescend to sleeping with the boss in hopes of getting on the air. Then along comes Moon Lady, and poof! The end of her dream. Of course, that didn't prevent you from sleeping among the upper echelons yourself—''

"Larry, shut up!" She brought her hands to her ears just as Larry rammed the brakes and jerked the car to a sudden stop, slamming her against the front seat. He whirled around, leveling the gun directly below her ear.

"Don't ever tell me to shut up. Is that clear?"

"P-perfectly." What on earth had possessed her to make such an issue of her virtue? It was her life he was holding in his hands—not her reputation!

"Good," Larry said, smiling almost benignly. "I am a rather splendid actor, don't you think? A master of many voices, excellent with disguises—and improvisation! You know, many in my profession have great difficulty mastering the art of improvisation."

Dear God, was this agonizing drive going to continue forever? "You were...remarkable," she agreed as she tried to think of ways to escape.

"I especially enjoyed my little caper with the menu card—my finest hour, perhaps." Larry was admiring himself in the mirror, but Kaitlin had no doubts that he knew precisely where the gun was at any given moment. Besides, she could hardly make a run for it with the back door handles missing. Her only hope was to persuade him to change his mind and free her willingly.

"How did you manage the card trick?" she asked with as much enthusiasm as she could manage. "I've always been intrigued by that."

"I was wearing a disguise, of course, so that even if you'd seen me, you'd never have recognized me. Great handlebar mustache, black wig... Anyway, I followed you from your apartment after waiting all day for you to come out.''

"But how did you know which restaurant I'd choose?"

He grinned, and for a moment, he resembled the Larry of old, friendly and a bit self-effacing. Except for the hard cold glitter in his eyes. "That was the simple part. I only had to study your expression to determine which place you'd selected. Then, an instant before you reached the entrance, I cut in ahead of you and picked up the top menu from the pile as if to examine it. The maître d' was busy seating somebody else, and no one even batted an eye while I stood there, pretending to scan the selection—and used the opportunity to exchange cards. It was a long shot, by the way. If you hadn't stopped for a drink, I'd have left the card in your door. By the time the maître d' returned to his post to greet you, I was out of sight. But I was watching you. Your expression was unforgettable."

Kaitlin fought to keep her breath even. Somehow she felt that Larry would be calmer if she, too, were in control. "Well, you certainly had me convinced of your...integrity."

"Then, by all means, hold on to your ticket, my lovely. The best performance is yet to come. When I put this gun to your lovely neck and pull the trigger—"

"No, Larry, please. You need help—"

He jammed the barrel of the revolver against her throat. At that moment, she'd have sworn it was all over. Suddenly, sirens and the squealing of tires seemed to come from everywhere at once. Through her fog of terror, Kaitlin took a moment or two to realize what was happening. When she did, she was far from relieved at the appearance of a squad of police cars.

Larry was a desperate, sick man. In his twisted mind, arrest and conviction in a court of law were little more than scenes in a play. Her desolation was overwhelming.

Just as she'd feared, he didn't lose his composure. The gun was still expertly poised in his hand, and his emotional detachment was total. "How appropriate," he mused aloud, "to have the rest of the cast show up on cue for my final scene with Moon Lady. I've written it all down, you know, all the things you and I experienced together. They'll all marvel at how brilliantly the production was staged when it's over."

Kaitlin didn't answer. From the corner of her eye, she saw several officers emerge from their cruisers, lying low, their revolvers aimed. *Great,* she thought, *an ambush.* Her chances of survival had probably just diminished tenfold. She had to try to talk Larry down. It was her final hope.

"You were brilliant—" she began.

From outside, a deep voice shouted. "Come out with your hands up! We've got you surrounded!"

Kaitlin groaned inwardly. This wasn't a gangster movie, for pity's sake. Larry didn't seem to be paying any attention to the warning. He was in seventh heaven, acting his little heart out, though she had no doubts he believed in his role to the fullest.

"That's precisely the line I wanted them to deliver," he said, cocking the trigger. "I think I'd make a fine director, as well."

"L-Larry, be careful..." Her breath threatened to lodge in her throat. She'd seen enough movies and cop shows to know the gun could now go off at any second.

He bared his teeth in a grimace. "Would you like to find out what happens next? There's been a last-minute rewrite in the script—something a touch more heroic. I think you're going to like it. I know I will . . ." The next thing she saw was the gun being lowered, the barrel aimed. He fired a single shot, and Kaitlin slumped in a heap to the floor of the taxi.

Ignoring the policeman's warnings, Elliot ran to the taxi and threw open the back door. He took Kaitlin's limp body in his arms, and as he lifted her out into the cool night air, he saw Larry leaning against the steering wheel, his eyes closed. Blood oozed from his temple, staining his button-down shirt. His fingers were still curled around the weapon that had ended his life.

Kaitlin's eyelids fluttered open to find Elliot's face above hers. "What happened?" she asked.

He gazed down at her, and his tears stung her cheeks as he held her close. "Thank God," was all he could say.

Epilogue

It was the height of the theater season in Stratford, the picturesque town a few hours' drive west of Toronto. The maple-lined streets, so quiet the rest of the year, were filled with tourists, gathered to see Shakespeare performed. The Bard himself, no doubt, would have approved. Only the swans on the Avon seemed to resent the influx, peering down their haughty beaks at the boaters and picnickers and the lovers strolling along the willowed riverbanks. Still, for Kaitlin, the town retained its gracious, unhurried life-style, an eternity away from the painful memories of a year ago.

She hardly thought about Larry anymore, even when she attended the theater, which she did at every opportunity. So much had happened in her life since then. And there was so much still to do before her guests arrived. Her home was a pale yellow Victorian-style clapboard with forest-green gingerbread, set back from the street and bordered by majestic red maples. From the first moment she'd laid eyes on the place six months earlier, she knew it was home.

The first guests to arrive were her former boss, Mike Andretti, and his new bride. Her name was Angela, and she was the widowed cousin of Rosa Santini's. Plain and stout, Angela was a delightful woman whose only ambition in life was to keep her man and her four grown children happy. Mike had sold CSKY and was concentrating on real estate these days, and though he'd been unsuccessful at losing weight, thanks to his wife's Neopolitan cooking, Kaitlin had never seen him looking happier. She'd heard through the grapevine that Lorna had resigned some time back and was now doing traffic reports for an AM station in Toronto.

The Duke showed up in style in a low-slung burgundy Jaguar, accompanied by the statuesque blonde he'd met at the Exhibition rock-concert party. He was producing videos full-time now, thanks to his lover's generous cash flow and his contacts in the record business. Rumor had it that the Duke was getting offers to move to Los Angeles where real money could be made. Of course, it didn't hurt that Sasha, his girlfriend, was American and knew everyone worth knowing in the business.

The party was in full swing by the time Charlie and Edith Carr arrived. When Kaitlin saw them come in, she set down the tray of hors d'oeuvres and rushed to the door to great them.

"I'm so pleased you could come," she exclaimed, hugging them both. "You two look wonderful!"

"So do you!" said Edith, elegant in a rose silk dress. "Obviously small-town life agrees with you."

"Thank you, it does," Kaitlin said. "And what about you, Charlie? How does it feel to be CSKY's new manager?"

He tucked his thumbs into the vest of his new checkered suit and beamed. "Can't complain. The new owners don't know a hoot about radio, so they pretty much let me run the show."

"And well they should," Kaitlin replied, ushering them into the spacious living room where the other guests were mingling. "What can I get the two of you to drink?"

"Don't worry, I'll take care of it," Charlie said. "Just point me to the bar. Edith can't wait to get caught up on the latest scuttlebutt."

The two women found a quiet corner where they could talk. "I was so thrilled," Edith said, "to hear that you and Elliot bought the station here in Stratford. Classical music and jazz are my absolute favorites, and fortunately I've been able to pick up the signal from our place. Your format is divine."

Kaitlin flushed with pleasure. "I'm glad you like it. Word is starting to get around, and we're hoping to become profitable soon. In the meantime, we're determined to enjoy the struggle."

"That's the spirit. We all started off humble, and it doesn't matter in the least when you're young and in love."

"I suppose not," Kaitlin said, laughing.

"I imagine Elliot has told you that owning his own station was a lifetime dream of his." Edith's eyes were twinkling with delight at the rare opportunity to chat with her friend.

The younger woman nodded. "Yes, I know. He'd been all set to purchase a station years ago until his father lost his farm and declared bankruptcy. Elliot poured all his assets into a retirement home for his parents, even though it meant he had to start from scratch again. We visited them in British Columbia last winter, and they have a terrific place. There's enough land for a huge garden and livestock; there's even a trout pond on the property."

Edith clasped Kaitlin's hands warmly in her own. "It sounds heavenly. But tell me, where is that charming, unselfish husband of yours?"

"I'm right here," a familiar voice said behind her. Elliot came around to greet Edith with a kiss. Then he went to his wife and did the same. "I could feel my ears burning so I thought I'd rush right home."

Kaitlin's eyes lingered a moment on the handsome loving face of her husband. It still amazed her that happiness could be so consistent and fulfilling. "How's the new announcer working out?" she asked him, slipping her arms around his waist.

"He's perfect. He knows more than either of us about classical music, he has a great sense of humor, and best of all, he hates theater."

Kaitlin and Elliot laughed, while Edith looked puzzled. "Mightn't that be a problem, considering this is Stratford?"

Elliot turned to his dear friend. "In this case, Edith, it's a blessing. The person I had intended to use for the evening show threatened to quit and leave town when she learned she'd have to miss theater performances. I had a devil of a time finding a replacement."

Mrs. Carr nodded in sympathy. "I understand what you mean. Announcers can be a prickly lot, at times."

At this, Elliot threw back his head and laughed uproariously as he drew Kaitlin closer. "They certainly can, and they're that much worse... when you're married to them."

WHAT READERS SAY ABOUT HARLEQUIN INTRIGUE . . .

Fantastic! I am looking forward to reading other Intrigue books.

*P.W.O., Anderson, SC

This is the first Harlequin Intrigue I have read . . . I'm hooked.

*C.M., Toledo, OH

I really like the suspense . . . the twists and turns of the plot.

*L.E.L., Minneapolis, MN

I'm really enjoying your Harlequin Intrigue line . . . mystery and suspense mixed with a good love story.

*B.M., Denton, TX

*Names available on request.

IQ-A-

Take 4 books & a surprise gift FREE

SPECIAL LIMITED-TIME OFFER

Mail to **Harlequin Reader Service**®

In the U.S.	In Canada
901 Fuhrmann Blvd.	P.O. Box 2800, Station "A"
P.O. Box 1394	5170 Yonge Street
Buffalo, N.Y. 14240-1394	Willowdale, Ontario M2N 6J3

YES! Please send me 4 free Harlequin Superromance® novels and my free surprise gift. Then send me 4 brand-new novels every month as they come off the presses. Bill me at the low price of $2.50 each—a 10% saving off the retail price. There are no shipping, handling or other hidden costs. There is no minimum number of books I must purchase. I can always return a shipment and cancel at any time. Even if I never buy another book from Harlequin, the 4 free novels and the surprise gift are mine to keep forever.

Name _____ (PLEASE PRINT)

Address _____ Apt. No. _____

City _____ State/Prov. _____ Zip/Postal Code _____

This offer is limited to one order per household and not valid to present subscribers. Price is subject to change. DOSR-SUB-1R